Ten Thousand Islands

Ten Th

ousand
Islands

Randy Wayne White

G. P. Putnam's Sons
New York

G. P. Putnam's Sons
Publishers Since 1838
a member of
Penguin Putnam Inc.
375 Hudson Street
New York, NY 10014

Library of Congress Cataloging-in-Publication Data

White, Randy Wayne.
Ten thousand islands / by Randy Wayne White.
p.   cm.
ISBN 0-399-14620-2
1. Ford, Doc (Fictitious character)—Fiction.   2. Marine biologists—Florida—Fiction.
3. Florida—Fiction.   I. Title.

PS3573.H47473   T4 2000   99-089808
                   813'54—dc21

Printed in the United States of America
1   3   5   7   9   10   8   6   4   2

This book is printed on acid-free paper. ∞

BOOK DESIGN BY RENATO STANISIC

For Renee

These are the clouds about the fallen sun,
The majesty that shuts his burning eye.
—W. B. YEATS

They (the Calusa) said to me that their forbears had lived
under this law from the beginning of time and that
they also wanted to live under it, that I should leave them,
that they did not want to listen to me.
—FATHER JUAN ROGEL, MISSIONARY TO FLORIDA, 1567

Author's Note

The gold medallion as described in this novel is
real, but the characters have absolutely no relationship in fact
or fancy to the good people who suffered the tragedy associated with the medallion's discovery.

This much is true: in 1969, on an island off Florida's Gulf
coast, a fourteen-year-old boy was sifting for Indian artifacts
when he found human bones. Among the bones were many
Spanish glass beads and a small, oddly designed pendant
made of gold. On the face of the pendant were etched cryptic
designs.

Picture a metal object about the size of your palm and

shaped like a miniature shield. On the upper half of the shield are concentric circles upon a cross. The circles are intersected by three lines. A rifle target as seen through the crosshairs of a scope would be similar.

Midway down the medallion are two square holes cut through the gold. They are placed in a way to suggest eyes, though that may not have been the intent. Below the holes are a pair of inverted teardrop shapes and several half-rectangles, like doors within doors on the spatulated bottom half. On its back are two perfect and delicate crescent moons, one above the other.

In Spanish journals from the sixteenth century, a medallion of this design (a *chaguala* in the literature) is mentioned in association with the chief who ruled southwest Florida's indigenous people, a powerful and advanced society, the Calusa. It may have been worn on the chief's forehead or around his neck. No archaeologist doubts that the symbols are significant or that the medallion was once worn by Calusa royalty.

Some say the medallion resembles an alligator's skull. Others describe portions of the etchings as a "spider" design or "doors of infinity," or "roots of a sacred tree." To this day, medicine men of the Everglades tribes will perform certain ceremonies only on a crescent moon. That may have been true of Calusa shamans as well. No one knows.

All interpretations of the symbols are conjecture, for the knowledge has been lost. The importance of the symbols, however, cannot be doubted, for they were repeated in carvings over thousands of years of Calusa hegemony. As Tomlinson might say, symbols have energy. Judging from their centuries of dominion, the medallion's symbols demonstrate that a powerful people once believed it was so.

Everyone who's held the medallion has puzzled over those symbols. The boy who found it was no different. Years later, his mother would tell me: "D— read everything he could about the history of the Calusa, and he liked to hunt for artifacts. It was uncanny the way he could find things. Like the medallion—he was digging in a place no one would think to look."

Archaeologists who later authenticated the boy's discovery were also impressed.

The late Dr. B. Calvin Jones of the Florida Bureau of Archaeology wrote to me, "D— was a bright young man and had a natural gift for understanding what lay beneath the earth. To this issue, he was the most gifted child that I've ever met. Yes, he did make a major discovery, one I think marks the burial site of Chief Carlos and his subordinates."

In conversation, another archaeologist told me, "The child had a genius for finding things."

According to his mother, though, the boy was troubled by his discovery. "He seemed to grow increasingly nervous as the weeks passed," she said. "I know that he was having nightmares and he seemed to become obsessed with thoughts of Indians. It bothered him that he'd dug up a grave."

The mother also had nightmares. In one, she and her son were standing in water that was neck-deep. The boy had the medallion in his hand. He dropped it. In the dream, the mother begged him not to go after it, but he laughed and disappeared beneath the water.

Three days later, the boy was found dead, hanging from a very low tree branch—perhaps a fatal attempt to "experience unconsciousness" as his mother believes.

This is also true: shortly after her son's death, the mother was contacted by a stranger who offered to hold a seance in which she might speak to her son from the grave. Nearly crazed with grief, the mother agreed.

At the seance, by candlelight, the dead boy "spoke" through a series of raps on the table. He told his mother to give the gold medallion to the man who'd organized the seance.

The mother did what her beloved son instructed.

This novel is fiction, entirely fiction, created in the mind of the author, although some of the events herein are based on actual events. For instance, looters actually did transport a backhoe to a deserted island to hunt for treasure. They decimated an important archaeological site, yet found nothing.

It is sad but not surprising. Florida is a transient state in which too many rootless people care nothing for the past nor this state's future. Florida is a vacation destination or a retirement place, as temporary as time spent in a bus station.

Like a bus station, Florida attracts con men and predators. It always has. Florida always will.

Randy White
Pineland, Florida

Acknowledgments

The islands of Sanibel, Captiva, Marco and Key Largo are real places, and, I hope, faithfully described, but they are all used fictitiously in this novel. The same is true of certain actual businesses, marinas, bars and other places frequented by Doc Ford and his friend Tomlinson. In all other respects, this novel is a work of fiction. Names, characters, places and incidents are either the product of the author's imagination or are used fictitiously. Any resemblance to actual persons, living or dead, or to actual events or locales is entirely coincidental.

The author would like to thank Commander Larry Simmons, formerly of SEAL Team 1; Captain Peter Hull, Dr. Ken Leber, Dr. John Miller, J. Robert Long, Dr. Richard Pierce, all of Mote Marine Laboratories; Mr. Troy Deal, Sybil Bailey and especially Renee T. Humbert for her assistance. I would also like to thank Dr. Bill Marquardt, Dr. Robin C. Brown and Corbett Torrence for their expertise on Calusa archaeology; Amy Massey, Capt. John Martinez, Jack Webb of Key Largo, and all the Mandalites; Dr. Thaddeus Kostrubala, who provided invaluable scientific fabric as well as case histories to support the premise that there are politicians who lie without remorse, there are human anomalies who prey on women and, sometimes, they are one and the same.

These people provided valuable guidance and information. All errors, exaggerations, omissions or fictionalizations are entirely the responsibility of the author. An example: the Calusa king, Carlos, and the man who betrayed his people, Filipe, actually existed, as did Father Juan Rogel and Juan Lopez de Velasco. They are accurately quoted or paraphrased. Salvador and Tocayo are fictional characters, although their lives parallel those of Carlos and Filipe, even to some translated passages from letters written by priests who lived among them.

Prologue

There's something sinister about the
sound of a big man trying to sneak through mangroves. On
the foggiest night of the year, standing alone on the porch outside my lab, I heard the crack of a branch, then silence. Heard
the rustle of leaves. Then I strained to hear through a longer
silence that implied observation and careful breathing.

The platform that supports my house and laboratory is
built on stilts over the water, thirty yards from land, Dinkin's
Bay, Sanibel Island, Florida. The only way on or off is by a
rickety boardwalk. Someone was working his way toward
that boardwalk, getting closer.

I waited, head tilted, and heard branches move once again. The sound of a snapping twig is an ancient alert. It fires all the limbic alarms that enable direct communication between the ears and eager feet. An unknown primate was out there in the gloom.

I touched a button on my watch and saw that it was 2:07 a.m., 2 October. Very, very late for a friend to come a'calling. Very, very late for me.

I was awake because I couldn't sleep, and I was outside because I was restless—neither particularly unusual. What was unusual was the weather. An abrupt and windless cold front had drifted in that night. It brought a sea change. Fog descended as if the island had slipped its anchor and drifted into a mountain cloud. Fall and spring are the seasons. If you have the misfortune to be on the water when the silver shroud arrives, your best bet is to flee the channel, drop the hook and wait it out.

Sitting in a rocker on the porch, looking out into the mist, however, is very pleasant. That's what I chose to do. I'd lain in bed, listening to silence and dripping water until I couldn't stand it anymore, then pulled on a pair of shorts and went out the screen door into the haze.

Amazing. I stood at one end of my deck and couldn't see the railing at the other end. I swung down to the lower platform to check my fish tank, and could just barely see the edge of a tin roof through the swirling mist.

My house was gone.

Dinkin's Bay Marina is just down the shoreline. The

lights of the marina created a surreal van Gogh sky: swirling stars and corridors of light on a white canvas.

I found a rocker on the porch and sat there listening. Fog is condensed water vapor and conducts sound far more efficiently than air, so it seemed as if the old wives' tale was true: Blind people have a heightened sense of hearing.

I was certainly blind in that fog. From the direction of the marina, I could hear the click of every auto-switch, the whir of every pump, the groan of straining dock lines and the steady gurgle of bait tanks.

Then I heard it, a sound that didn't belong, a sound that didn't fit. It was the careful closing of a car door. It is a distinctive latching of metal on metal made when a door, half closed, is pressed with the hip.

A moment later, I heard the same sound again.

I sat a little straighter, trying to peer through the fog. It was blinding, dizzying. The sound came from the direction of the mangroves where the shell road, separated by the marina's gate, becomes Tarpon Bay Road. I could only occasionally see the mangrove fringe. Black limbs reached toward me, then vanished in a smudge of white.

It's not unusual for insomniac tourists to turn onto the marina's dead-end road to see what there is to see, but there's a pattern. I've heard it too often not to know. They stop at the gate where business hours are posted. They read the sign. Then they back up and leave.

The shell road also attracts lovers. But people who stop for a roadside encounter don't get out of the car unless it's to urinate, and there is a pattern to that, too. Doors open, there's a short pause, doors close.

I sat waiting to hear the doors again.

Waited two minutes; five minutes. Nothing.

Then I heard that distinctive sound in the mangroves. Heard the snap of a limb; rustle of leaves. Then: *silence*.

Thus I knew that two or more people had exited a car, and at least one of those people was trying to find the path to the boardwalk that leads to my house.

I stood. Listened for another moment. Then, very quietly, I began to move.

I get the occasional late night visitor. It was bar-closing time on a nasty, foggy night. Stumbling toward me was probably one of any number of my drunken friends with a couple of friendly drunks in tow. I could hear them explaining to me, Doc, it was just too damn foggy to run the boat home, so I caught a ride to your place. I'll sleep on your porch, you don't mind.

It's happened before.

I stepped into the house, left the lights off. In any emergency situation, a man wants two things covered: his testicles and his toes. I was already wearing shorts, so I slipped into my running shoes, then fumbled around in my dresser drawer until I found my old 9mm Sig Sauer pistol wrapped in oil-cloth, always loaded, always ready.

I shucked a cartridge into the chamber . . . then I stopped, remembering a recent letter I'd received from a lover, the tall and articulate Dr. Kathleen Rhodes.

Correction, *former* lover.

Among other things, her letter had described me as a man whose heart and head weren't connected, that I was capable of violence without emotion. I'd been fretting over the damn thing since I'd received it. While it's true I'm not overly emotional, I still have feelings, and her words had struck a nerve. Was I really so heartless, so insular? Now I had to admit it— she was *right*. That's precisely how I was behaving. I'd automatically assumed I was being targeted for attack. Those were probably friends of mine out there! And here I was already arming myself with deadly force.

I see my life as divided into two distinct rooms. One of those rooms is forever locked, as it must be. Inside are too many jungled nights; too many nights spent moving quietly in darkness. The second room is brighter, simpler; my life as it is now. I am the owner and sole employee of Sanibel Biological Supply, purveyor of marine specimens to labs around the country. It is a straightforward, constructive life that I tend carefully and reinspect often. The reason is simple. Once the door to the darker room has been opened, the creature therein is forever alive.

I was sweating despite the cool air. Sweat dripped down my forehead. I took off my glasses. I didn't need them. They'd be a liability in the fog.

I hesitated, undecided. Then I put the Sig away.

Still . . . some atavistic sense refused to allow me to go lumbering down the dock with my big hand of friendship extended. Boat theft is a thriving business. Thieves carry cable cutters and crowbars, ready-made clubs. Only a fool would walk into something like that.

And if they were friends? Well, the only reason a friend would sneak around at 2 a.m. is to play a practical joke.

Friend or foe, I decided to turn the tables.

Let the joke be on them.

I stood in the shadows of the deck, peering into the fog. Mangroves disappeared and reappeared before me and to my left. The van Gogh lights of the marina were to the right. Even in fog, if I crept along the walkway to shore, the lights would isolate me in silhouette.

The best option was to swim along the shoreline, then come up behind them. *Surprise, surprise! Guess who!*

Some part of me was glad that it was my only choice. I like black water. I like swimming at night where creatures of purer instinct cruise. There must be a compelling reason to swim, though, or else it is cheapened. It becomes a puerile device, like bungee-jumping or the craps tables at Vegas.

People naturally think that Sanibel runs north and south, like most barrier islands on Florida's Gulf coast. It doesn't. It curves from east to northwest. The north windows of my house look over the bay, and that is where I went. Putting one hand on the deck, the other on a floorbeam beneath the house, I lowered myself into the water. The water was warmer than the air; a mixture of salt and fresh.

I released air until my feet touched bottom a few feet below, leveled off, and used the pilings to pull myself along. I did everything by feel, seeing only the bioluminescent streaks of fish as they spooked away; hearing the crackle of their fast-twitch muscle fiber as they exploded to speed.

Unexpectedly, my face pressed into thick netting. It took me a moment to realize that it was the deep-water pen where I keep big fish. Already, my navigation was off.

I used the netting to pull myself along. Took my time, moving slowly to conserve oxygen. I'd been down for less than a minute. I wanted to surface far from the house.

The darkness of the innermost core of the brain would be a similar darkness. It was a darkness given occasional dimension by sparkling green light: bioluminescent plankton.

How many times had I used that darkness to travel unseen? The unexpected is defined by the fears of our enemies. Always choose the unexpected route.

THUNK

I nearly panicked when I felt a creature of great mass punch me in the side. I floundered momentarily for control, then it hit me again, *thunk*. Not hard, but in a measuring, experimental way.

It took a moment for my brain to compute what had happened.

On the other side of the thick mesh I kept two big bull sharks. There was a torpedo-sized female over two hundred pounds, plus a male close to a hundred. I do ongoing research on these unpredictable animals; animals that can be found three hundred miles up a freshwater river, or a mile below in the purest blue sea.

Now they were doing their own investigation. I could picture them circling inside the mesh, pectoral fins drooping into attack position as they touched deticles to flesh. It was an ancient interrogative: Was the thing alive? Was the thing edible?

True predators prefer darkness.

I pushed away from the netting, toward shore.

I was no different . . .

When I surfaced, someone was whistling . . .

It wasn't a normal, cheery kind of whistle. It was a thin, absent-minded sound, made through clenched teeth, no louder than a series of harsh breaths.

We all do it. A tune gets into our brain. We don't know it's there. During moments of deepest concentration, it slips out, a subliminal backdrop to the work at hand.

This man must have been a romantic. It was one of those old country-western torch tunes. I could hear little bits and snatches of it, as I drifted toward him through the fog. Couldn't identify it. Kept listening.

He was standing on the bank, near the steps of the board-walk. He was a black, vertical shape in the drifting plateaus of mist. I knew he was trying to decipher the obvious: Was the house occupied? Would someone awaken if he crept out, cut the lines to one of my boats and paddled it away?

Was he wearing something over his face?

The cloud parted momentarily. Yes. A tall man. Perhaps wide. A ball cap backwards on his head, a dark scarf tied over his nose.

The curtain closed and he vanished.

But I could still hear his absent-minded whistling . . .

The reason we remember song lyrics more easily than

poetry is that music is stored in the cleaner, mathematical side of our brains. Poetry is shoveled into the cluttered, creative side.

Some of the lyrics came to me as he whistled: *In the dah-dah glow I see her, dah-dah cryin' in the rain. . . .*

It took me a moment. *Blue Eyes Crying in the Rain.* That was the song. Willie Nelson sang it; maybe a woman country singer, too.

My hands were on the bottom now, pulling me along toward my visitor. Fingers touched muck and broad-bladed turtle grass. Only my back and the top of my head were on the surface of the water. I knew the silence of a saltwater croc; knew expectations no croc would never comprehend.

Love is like a dyin' ember, only dah-dah remains. . . .

Now I was nearly under the base of the boardwalk. Only a couple meters from the man. Staring up at him in darkness, he was still a charcoal shape. I floated there, belly touching the warm bottom, the toes of my shoes dug into the mud for quick traction.

I waited. I waited.

On the banks of billabongs in Australia's Northern Territory, I'd watched massive crocs wait for feral water buffalo to take just one step closer. Move too soon, the quarry runs free.

I'd learned from the best.

The whistling stopped. I watched the man take a step toward me; saw him turn slowly, slowly to check his backside. Watched him stumble slightly, disoriented by the fog, perhaps.

At that instant, I lunged from the water in one smooth motion, grabbed him chest high and held him, consciously

fighting the urge to slam him to the ground. He made a screaming, gurgling sound; a cry of pure terror. Screamed loud enough to
awaken people at the marina a hundred yards away. It was such
a frenzied, feminine sound that it froze even me momentarily.

I released him; pushed him away. "Take it easy, fella." I
squinted at him through the mist with my poor eyesight. The
screaming stopped, punctuated by a series of rapid, suctioning
breaths. He began to back away from me.

I dismissed the old, old voice in my head which told me to
immediately take physical control, to force him into some kind
of painful come-along hold, bury his face in the mud and lock
his arm up behind his shoulder blade until the bone grated.
Instead, I took a long, slow breath and said, "A little early to be
playing Halloween, isn't it?" Meaning the scarf over his face.

No reaction.

"Okay . . . let's make it real simple. You picked the wrong
place to rob. But we talk it over, I get the right answers, maybe
I won't even call the police."

Kathleen Rhodes would have been surprised and pleased
by that.

The dark shape continued to back away slowly. I kept pace
with him for a few moments, but then I stopped. "Hey—listen to
what I'm saying. If you run, I'll catch you. So what you're going to do right now is follow my orders. You're going to throw
your wallet on the ground; put your hands behind your head
and drop to your knees." I gave it a few seconds. *"Do it!"*

Nothing. Which is how I knew he was going to make a
break.

He backed away two more steps, then crouched slightly. It was like a telegraph signal. I was already moving when he pivoted. I jumped onto the boardwalk to cut off his angle of escape . . . and saw him stumble when he realized that he couldn't get past me. I stood there looking down at him, and heard a falsetto whine of frustration, a precursor to his shriek.

People on the verge of panic are more apt to react to words spoken softly. Nearly whispering, I said, "If you scream again, I'll shut off your air."

The whine became a sob, nothing more.

I stepped down and reached for the scarf that covered his face, then grabbed him roughly by the shirt when he stepped away . . . which is when I sensed a tremendous rush of wind from behind me that culminated in a withering impact. The force of it drove me away from the boardwalk into the water.

I rolled groggily, feeling starbursts in my head, expecting to be stomped at any second. I was down. I was hurt. They'd certainly come after me.

I pulled myself toward deeper water. For me, there is always safety in deep water. I lunged and dolphined until I was underwater, swimming hard. Then I surfaced.

He was gone. They were gone. . . .

Sculling on the surface near my shark pen, I heard an automobile engine start and tires spinning in the loose shell.

I pulled myself up onto the dock, found my glasses and took a towel from the stack near the outdoor shower, then I went into the lab and switched on a light. I thought about calling the Sanibel police, then decided against it. No laws had been broken; I hadn't given the intruders time even to get to my boat, which had certainly been their intent. I couldn't blame them. I've got a great boat.

Or was there another possibility?

I stood there for a moment, letting my mind clear. I took my glasses off and cleaned them. Along the west wall of my lab, there is a stainless steel dissecting table. Scattered on the table were the contents of a box recently delivered by a friend. There was a package of blue glass beads, dozens of arrowheads and a stunning impressionistic wooden carving of a cat; an Everglades panther, perhaps. The cat was upright in a kneeling position, its front legs pressed into its lap. The legs were suggestive of human arms. The carving was surprisingly heavy and there were still traces of paint to be seen if you used my good magnifying glass.

Only traces of paint because the thing was ancient, made by an American Indian artist many centuries ago, then found in a recent decade by a gifted child.

The child was the daughter of a friend of a friend who was now in trouble.

Okay, so what if the guys I'd surprised hadn't come to steal outboard motors? Was it just possible they knew the artifacts had been mailed to me, and they'd come to take them?

No, not likely. The artifacts were valuable, but not *that* valuable. To try something so risky for so little return wasn't rational. Even thieves tend to behave rationally.

Right?

Right.

One

The lady came asking for help on one of the most glorious autumn Fridays in the history of Sanibel Island. I was hunkered down, working in the engine well of my 24-foot trawl boat, up to my elbows in gas and oil and goo, when the familiar vibration of piney wood told me that someone was clomping along the dock, approaching my little house and lab.

It was just past noon. The September sun was bright overhead. I squinted upward to see chunky legs metronoming from within khaki safari shorts and the shampoo bounce of copper hair. Then a familiar silhouette was standing above me, hands on hips, boat shoe a-tappin'. So say hello to JoAnn Small-wood, part owner of the old Chris Craft cruiser, *Tiger Lily,* one of Dinkin's Bay Marina's gaudier floating homes. JoAnn is a heavy-hipped, busty lady with the sort of wide, handsome face that I associate with wheat fields or Wisconsin steetlights. She was already talking before she reached the mooring dock.

"I've got a problem, Doc. Can you spare me a minute or two?"

JoAnn's voice modulates an alto clarity. Women who are successful in business, trusted in politics, or who are very, very good teachers, speak with similar definition. But there was lots of anxiety in there, too. She was upset. No doubt about that.

I had a ratchet in my hand, and I was cleaning the ratchet head with a towel. As I fitted a spark plug into the rubber gasket, I said, "Mind if I finish this first?"

"Take your time." She looked toward the house. "Is Tomlinson inside?"

"Yeah. He's going through his record collection. He stores it here because he says his boat's too damp."

"Good. I'd like him to listen, too. He's weird, but he's smart."

"Right on both counts."

"No kidding. Did I tell you this? Rhonda and I cruised by his boat the other night and he had candles sticking out of each ear. Lighted candles. He was sitting naked on the bow, flames shooting up, his legs crossed. Inner ear purification, he told us. They were special hollow candles. The heat melts the earwax, or maybe it's the smoke that purifies the inside of his brain. Who knows?"

I said, "You just explained his sudden interest in listening to old records."

My net boat has an old standard six-cylinder engine. The name brand is "Pleasure Craft," but it is actually made by Ford. Plugs and points, and no computer gizmos of any kind. The engine had developed a nasty little miss and the habit of stalling when I attempted to dock. Boats that stall around the dock cause irritation and embarrassment, particularly flat-bottomed boats with wheelhouses and nets that act like sails in a wind.

This one was built of heavy cedar planking and brass screws; an old workhorse that I'd bought in Chokoloskee a couple of years ago and chugged up the inland waterway and used to dredge specimens for my business. She is solid as a slab of concrete and just about as nimble.

Thus the ratchet and a box of brand-new spark plugs.

I threaded the plug carefully, gave it just a tad of torque, swore softly when I clunked my head on the starter motor, then found the towel and began to wipe my hands.

"You're bleeding."

I looked at the rag. "Um-huh. Blood and oil. Mexicans say it's good luck. The blood, I mean—if you scrape your knuckles or something when you're working on an engine. So I'm lucky."

"And I called Tomlinson the weird one." The woman had a nice smile. "You two guys, you're really characters. You hold this whole crazy marina together."

I swung out of the boat and headed up the steps. "So come tell a couple of characters your problem."

Dinkin's Bay Marina does, indeed, attract its share of characters. Most of them arrive by boat, turning south off the Intracoastal at Marker 5 just west of the Sanibel Causeway and past the power lines. By car, they follow Sanibel's Tarpon Bay Road into the mangroves, through the gate to the bay.

Beyond the gate, in the shell parking lot, there's a community of wooden buildings that extends out onto the water via a latticework of wobbly docks. It is an unexpected anachronism on an island known for designer homes and elegant restaurants. There are plank tables for cleaning fish, a bait tank, and benches beneath a tin roof, so visitors have a place to sit while they eat the marina's sandwiches and chowder.

There is a gift shop, the Red Pelican, that offers sarongs and knickknacks and paintings by local artists. There is the marina office and store. Along with items that you might expect—fishing tackle and suntan oil—there are also items for sale that may be unexpected: strange ball caps in the shape of sharks or manatees, used books, foreign beers.

Inside the office, behind the glass counter, you will find stocky, pragmatic Mack, owner and manager. Jeth Nicholes, the fishing guide, lives alone in the efficiency apartment upstairs.

The other fifteen or twenty full-time residents live aboard boats: a garden variety of sailboats, cruisers and chunky little houseboats. They are umbilicaled to civilization via hoses and electrical conduits, and a couple have tiny satellite dishes. Toss off the umbilicals, though, and they are free again, alone and underway.

That is the illusion, anyway, and one reason they probably live aboard.

There are two exceptions: Tomlinson and myself. Tomlinson anchors his sailboat away from the docks, refusing what he calls "the poisonous delusion of self sufficiency." I live on the other side of the channel, occupying two weathered cottages under a single tin roof and separated by a breezy throughway, all built on stilts and connected to shore by ninety feet of old boardwalk. One house is my lab. The other is where I live.

Toss in a couple of other fishing guides, Captain Nels and Captain Felix, a cook, two clerks, plus a fluctuating number of wives-boyfriends-girlfriends-lovers, and you have the entire population of Dinkin's Bay.

The point to all this is that the marina is small enough to create the same dynamics and interdependencies as an extended family. The men are protective of the women in a brotherly way. The women chide or organize or comfort the men, depending on the situation or their sisterly mood. The metaphor is carried to the logical, responsible conclusion: romantic involvement is discouraged.

It is a common-sense rule and so never mentioned openly.

A short time back, Jeth and Janet Mueller broke the rule. They began a relationship: two shy people in love. It should have worked. Everyone expected it to work. But it didn't work, and the gradual collapse of the affair created an escalating uneasiness among the marina family.

Which is why Janet moved her houseboat up to Jensen's Marina on Captiva Island. Jensen's is a great place, just as quirky and kicked back as Dinkin's Bay, but her decision to move still left a cloud.

The point being, JoAnn seldom came alone to my house. Over the years, I'd felt an increasing sexual interest in her; she felt the same for me. I liked her plain looks and no-nonsense manner. She knew it. We'd discussed it. Which is why we took pains not to be alone together.

So, for the lady to come running to me, I knew that she had to have a very good reason. In her mind at least, whatever the problem was, it was serious.

Tomlinson was in my lab, futzing with my equipment, peering into the rows of jars that contain chemicals and preserved specimens: the nudibranches, sponges, octopi and unborn sharks that I collect, prepare and then sell to schools and research facilities around the country.

When I opened the door, he looked at us and said, "Today's the equinox, you know."

I said, "Huh?" Then I said to JoAnn, "Oh. He's talking about astronomy."

Tomlinson was wearing a Cubs baseball jersey and patched surfing shorts. He had a plastic bottle of sodium hydroxide in his hand, tossing it in the air like a baseball. The moment I realized what he was playing with, I glanced at the other chemicals on the shelf. Volatile, accidental combinations are easily made. But nothing else was missing.

He said, "Yeah, the autumnal equinox, just two days before the full moon. It makes me restless as hell, man. Add a full moon and I go damn near goofy. Nothing helps. I spent all morning meditating"—he shrugged—"whacked off a couple of times. Didn't dent it. It may be time for some serious medication."

JoAnn said uneasily, "I'd see a doctor about that. Yeah."

Now we were in the living room. JoAnn had a glass of iced tea. Tomlinson was on his third or fourth Amber Bock, sitting cross-legged on the tattered gray rug. I was in the chair by the north window where I keep my telescope and short-wave radio.

The ladies of the *Tiger Lily* do not posture. They are tough, direct women who speak their minds. It didn't take JoAnn long to get to the point. "Doc, I want you to do me a favor. I want you to listen to a story and tell me what sense you can make out of it."

"I'll do what I can."

"I want to hear your opinion, too, Tomlinson. That surprised look on your face, I know why. Let's be honest: you and me, we've never been what I'd call close buddies or *sympatico*. To each his own, right? But I know you've got a good brain in there somewhere. That's what everyone at the marina says, at least. So, yeah, I'd be interested in your opinion, too."

Tomlinson's stringy blond hair had recently been braided Rasta-style during what he called an "herbal research mission" to Belize. It might have had something to do with collecting chili seeds, but probably didn't.

Now Tomlinson tugged at one of the beaded ropes and

said, "Odds are good, sweetie, that the goods are *bound* to be a little odd when you meet a guy like me." He smiled his Buddha smile.

JoAnn looked at him blankly for a moment before deciding to refocus her attention on me. "It concerns a friend of mine, Doc. Her name's Della Copeland, but it used to be Smith before she married, back when our folks lived next door to each other on Marco Island. Della was like an aunt to me or an older sister—she was a junior in high school when I was in fifth grade. I didn't get along very well with my mom, so Della sort of played that role. We became very close and we've always stayed in touch, like family.

"Now Della lives in a trailer park down on Key Largo where she works, tends bar at a funky little place called the Mandalay. A good woman who's had a hard life, but she's making it okay. She's about forty-five or so now, but still attractive. Least, I've always thought so."

JoAnn must have noticed me glance at my watch, because she added quickly, "You need to know a little background first for you to understand the whole story. That she's no neurotic goofball. She has a steady job, she's good at what she does. Della's a woman who deserves to be taken seriously."

I said, "I will take your friend seriously, JoAnn, because I trust you and take you seriously."

I received a private little smile, those sharp green eyes intent.

"Fair enough, Doc. So I'll skip straight to the problem. Twice in the last couple of months, someone broke into

Della's trailer while she was working. They didn't steal anything, but they went through her stuff and all of her daughter's stuff. Della is very prissy neat. Anything gets moved,
she'd notice. Whoever did it must be good with locks because
they didn't break anything going in."

"She contacted the police?"

"Of course. That's the first thing she did."

I said, "But the police had no interest. If there's no sign of
breaking and entering, if nothing's been taken, what can they
do?"

"Exactly, that's just what happened. They told her to get
new locks, maybe install an alarm system. But, yeah, that was
it. In other words, don't bother them again unless something
really happened."

Tomlinson was following along closely, I could tell. He is
a fidgeter, a sky-gazer. There was a dazzling blue day through
the window, with smoky thunderheads forming beyond the
marina. The cloud towers were motionless, tinged with pink
and purple, so they seemed as permanent as an Arizona
canyonscape. Even so, Tomlinson was focused, intense, chewing at a strand of hair. He said, "Has your friend had any
hang-up phone calls?"

JoAnn seemed surprised by the question. "Why, yes. She
told me she'd received several calls like that. Phone rings, no
one there."

"She doesn't have caller ID?"

"Della does, but whoever called, it came up 'private number' or something like that. 'Shielded'? I can't remember the

exact wording, but she couldn't get the caller's number because I asked."

"Did they go through her clothing? Her personal items like her underwear?"

"Her clothing drawers, yes, and her daughter's. The underwear, I don't know about. You're thinking like this is some kind of sexual kink, right?"

Tomlinson was silent for a moment, eyes closed, before he said, "Your friend's daughter, she's dead, isn't she?"

JoAnn looked at me, surprised. She couldn't speak for a moment, but then she said. "How does he know that? There's no way he could know that. I was just getting ready to tell you."

I said, "It was the way you said, 'daughter'. The intonation. I got a sense that something was wrong, too. Not that she was dead, but that she was sick or in trouble or something. Don't let it bother you. Tomlinson specializes in the unexpected. Finish your story."

JoAnn was shaking her head. "If you say so, Doc, I will."

Tomlinson's eyes were still closed. He said very slowly, "This girl . . . this child? She died unexpectedly . . . and tragically." He paused, thinking. Then he said, "It was unexpected by everyone, including the child who died. Her last cognitive thought was surprise."

I said to JoAnn, "Relax. The guy's very good at making accurate inductions from simple things most people wouldn't notice. Think about it: It's unexpected and tragic whenever a child dies." Meaning that there was nothing to be surprised about.

He added, "In her way, she was gifted. Perhaps brilliant."

My explanation had done nothing to change the expression of astonishment on JoAnn's face. "Yes, she was very gifted. Dorothy, that was her name. She died fifteen years ago. I'd moved away from Marco by then." Now JoAnn returned her attention to me. "But how Dorothy died and why she died, that's another story. Della thinks the break-ins have something to do with her daughter's death, even though it happened a long time ago. That's why you need to hear the whole thing."

I got up, went to the little ship's galley, which is my kitchen, and got the jar of iced tea out of the fridge. I carried it into the living room as I said, "So tell us what happened, JoAnn. Me and the friendly witch doctor here, we're both at your disposal."

She grinned, then chuckled. Her face was attractive in an unspectacular way: a successful woman with her own life, her own mind and way of doing things.

Two

Della Copeland came from a family of fishermen and clammers, people who lived in tin-roofed houses and built their own boats. Like JoAnn's people, the Copelands and Smiths were spread around South Florida from Flamingo to West Palm. Della's parents had settled on Marco Island before the Mackle brothers turned it into a famous resort and forced land prices sky high.

When Della graduated from high school, college was not a consideration. Who had money for college? Instead, she went to work waitressing at the Marina Inn in Goodland, where she met a forty-year-old pompano fisherman out of

Upper Matecumbe, though his people were from Devil's Garden, north of the Big Cypress Indian Reservation. He was part Cracker, part Miccosukee and he looked a little like Clark Gable.

"His name was Darton Copeland," JoAnn told us. "He was a strange one, Dart was. I was just a girl, but even I could tell there was something unusual about him. The way he'd look at you, his eyes had this kind of . . . I don't know, like a glow to them. Have you ever seen a wolf?"

I said, "Photographs, that's all."

"They were like that. His eyes. They were a sort of brownish yellow. They had a light to them."

One thing about Della, JoAnn told us, she'd always had perfect judgment when it came to men. "Put her in a stadium full of a thousand guys and she'll pick the biggest loser and abuser every single time. Why some women are like that, I don't know. Sad thing is, they're usually the talented girls, the ones with a lot to offer. Maybe deep inside they're afraid they'd soar away if some jerk wasn't there to drag them down and make things ugly and safe."

Two months after meeting Copeland, Della was pregnant. She was eighteen years old. Copeland married her in a drunken wedding ceremony and vanished one month later, and four months before his daughter, Dorothy, was born.

"We heard rumors that Dart was living back on the Keys with one of his wives. He had several wives, it turned out. Della's daddy went looking for him a couple of times but never found him, so Della raised Dorothy on her own. This little blond-haired child, she looked like an angel, she really did. Big blue eyes and very, very long, delicate fingers. That's what I remember best about her. Her eyes and those fingers of hers, like stems on flowers.

"I was twelve when Dorothy was born, and mature for my age, so I baby-sat her lots of nights while Della did her waitressing. One thing I can tell you from personal experience, that child was different. I think you've been around me enough to know I'm the solid type, Doc. I'm a show-me person. I believe that when we die, we die, and that's all there is to it, and I've never bothered reading a newspaper zodiac column in my life. What a racket. But this child was different. I don't know what caused it or why, but she was."

JoAnn swirled the ice in her glass, looking to me for some reassurance. Tomlinson spoke before I had a chance. "You and Doc are a lot alike, no argument there. Branches of the same tough tree. And this guy"—he hammered his thumb at me—"is straight as cable. Or Wally Cleaver. You say the baby was different? We believe you."

"But how?" I asked.

"One thing was, she was always so . . . distant? Yeah, like only part of her was in the room with you. Only part of her heard what you said. Like most of her, maybe the most important part of her, was in an entirely different world."

Tomlinson was nodding, like he was enjoying the story but already way ahead. He asked, "Did the child tell you what she could hear?"

JoAnn paused for a moment, then said very carefully,

"She told me that she could hear voices. She told me that herself. One night she looked out the window—this was down on Marco Island; she couldn't have been more than six—Dorothy looked out the window and she said, 'There are so many people trying to talk to me, JoAnn. All the talking, it makes me so tired. They won't let me rest.' She was crying. Very upset."

Tomlinson said, "When you looked out the window, no one was there. It was dark. You were on an Indian mound or there was a shell mound near by."

She said, "You're doing it again. That's one of the things that irritates me about you, Tomlinson. I know you're smart. But the tricky part of you, I don't like. I need some honesty. How do you know that Dorothy heard people that no one else could see or hear?"

Tomlinson seemed amused but also a little wistful as he said, "Because, all my life—" He stopped, thought for a moment before he continued, "Because I've known someone who's the same way. It's a very strange gig, like being able to hear through the walls of a busy hotel. People like Dorothy are born on a dimensional cusp. Half in this world, but half out, which means they're aware of other worlds as they spin by."

"Other worlds."

"Absolutely. You don't know what I mean?"

JoAnn gave a little laugh as I said, "No one knows what you mean, Tomlinson. Let her finish the story."

"Okay, okay, but keep in mind a simple truth: classic physics has no explanation for randomness. The existence of many worlds is the only explanation for what appear to be random events. You get some time, read a paper called *The Copenhagen Interpretation of Quantum Mechanics*. It explains it all."

I rolled my eyes, but she was nodding. "Okay, different worlds. I thought you meant like ghosts."

"Yes, ghosts, too. Dorothy could probably hear ghosts. And believe me, ghosts are no different than people. Lots of loud, self-centered shits. They're worse than drunks."

"Ghosts, uh-huh." She looked at me. "Do you believe any of this?"

I said, "No, of course I don't. Half the time, he says things like that just to irritate me. Certain people are more perceptive than others, I believe that. I also believe that some people have a tough time dealing with their own imaginations."

Tomlinson tilted his bottle of beer upward, drinking, a familiar smile on his face as JoAnn said, "Whatever the reasons, Dorothy was different. The voices, the way she behaved, all sorts of things. But the main way she was different—and no one ever has explained this—the way she was most different was that she was good at finding things. Old stuff, stuff made of metal. Dorothy would go right to it. Lose your keys? A diamond ring on the beach? People would call Della and say, 'You mind if we borrow Dorothy for an hour or so?' She became kinda famous on Marco Island."

"That's a great gift," Tomlinson said. "Extraordinary."

"Yeah. I used to think so. But then, this gift of hers, her gift for finding things, I think that's what went and got that little girl killed."

JoAnn didn't know all the details. She'd been in her twenties when Dorothy died. She'd already moved away from Marco Island, but stayed in phone contact with Della Copeland.

"I knew that Dorothy made good grades in school, but that she was kind of a social outcast. An oddball, the other kids probably figured. Della worried about that. It hurt her that the girl didn't have friends. And there were always people around trying to get Dorothy to use her gift for reasons Della didn't like. I know she worried about that, too. As I said, Dorothy got kind of famous on the island."

Something that contributed to the girl's notoriety was her discovery of several pre-Columbian wooden artifacts. She found them in the muck of what everyone thought to be a mosquito drainage ditch. The ditch turned out to be a canal that had apparently been dredged by the Indians who'd once lived there, the Calusa.

"They figure the Indians dug the canal a thousand years ago for their canoes. So they could cross the island and not have to go off-shore."

"Marco Island?"

"No, it was a little island right next to Marco. I've forgotten the name of it. Anyway, Dorothy, she figured it out about the canal. Della was very excited, because the state archaeologists got involved and there was some talk of giving her a scholarship to college when she got old enough because of all the help she'd been to them. You can imagine what that meant to a single woman raising a daughter on waitress pay.

"The stuff Dorothy found was real valuable. There was a carving of a cat and two of these horrible-looking masks with real long noses. Because of the muck, they were in perfect condition; still had paint on them. I guess because they hadn't been exposed to air, or something. Also, there was this small wooden carving shaped like a paddle blade. About the size of both my palms together with very odd designs on it. Teardrops and a cross and circles within circles."

Tomlinson got up, found pencil and paper and drew what looked to be a bull's-eye over a Gaelic cross. "Was it like this?"

JoAnn squinched her jaw, thinking. "Maybe. I can't remember. The newspaper did a story on what she found, with photographs and everything. I might have it in a box if I can find it. I remember thinking that the cat looked Egyptian. You know the one I'm talking about? The tall one with its eyes closed and paws folded up. It was very strange stuff and Dorothy gave some of it to the archaeologists. The title was 'The Girl Who Finds Things.' The newspaper story, I mean."

That was just the beginning, JoAnn told us. Less than a year later, the child made another discovery. Digging near the edge of the same canal, she'd found human bones, a skull, several hundred blue Spanish chevron trade beads and what JoAnn called a golden tablet. It was the only one like it ever found. The Florida Indians weren't supposed to have had gold, but there it was, the child had uncovered it.

"Della was so happy, it breaks my heart now. She didn't know how much sadness that damn tablet was going to bring her. At the time, I guess it represented a little break in all her bad luck. The things Dorothy had found before were valuable, but the golden tablet was worth a bundle. It was her ticket to college, that's the way Della saw it."

Tomlinson said, "How big was the medallion?"

"Not big. Three or four ounces of gold I think Della said. About half the size of a postcard. Beautiful, very intricate, that's the way I remember it. But its real value was historical. I guess those things, the rare Indian stuff, sell for a lot."

"That's true, I'm afraid. The designs, were they similar to the designs on the wooden totem?"

"Totem? Oh, you mean the paddle. I never saw the totem in person, but I did see a picture. It was a good picture, but I really can't remember. The gold tablet, though, wow! I remember that. Really beautiful. Maybe they were kind of similar."

Tomlinson was nodding as if he'd expected it to be so. "What makes you think the medallion had something to do with the girl's death?"

"She began to have bad dreams. Nightmares, Della said, almost every night after she found the thing. The tablet was in the dreams. I don't know what the dreams were about. You can ask Della if you want." JoAnn placed her glass of tea on the hatch cover beside her. Her voice had reminded calm, but I noticed that her hand was shaking.

I said, "You're still upset by this. It happened, what? fifteen years ago?"

She was nodding. "I helped raise Dorothy, Doc. I carried that little girl around and burped her and did all the stuff that mothers do. She was a sweet kid. Very gentle and quick to cry at another person's pain.

"It rained the day of the funeral. One of those gray drizzles. It made her casket look so tiny and alone. I've never had children. Dorothy was about as close as I ever came. So, yes, it still hurts and it's still hard for me to talk about and it never goes away."

"How did she die?"

"The coroner ruled it a suicide, but Della still believes it was an accident. What happened was, one of the island teenagers found Dorothy hanging from the limb of a low tree. This was on Marco, way back on an Indian mound behind the house. Her hands weren't tied, her feet were touching the ground. So Della thinks maybe she was experimenting with unconsciousness. You know how kids will hold their breath, hoping to pass out, maybe have an out-of-body experience? Della thinks it was like that. But I don't know. I think the child was probably so scared by the demons she couldn't take it anymore."

"Her mother wants to believe it was an accident?"

"I think so."

"These break-ins," Tomlinson said, "it must be very hard on your friend, someone going through the clothing of her dead daughter."

JoAnn was nodding. "Della's a wreck. An absolute nervous wreck. It's brought all those old emotions back, all the pain. Someone is violating her daughter. That's the way Della sees it. All she has left is Dorothy's clothing and some photos, and last night it happened again.

"She got back from work and realized someone had taken out the drawers where she hides her keepsakes and very carefully slit open the sealing paper on the back of the drawers. You know that brown paper I'm talking about? She called the police—third time it'd happened, and by now they think she's a nut case, which she practically is after all she's been through."

"Was anything missing?"

"Some photos, she thinks. Maybe some of the Spanish beads that Dorothy found. She'd found a lot of beads and that's where Della hid some of them, in the little space between one of the drawers. But the point is, fellas, the woman is in trouble and needs a helping hand."

Meaning us.

There was no one else to choose from. Della had an estranged boyfriend who was an abuser. He couldn't be trusted. And her taste in men was so consistently bad that JoAnn had taken it upon herself to find a brotherly protector.

"What she could really use is a friend. Someone to stay there for a week or so, so she can at least get some sleep at night. As it is, she's terrified of every sound. If our magazine wasn't right on deadline, I'd be down there now. It's gonna be another week or so before I can get away, and she can't come up here because she's gotta work."

Years ago, recently divorced and broke, JoAnn and Rhonda Lister had founded a single-sheet weekly "newspaper" that they called *The Heat Islands Fishing Report,* and sold advertising. Within two years, it was a full-sized magazine and hugely successful. They'd both made a lot of money but they still ran every aspect of the business themselves. Busy ladies.

"Something else, Doc. It wouldn't hurt for someone to ask around, talk to the police and give them a nudge. The jerk who's scaring her needs to be caught. That's the only way she's going to feel comfortable living there."

I said, "That's not exactly my line of work."

"I know that, but a guy like you—kind of big and bookish and solid—the cops will pay attention to a guy like you. Plus you're smart. All I'm asking is, drive down there, talk to Della. Maybe you can help, maybe you can't. Spend a day or two. Are you that busy?"

Yes, I was that busy. I was under contract to collect for Mote Marine Laboratory, near Sarasota, one of the world's great research facilities. After months of paperwork and genuinely asinine government red tape, I'd finally received a Scientific Collecting Permit from the great state of Florida that allowed me to net and transport brood snook, a favorite game and food fish.

Getting the permit had been a bureaucratic nightmare. Never mind that the snook I caught would be released unharmed after we stripped them of milt and eggs. And never mind that Mote is the first to successfully raise snook in large quantities, then reintroduce them into the wild—something state biologists had tried but failed to do.

In the bowels of certain agencies, Florida's bureaucrats maintain a superior attitude of bored disapproval. I wanted to help save the snook population? Well, I'd have to jump through their silly hoops first! Which is why I'd missed the annual June spawning run and would now have to hustle to catch up.

I told JoAnn, "I'm supposed to deliver twenty brood snook to Mote by Saturday and, this late in the season, they're going to be very hard to find. I'll be working day and night. But if you want, I'll drive down to the Keys after that."

"I'll go." Tomlinson was standing. He found the trash bag nailed to the wall and carefully placed his empty bottle therein. "*No Más* is loaded and ready. I'll leave this afternoon with the outgoing tide. I'll need Della's phone number. There's gotta be a place to anchor near her trailer park. You said she lives on Key Largo? That's a pretty big island."

JoAnn gave me a searching, nervous look. One more private little exchange. "But Tomlinson, you've probably got stuff to do, too. Why don't you wait until Doc—"

"No reason to wait. I've been wanting to take a trip, just couldn't decide where. Now I know. Besides, I'm restless as hell. The equinox, that's the problem. And now I've got this full moon thing to deal with."

"I don't know. . . ."

"Only plans I had was playing harmonica for Jimmy Louis at the Hardware Store, then spend Sunday sitting around the pool bar at 'Tween Waters. So what else is new? That and I've got a monograph due to the International Academy of Sociology and Science—but screw it, they waited this long, they can last another month."

I received another visual inquiry. What should she do?

I told her, "You can trust Tomlinson. If he leaves today, he

can be on Key Largo by tomorrow afternoon. Let him check
it out, talk to people. If he thinks I can help, I'll drive down
next week."

"You're going to sail all that way? It's got to be a hundred
miles down to the Keys. I'll pay for a rental car if that would
be easier."

Tomlinson was looking around, seeing if he'd forgotten
anything, patting his pockets for sunglasses, getting ready to
leave. "Nope, a thousand miles of water is easier than a hundred miles of land. Know what? It's exactly what the doctor
ordered. Blue water, lots of clean air. Get some boat beneath
my feet. Yeah, that's the ticket. Then roll a couple of Maya
Mountain fatties to cleanse the receptors." Now he was going
out the screen door. His John Lennon sunglasses were still lying on the bookcase in plain sight. "I'm already getting some
very strong vibes about this one, and not totally unexpected.
Della and Dorothy, those two ladies have both keyed into
Karma 9-1-1. As of now, I'm on the job."

JoAnn was watching, listening, trying not to seem worried. *"Jesus."*

I told her, "He's actually not as airheaded as he seems.
Your friend will love him. Almost everyone does."

"If you say it's okay, Doc, I guess it must be."

"Then you'd better call Della. Tell her she's about to get
company."

Three

I spent the next three days working fourteen hours a day, trying to fill the order from Mote. I was up every morning before first light, cruising the beaches of Captiva Island and Cayo Costa, looking for spawning snook. They are a hardy species but delicate in their way. Most conventional nets will injure them, so I had to use a castnet. A castnet is a circular web of monofilament with lead weights seeded along the perimeter. It is ancient in its design and very effective. Three thousand years before Christ was born, men wading in water were throwing castnets at fish, and we still throw them pretty much the same way.

I'd had this net custom-made just for snook. It was huge: twenty-four feet in diameter. It was woven of much heavier, finer mesh than most nets. Because there was more mass and resistance, the net required twice the lead weight to make it sink fast enough. Throw a castnet properly and it will open like a parachute, trapping everything beneath. Throw it improperly and it will spook every fish around. A standard bait net weighs maybe fifteen pounds. This monster weighed nearly thirty pounds dry, and so, good throw or bad, it was like tossing a small refrigerator. And I was making forty to fifty throws a day, without much success.

It's tiring enough to spend all day in the heat of a September sun, poling a boat, stalking fish, anchoring and re-anchoring. Add this man-killer net to the equation and you are toying with debility.

So, at the end of each day, when the work was finished, I would limp up the steps to my little house, strip off my sodden, filthy shirt and shorts, and stand under the outdoor shower for half an hour, my muscles quivering, threatening to cramp. Then it was into fresh clothes, maybe some snapper or grouper on the grill if I could manage, or else hobble over to Timber's Restaurant for dinner. After that, I would sit on the porch, my feet propped up on the railing, beer in hand, and wait for sunset, because it is inappropriate for a grown man to go to bed before it's dark, and I do have some pride.

A couple of days after I watched *No Más* make the tricky jibes out the channel, bound for the Keys, JoAnn stopped by with a snack of sandwiches and one of those collapsible coolers filled with ice and bottles of beer.

It was a Sunday. Beyond the mangroves, the sunset horizon was a lemon sphere streaked with blue. On Sanibel's beach side, the Gulf of Mexico absorbed light and deflected colors skyward.

She asked me, "Did you talk to Tomlinson last night?"

I was in a porch chair as usual. One more tough day behind me in which I'd managed to fall off the poling platform and damn near drown with thirty-some pounds of net tied to my wrist. But I'd also added five good brood snook to my holding tank.

I sipped the bottle of beer she'd placed in my hand and said, "For the last three or four days, I haven't answered the phone, returned messages, nothing. Haven't checked my mail or paid bills. I'm on autopilot. So the answer is no."

"He said he was going to try and call. Something else, he took the other stuff Dorothy found, all the remaining artifacts, put them in a box and mailed them to you. So the thieves wouldn't know where to look. So now I understand why you haven't gotten it yet."

"Like what?"

"That Egyptian-looking cat I told you about? He mailed it insured, priority, plus some other things Della wanted to protect. Nothing really valuable, except for maybe the cat, but Della's lost enough. You don't mind, I'll stop at the post office tomorrow and pick it up. I'll get your mail while I'm at it, drop it all by tomorrow morning."

"Does he want me to open the box?"

"You can ask him when he calls. But I wouldn't mind seeing that cat again."

"If I talk to him, I will. Just before I fall into bed, I unplug the phone. The idea of waking up to Tomlinson on a talking jag is not pleasant. I've been through that too many times."

She pulled a chair close enough to the railing so that she could prop her feet up beside mine. I got a whiff of shampoo and subtle, indefinable female odors.

It was a calm evening. The saltwater lake that is Dinkin's Bay spread away in shaded increments of brass and pewter and pearl. Pelicans roosted heavily in nearby mangroves, while white ibis crossed the bay in gooselike formation.

The moon, one day past full, would soon balloon up over the bay.

She watched the ibis for a moment before she said, "I figured there was a reason he couldn't get you. Last night, he kept me on the phone for more than an hour. And it's not easy to call him because he and Della are either at the bar where she works or he's aboard his boat. There's a lot of stuff he wants to tell you about the gold medallion that Dorothy found. The wooden paddle thing, too. What he calls the totem. The medallion and the totem, that's all he talked about. He says it's related. The break-ins, Dorothy's death, everything. There's some books he wants you to find and read."

"I barely have time to eat. If I don't get those snook to Mote by Saturday, they may not renew my contract. Getting permits from the state was a nightmare."

"Then I'll go to the library for you, maybe tell you about it. The history stuff, I think it's interesting."

I nodded, staring at JoAnn's profile. It's surprising, but if we interact with a person day after day in a benign setting, we cease to see them as a specific, physical being. Their physical characteristics are blurred by familiarity.

Now, for the first time, it seemed, I noticed that JoAnn had an elegant nose and chin. In the sunset light, her eyes were iridescent jade and she had good, clear skin beneath the smile lines and wrinkles of thirty-some years in the Florida sun.

I believe that sexual awareness is chemically induced and the dialogue necessary to catalyze that reaction takes place on many levels. Through eye contact or body positioning, an interrogative exchange takes place: *Are you? Would you? May I?*

But first, the synapses must open the door to whatever chemical it is that keys sexual interest.

I sat there staring at her, then she was staring at me, her eyes making cursory contact, then deeper contact. We sat there in a momentary trance, the two of us, before we realized what was happening. Still looking at me, JoAnn touched her fingers to my wrist. "Doc? I think I probably shouldn't stop here for a while."

I smiled; leaned to kiss her, then paused, undecided. Then I kissed her on the forehead and stood quickly. "I'll make it easy on both of us. I'm taking my boat up to Mote tomorrow. It'll give us both a break."

The next morning, a Monday, I packed my skiff with

castnet, ice, food, water and beer, plus a tent with sand fly netting, just in case, and set off on what might be a two- or three-day expedition.

To paraphrase an old-time Key West writer and fisherman, Florida's hurricane months, June through November, have the finest kind of weather when there's not a blow. The weather during this particular autumn was fine, indeed. So why not vanish for a little while? Furthermore, to quote Tomlinson, I needed to get some boat beneath my feet.

Just after first light, I idled into the marina docks and kibitzed with the skiff guides as I topped off the oil reservoir and fuel tank.

Captain Felix called over that he'd found some small chunk of wreckage about seven miles off the lighthouse. "Maybe some old World War Two plane, one of the trainers they used to fly out of Buckingham," he said. "We'll have to dive it when the water clears."

Dieter Rasmussen, a retired Munich psychopharmacologist, was up early as usual. He and his gorgeous Grand Banks trawler, *Das Stasi,* were a recent addition to A Dock. He's a big guy with a shaved head, good-looking—judging from the reaction of local women—brilliant, rich, and he apparently loves the kicked-back, happy life of Dinkin's Bay. He called out a greeting. I nodded in reply.

Then Jeth stopped to talk. Recently turned thirty, he's a big, good-looking guy with straight black hair, all shoulders and narrow hips. He'd just taken delivery of a 20-foot Shoalwater with a console tower that was light years nicer than any-thing he'd ever run before.

I complimented him, adding, "From the tower, I bet it's a lot easier for you to spot fish."

"Man-oh-man, that's the truth! Dave Godfrey, up to Cap-tiva, he told me this boat would increase my fish production thirty percent and I bet he's right!"

Early morning at a fishing marina has a fresh, anything-can-happen mood that is cheerful and frantic and full of ex-pectation. The guides hosed their skiffs after catching bait, then loaded on drinks and ice for their anglers, while coffee in big Styrofoam cups steamed within their hands.

One by one, they waved at me as I idled toward the channel.

I should have felt better than I did, but I was still fretting about how close I'd come to kissing JoAnn. That was a line not to be crossed, and we both knew it. I told myself that the uneasiness between us was temporary, but I knew that it was a lie and that it would be awhile before JoAnn and I would feel comfortable together. There is no such thing as casual sex. It can elevate one's sense of self-worth or diminish it pro-portionally. It always, always changes a relationship, some-times for better, often for worse. Each and every new partner extracts some thing from us; a little piece of something that is innermost and private. Sadly, it is one of the most common ways of ending a friendship.

Four

Water is a dependable antidote for nearly anything that is troubling, including regret, so I did not stay upset
at myself for long.

I flew my little skiff out the channel from Dinkin's Bay,
past Woodring Point, then banked northwest into Pine Island
Sound, running a golden rind of sandbar that was the demarcation of mangrove and turtle grass.

It was a powder-blue morning, summer-slick but with a
September horizon. The meld of sea and sky created a translu-
cent sphere into which I seemed to be traveling at speed; a liquid void on which floated dark islands that were as solitary as I.

Before me, black diving birds flushed to desperate flight while, behind, an arrowing wake expanded in slow proportion to the velocity of my fast boat. I stood at the wheel, feeling the wind, feeling the water beneath me.

Water is a mirror until you learn to use it as a lens. Through Polarized sunglasses, the sea bottom was iridescent. Beneath and beyond me were green fields of turtle grass that were vein-worked by riverine trenches of deeper water and craters of sand. On a low tide, I could use those submerged creeks and rivers to cross the flat as if traveling a mountain road.

There were valleys and hills and ridges below me, too, where lives were being lived. Tunicates and sea hydroids and sponges flew past in a blur. I spooked a school of redfish that angled away as a herd, pushing an acre of waking water. A stingray flapped off in an explosion so abrupt that I could feel the shock wave through the fiberglass skin of my skiff.

I stood for a while, then I sat behind the wheel in the heat and light, comfortable and alone, on the move.

Jeth was not the only one at the marina who'd recently taken delivery on a new boat. I am not a gadget person. No one has ever accused me of being faddish, nor am I normally attracted to gaudy, big-horsepower machinery. My old Chevy pickup truck has a tough time making it up steep hills and it may be one of the last vehicles in Florida that doesn't have air conditioning. I am, however, very picky about boats. So when it came time to get rid of my old skiff, I researched my options as carefully as I would have researched fine optics before buying a microscope.

There is no such thing as a perfect boat, so selection is a process of reasonable compromise. There were my own quirks to consider. The number of cars in Florida has nearly doubled in the last ten years, and many of those vehicles, it seems, end up touring Sanibel and Captiva. Traffic is terrible and I hate to drive.

As a result, I use my boat the way most people use their car. Nearly all of my shopping is done through the mail or a couple of blocks from the marina at Bailey's General Store. Otherwise, if I can't get there by water, I usually don't go.

So I needed a skiff that could take a sea. It had to be comfortable, dry and fast. Because of my work, it also had to be capable of running in very shallow water.

I spoke to a bunch of fishermen, I test-drove dozens of hulls. I ended up buying one of the great little boats in the world, an 18-foot Maverick, which is built over on the east coast, Fort Pierce. For power, I added an equally classic engine, a 200-horsepower Yamaha V-Max. To avoid attention from the Marine Patrol, I'd opted for a cowling that read: *150*. Why advertise?

The stunning and sometimes scary result of this volatile combination was an engine that was ghostly quiet on a boat that steered like a BMW. If the crunch was every really on and I needed to get someplace in a hurry, I could run seventy miles an hour in a foot of water. Which I sincerely hope never happens. At fifty, my eyes begin to water; at sixty, the world begins to flutter like film from a bad projector. But seventy-plus was there if I had to outrun a storm or if there was an emergency.

On this calm Monday morning, though, I ran north at a comfortable forty miles per hour, enjoying myself, taking in the scenery. I stopped and took a quick swim at Useppa Island. Stopped in at the Temptation Restaurant on Boca Grande for lunch; sat at the bar and talked with Tina while Annie the fortuneteller read my Tarot cards.

"Says here, you're due to have some women problems," Annie told me.

I replied, "Really? Gee, that's uncanny. Those cards say anything about me getting another beer?"

The weather held, so I cut through into the Gulf at Gasparilla Pass and ran the outside beaches along Don Pedro Island. Just south of Englewood, off Stump Pass, I got very lucky and spotted two large balls of spawning snook working their way up the beach.

The word "ball" is appropriate because the spawning ceremony consists of many, many male fish twisting and turning around one or more much larger females. These fish were so focused on their reproductive mandate that they didn't notice as I used the push pole to swing my skiff into position above them.

I made two throws of my gigantic cast net and put six fine gravid females into my live well. Just looking at them gave me pleasure. A snook is an impressive animal, both in terms of behavior and physical beauty. It has a cartilaginous jaw that flares anvil-like beneath black carnivore eyes. The eyes are ringed with gold, its skin is pewter-bright, fringed with yellow, and there is an armorwork of scales covering a dense coniform body. It is a heavy, functional, predator's body. Beauty is secondary; a stroke of hereditary luck. Such creatures evolve over thousands of years, refine a perfect genetic design, then prosper for thousands of years more, unchanged. The black lateral line is a sporty touch, not unlike a racing stripe. It is appropriate for this very fast animal.

Trouble is, snook are not fast enough to outrun nutrient pollution from thousands of Florida golf courses. They are not fast enough to outrun illegal stop nets. They are not fast enough to outrun high-tech fishing machines such as mine. A million years of evolution did not anticipate the previous busy, brilliant and sometimes destructive century. Which is why I was so pleased to play a role in Mote's superb stock-enhancement program.

So I was feeling pretty good as I sped along the beaches past Englewood, Siesta Key and Lido Beach on my way to the docks of Mote Marine. Every now and again my mind would slip and I would think about JoAnn, the unexpected sexual charge at her touch, and I would scold myself, using Jeth and Janet as an example. See what happened when marina people dated?

I also thought about Tomlinson down there on Key Largo. Someone had been breaking into the trailer of a waitress to loot the mementos of a child. The mother had been sufficiently upset to allow Tomlinson to box her remaining valuables and ship them to a stranger.

It couldn't be important. Some freak on the prowl. There

are so damn many freaks on the prowl these days. Still, I have a logical mind that probes and prods when behavior, human or otherwise, does not follow sequential, rational patterns.

I kept asking myself a simple question: *Why?*

Three days later, I would ask it again when I learned that someone had dug up the grave of the late and long-dead Dorothy Copeland.

Mote Marine Lab is one of a very few independent marine research facilities that still survive in the U.S. The lab and aquarium consist of a half-dozen modern buildings and several deep-water holding pools on an eleven-acre campus fronted by sea grapes, palms and Sarasota Bay. About fifty scientists work at the lab, plus hundreds of volunteers. Because it is privately funded, the imperative of private enterprise is very much in effect: if Mote Marine does not excel, it is out of business. If Mote Marine's employees do not excel, they are out of a job. As a result, this unusual lab is a busy and productive place.

But it wasn't the lab that was on my mind.

Kathleen Rhodes's pretty trawler, *The Darwin C.,* was moored at Mote's L Dock, just down from the Salty Dog bar and restaurant. The windows of its mahogany wheelhouse were dark: no one home. Tied astern of the trawler was Capt. Peter O'Rourke's collecting boat, *Ono III.*

I thought I'd put Kathleen out of my mind and out of my life. If she wanted to take a break from what had become an intense physical and emotional relationship, that was just fine with me.

Or was it?

Seeing the trawler brought back memories of the nights I'd spent aboard. It brought back the shape and scent of her; the memory of her intellect and her lucid, scientist's view of life. Independent people seem to be increasingly rare. She was one of the few.

Add self-reliant to the list, too.

After getting her Ph.D. from Stanford, Kathleen had spent two years bringing her trawler down Baja through the Sea of Cortez to the Panama Canal, then along the Gulf of Mexico to Sarasota. It is not an easy trip for a single-handed sailor, female or male, but she'd made it without incident, collecting specimens and data the whole long way.

The sons and daughters of wealthy parents can be a troubled, undependable lot. An unfailing financial safety net does not contribute to character. But Kathleen was not affected by her family's money. She was a spectacular woman, indeed, and seeing her empty boat produced an unexpected stab of disappointment.

If I didn't care, why was I already inventing reasons to contact her while I was at Mote?

I tied off my skiff and found Pete O'Rourke in his funky little waterside office. Pete is in charge of collecting for Mote, and he is the perfect choice because he is an unusual combination: a first-rate fishing guide who possesses the clear eye and intellect of a scientist. His office reflects the same dual personality.

We sat talking for a few minutes amid stacks of fishing

gear, lures, stuffed fish, scuba tanks, test tubes and journals. Through the front window, beyond the file cabinets and ratty green carpet, I could see the New Pass swing bridge and the cabin of Kathleen's boat.

It took some effort to look away.

Then I didn't have to think of it because Pete and I were busy transferring the snook I'd brought. We put them into what is essentially an oxygenated wheelbarrow and rolled them, two at a time, to the massive brood tank. In the tank were male snook. By carefully controlling temperature and lighting, the Mote scientists could trick the fish's biological clocks into believing it was eternally spring with many, many moonlit spawning nights.

Before releasing the females, though, Pete and I carefully stripped them of eggs. A big female will carry a million and a half eggs, each not much bigger than the head of a pin. Touch their bellies, and roe flows as if from a dispenser.

We captured the eggs in bags of seawater, then mixed them with milt from male fish. Then we deposited the fertilized eggs into 2,000-gallon incubator tanks.

At some time during the next day, thousands of tiny snook would hatch, none much bigger than mosquito larvae. They would feed on algae and rotifers, then brine shrimp. In a couple of weeks, they would look like the truly remarkable animals they are.

Back in Pete's office, he caught me looking at Kathleen's trawler. By not mentioning her name, I had, apparently, underlined my interest in her, which is probably why he looked so uncomfortable. Finally, he said, "A guy as smart as you, it's hard to believe you can be such a big bonehead."

I said, "Pardon me, Pete."

"Don't pretend you don't know what I'm talking about. Kathleen. Or maybe you're back to calling her Dr. Rhodes now. A woman like that, a fine scientist and a hell of a talented musician. All the brains and class in the world, plus legs up to her shoulders and you're about to let her get away? Or maybe you already have."

I shrugged, letting him know that it was no big deal. "We decided to take a break, that's all. Give ourselves some time to think things over. It was mutual. Besides, I was already involved with a very nice woman when Kathleen and I met."

"The one from Tampa, you mean."

How did he know that? I said, "There aren't many secrets between you scientific types, I guess."

"You know better. But fishing guides tend to be talkative. The Tampa woman who was separated but ended up going back to her husband. I know the one you're talking about. You stopped seeing Kathleen for her?"

"There were other reasons, too."

"What bullshit." He was smiling, shaking his head. "The moratorium was all Kathleen's idea. She told me. She also told me that she hoped like hell you'd miss her and call and insist that you get back together again. It was a test. You don't know by now that people in love give each other little tests?"

"Nope. Apparently, it's not the sort of thing you can study for."

He said, "We'd sit here talking, Kathleen and me, and I'd catch her staring out the window, the same expression you had on your face a few seconds ago. Hoping to see you pull up to the dock, just like you were hoping to see her."

The man was infuriating, but he also happened to be right. I said, "Okay, so I was hoping to see her. I was also dumb and stubborn and not particularly perceptive. When it comes to women, what else is new? So maybe what I should do right now is stroll over to Dr. Rhodes's office and apologize. Then maybe Kathleen and I can take you and your pretty wife out to dinner. How's Chinese sound?"

O'Rourke wasn't smiling now. "It sounds great but you're not going to find Kathleen in her office. Or anywhere else around here."

I said, "Huh?"

"Just what I said. She waited, what, nearly three months? A couple times I told her, 'Hey, think of some excuse, drive to Sanibel and visit the guy! Let him know how you feel.' But you two, you're both so damn logical and analytical. She made me promise not to call you, either. So what I'm getting to is, she met a guy. He plays football for Tampa Bay. Not at all her type, but at least he was smart enough to figure out how a telephone works. He's on injured reserve, so they flew to Mexico last week for that sawfish project she's been doing, plus so steroid man can see what life is like in the true tropics. The football player, I'm talking about."

When I didn't say anything for a moment, he clapped me on the shoulder as he crossed the room. "Those two, they're not going to hit it off. So maybe it's not too late. Anyway, Kathleen told me to deliver this if you stopped being stubborn long enough to ask about her."

He held out a blue envelope, which was addressed to me in her tiny, precise hand. When I started to open it, O'Rourke said, "Christ, don't read the damn thing in front of me! I feel bad enough as it is. Go back to your boat, catch us some more fat brood snook. You still owe me five or six fish, right? We need them by Saturday, don't forget!" He pointed me toward the dock before adding, "That way you can suffer in private."

In the afternoon, I found a deserted stretch of beach on one of the barrier islands, Cayo Costa, and I camped between a fringe of coconut palms and the water. I stayed two nights.

By the end of the first day, all the beer was gone and most of the food. The morning of the second day, depressed and feeling sluggish with a hangover, I told myself that twenty-four hours of fasting and a marathon workout was not only what I needed but what I deserved.

It has been a lifelong practice of mine. When things are going badly, or when I'm dissatisfied with my own work or behavior, I devise a new and improved Dumb Ass Triathlon. The events are determined by my environment. There must be at least two different disciplines and three different punishing events.

For me, it's an effective way of stopping negative momentum and of jump-starting a change in personal behavior. It is also an effective way to give myself a personal kick in the butt.

Punishment is the order of the day.

So I punished myself.

I stripped down to Nikes and running shorts and lumbered along the beach to the north point of the island, then all the way back to my camp, about eight miles.

Then I traded in the shoes for goggles and swam almost to the south point of the island—three miles, and all the harder because, toward the very end, I was pulling myself along against an outgoing tide.

Finally, I jogged and hobbled barefooted back to camp, where I drank a half gallon of water, cleaned my glasses, then laid down beneath a sun tarp to read.

Kathleen's letter was troubling. It was troubling because she wrote without anger nor any attempt to manipulate. There is no criticism so unsettling as the truth, and her observations were logically presented. Perhaps they were accurate, perhaps not.

Certain sentences stood out. I read and reread them.

She wrote: *Marion, You have a wonderful brain and a heart that is bigger than you know, but you are a strange man. Your heart and your brain don't seem to be connected . . .*

She wrote: *I remember the look on your face when that drunk stumbled out of the bushes and surprised us. I learned something I couldn't have learned any other way. I learned that you have a capacity for violence without emotion. No emotion that I could see. No anger, no fear. The only primate who has that capacity is man, and very, very few of them. It frightened me. It should frighten you. . . .*

She wrote: *I've found few men as attractive as you, but neither have I felt so isolated during intimacy. As thoughtful as you are, part of you is always in some faraway place. I wish I knew that place. I would have gladly traveled there with you . . .*

She wrote: *Humans aren't driven to behavior for which we are not coded, nor do we long for something unless we've lost it. One or both may explain how you are different from other people. You have always been alone, Marion. I think you will always be alone. . . .*

The portrait that emerged wasn't very flattering. How long had Kathleen and I dated? Seven months off and on, then four months exclusively. Could she really have gotten to know me so well in so short a time?

As I lay on the sand listening to the respiratory wash of waves, the whistle of sea birds, I considered the validity of her observations.

I remembered the night that the drunk had come charging at us out of the shadows. We'd had dinner in downtown Sarasota and were walking along the waterfront to her car. We were talking, looking at the mast lights of sailboats. Unexpectedly, a big man was reaching for her, only a few meters away. Yes, he'd stumbled, but there was no way I could have known that.

I consider my reaction very practical, not extreme. I'd turned the man without much effort, then pinned him to the sidewalk until I was certain of his intentions. It had been methodical, not violent. Of course I hadn't been emotional. In such a situation, of what possible value was emotion? Yet, the woman found fault with my behavior. It made no sense.

I was also surprised by the depth of her affection. She mentioned her attraction and implied that she would have traveled with me anywhere. Yet, she'd never openly voiced her feelings, so how was I supposed to know? Had I missed some signal?

Perhaps. I thought about the night Kathleen had played at a big bayside folk concert, several hundred people listening. This was on the grass of pretty Coolidge Park, just across the bridge from Saint Armand's Key—could picture her seated, head tilted above guitar, lost in the music, brown hair hanging down over strings that her fingers touched knowingly, lovingly, long legs crossed, her face in the spotlight.

I thought about a particular song she'd played. It was a Judy Collins song or maybe a Joni Mitchell song, one of the vocal greats from an unstable decade. The song was wistful and resigned, something about a woman yearning to follow her cowboy lover. After the song, Kathleen had looked pointedly at me and nodded.

Was that the sort of cryptic message that I was supposed to process and correctly interpret? If so, I'd missed badly. It was surprising. Such silent dialogue is something that I'm usually good at deciphering. At least, that's what I've always thought.

Finally, there was her most troubling claim: that I was a loner and would always be alone.

No, that definitely wasn't true, I told myself. I liked people and people seemed to like and trust me. I had a family at Dinkin's Bay Marina. The point could not be argued. There were people there to whom I was dedicated and who reciprocated without question. There was Tomlinson, Mack and Jeth, Janet, Rhonda and JoAnn, plus several others.

See, I wasn't alone. No way. Not me.

Five

I found out about the grave robbery on Friday afternoon. I came cometing across the bay, doing sixty easy, a smoky, lucent veil of rain and electricity right on my tail. In hurricane season, squalls come blowing up out of nowhere.

I'd just dropped off the last of the snook to Mote. I came swinging up to the dock, to find JoAnn standing above me on the porch outside my stilthouse. She was wearing faded cotton slacks and a pale pink jersey banded with horizontal stripes that I associate with French painters or British seamen of long ago. Her eyes were red; she'd been crying.

As I tied my boat, she said, "They dug her up, Doc. I've

been trying to get in touch with you. The county people, the ones from Marco, they called Della."

I said, "They *what?*"

"Someone dug up Dorothy's grave. She was in the old town cemetery down on Marco Island. They dug her up and tried to get into her casket. Who knows what they took out? Tomlinson says it's time for you to get involved. He needs your help down there."

"Let me get the lines on my skiff," I told her, "then we'll talk."

Della had called that morning in hysterics. JoAnn could hear Tomlinson in the background trying to comfort her. "I picked up the phone and she's yelling, 'Oh, they've hurt my little girl again. They've hurt my baby!' Panicky stuff. Terrible, like after a car wreck. I thought she was drunk or the pressure had finally pushed her over the edge, until Tomlinson took the phone and told me what happened."

JoAnn and I were sitting in caneback chairs in the little roofed walkway between my house and lab. In gentler days, such passages were known as dog trots. Listening to JoAnn's story, I was reminded that the gentler days of Florida, if such days actually existed, were long gone.

Inside, on the hatch-cover table, was the opened box of artifacts that Tomlinson had mailed, with the beads, the arrowheads and the cat. The similarities to Egyptian art were not apparent to me, but then I know next to nothing about the subject.

"If you think that's pretty," she said, "you ought to see the medallion. The way I remember it, so intricate and beautiful, it takes your breath away. Maybe you'll see it if Della still has it or knows where it is."

"Maybe I will."

Beside the carving was a bushel basket of unopened mail, all delivered by JoAnn two days before.

My ability to ignore mail has grown stronger over the years. I view it as a sign of maturity.

It was dusk. The storm cell was a foggy mushroom cloud above us. Thunder vibrated in the windows; lightning popped and sizzled outside. Rain flowed down off my tin roof, so that the mangroves and bay beyond were blurred as if through a waterfall.

A waterfall is exactly what it was.

To take advantage, I'd slid open the cover of my thousand-gallon rain cistern so that it might fill faster, then, standing naked in the rain, shampooed and sluiced away three days of beach sand before joining JoAnn.

Because it seemed like a good idea to go to a primary source, I'd already tried to phone Tomlinson at Della's trailer. While JoAnn waited outside, I left a message on the recorder. I also called the place Della worked, the Mandalay, on Key Largo. They weren't at the restaurant, either, so I left another message: "Have him call, ASAP."

Tomlinson, apparently, was already a popular fixture on the island because the waitress who answered said, "You callin' for Tommy-san? Oh, I just love that guy! 'Course I'll give him the message if ya'll're a friend a' his."

Tommy-san? Tomlinson collected nicknames as quickly as house pets and small children.

So now I was sitting beside JoAnn while she told me what she knew, which wasn't much. Her voice provided a steady alto tempo to the lightning and chilly rain.

"Early this morning," she began, "one of the Marco Island cops was driving past the old town cemetery. It was still dark and he noticed some kind of light through the trees. How well do you know Marco, Doc?"

"Not well. It's changed a lot. Years ago, I spent some time on the island. It was already pretty heavily developed. My uncle had a ranch in Mango, south of there in the Everglades."

"Then you probably saw the cemetery but didn't notice it. It's a little tiny thing, real easy to miss. There're some pine trees and old tombstones. When we were kids, we used to say the place was haunted. There're all these old graves of sailors and fishermen, and we'd dare each other to walk through it at night. Which is what the cop thought, it was just kids playing around. So he shined his spotlight and saw at least two people run off, maybe more. He told Tomlinson he couldn't be sure, but didn't think it was important. He'd scared them, so the cop drove away."

At first light, though, the cemetery maintenance man found that Dorothy Copeland's grave had been exhumed. After a check of the cemetery records, they'd tracked down Della, who still paid a yearly fee to keep her daughter's plot trimmed and neat.

"What a nightmare for Della," JoAnn said. "The poor

lady's been through so much. The cops asked her for permission to rebury her, but Della said no. She wants us to meet there tomorrow and have a little ceremony. Say goodbye to her little girl one last time, plus she thinks something might be missing from the casket."

"So they *did* get the casket open."

"She's not sure. The guy from the funeral home, the guy who called Della, he didn't think so. He opened it with the some official what-a-ya-call-it standing by. The medical examiner? They opened it just to be sure and he said everything appeared normal. Whatever that means. But only Della would know, because of something she put in there when Dorothy was buried."

"Did she say what it was?"

"I didn't hardly talk to her at all, she was in such hysterics. Tomlinson, he's the one told me. You two—you and Tomlinson—he said you guys need to take a look inside the casket, because he doesn't think Della can deal with it emotionally. He said that's why you need to do some reading first. To understand what it is you might find."

I'd already noticed that, along with the blanket, she had a book and some papers in her lap. She'd been to the library.

Over the years, in different parts of the world, I'd dealt with enough drug people to know that they are prone to fixation. If the drug person happens to be dangerous, it is a wise thing to take his fixations seriously.

Tomlinson was a drug person, always would be. The difference was, he wasn't dangerous.

Hadn't been dangerous for many years, anyway.

I said, "Could you just paraphrase so I don't have to read through all that? I don't see the point. It seems obvious that the girl found something that someone wants badly enough to risk digging up a grave in a public cemetery. Financial gain, that's what robbery's all about."

"Tomlinson says no, that's not it. Money has nothing to do with it. He says it's a lot more complicated. Like an ancient-curse sort of deal, only it's not a curse. They're after things that will give them more power. That's why they're after what Dorothy found. I'll sum it up and make it quick. It can't hurt at least to listen, can it?"

Six

What Tomlinson had her find at the
Sanibel Library were a couple of books plus translations of
letters from Spanish Jesuits who'd been sent to what is now
the west coast of Florida. This was back in the late 1500s,
when missionaries were an important political arm of colo-
nialism.

When Europeans arrived in Florida, they found a complex society living on the Gulf Coast. The dominant tribe of
the region, controlling both coasts and what is now the
Florida Keys, had built great pyramids out of shell, ornate
plazas and a highway system of canals. Because Carlos was

ruler of Spain, or because the conquistadors misheard, they called the chief Carlos, although *Caalus* was probably closer. The kingdom and people over which he reigned was soon mispronounced, *Calusa.*

Physically, the Calusa were much bigger than the Spaniards and impossible to intimidate. A member of Ponce de Leon's crew described the men as being more than seven feet tall, though that was an exaggeration. The Jesuit missions all failed and Ponce de Leon was mortally wounded in battle and later died in Cuba. The Calusa never accepted Christianity, nor the Spaniards who came later. They had controlled the peninsula for several thousand years and would not submit. However, they had no way to fight European diseases, and they gradually vanished, leaving their cities abandoned.

At one point, from the work of an anthropologist, JoAnn read, "The Calusa operated as a conquest kingdom with a pattern of tribute collection that resembled that of the Aztecs and Incas. There are indications that the Calusa language originated in the interior of South America, around the Orinoco River, nearly 2,000 years ago." Then she added, "Tomlinson said that would interest you, because you've spent so much time in Central and South America."

I said, "Uh-huh. What I'm trying to understand is what any of this has to do with someone opening the grave of your friend's daughter."

JoAnn also read a series of letters by a Jesuit missionary, Father Juan Rogel, and also one written by Juan Lopez de Velasco, both of whom lived for a short time among the Calusa.

"You picture these guys with shaved heads, swatting mosquitoes, writing on parchment in the Florida jungle. I find it interesting as can be."

Some of it was.

According to the priest, Carlos was the most powerful man in Florida. His people didn't view him as a leader. He was divine, like a god. They believed that he controlled the heavens, and he had secret religious knowledge that he wouldn't share with commoners. He'd go to the burial areas at night and talk to ghosts. From those conversations, the priest wrote, Carlos could correctly predict the future. As a symbol of his divinity, the missionary described Carlos as wearing a golden medallion and carrying a wooden totem.

"Now we're getting to it," I said. "Pure Tomlinson."

According to the priest, Carlos enjoyed the absolute loyalty of his people. He hated the Spaniards, therefore none of his people would cooperate. So the Jesuits found a traitor, a Calusa they called Felipe. Felipe lured Carlos into a trap where the Spaniards murdered him. That was the beginning of the end of the Calusa.

At the same time, a similar drama was being played out in the Ten Thousand Islands, a region of mangroves, black water and swamp south of Marco Island. The ruling chief there was Salvador. Like Carlos, he was a human god, controlled the skies and storms, wore a royal golden medallion and carried a sacred totem. He, too, despised the Spaniards.

To illustrate, JoAnn read part of a letter from one of the priests who tried to convert Salvador: "When my fellow priest,

Fray Castillo, ordered Salvador to tell his people to pray to the True God, Salvador became angry. Salvador gave the Father a number of blows to the face. He then rubbed human excrement on the Father's face while he was praying. Then Salvador urinated on him, saying, 'Man boy, why are you so small?' He then told we religious many times that they did not want to become Christians and that we should go away."

JoAnn added, "Because the Spaniards couldn't make Salvador cooperate, they started recruiting a traitor. It solved the Carlos problem, so why not assassinate their second great chief?"

I said, "Religion had an edge to it in those days."

"Uh-huh. What's the biblical line? Something about a terrible swift sword." She paused for a moment. "Funny thing is, Tomlinson said you'd understand that part easiest of all. Deposing one leader to put your own guy in power. Political assassination, that sort of thing. What'd he mean by that, Ford?"

Very softly, I said, "One of Tomlinson's little jokes. He thinks he's funny."

The traitor selected to dispose of Salvador was an outcast shaman from a "distant land" they called Tocayo, a dangerous man, according to one of the priests, but potentially useful to the Spaniards' cause.

The priest wrote, "I believe that the devil is in Tocayo, yet he promises that he will accept the True God if we help him depose Salvador. Tocayo also promises that he will forsake witchcraft and burn his sacred idol and no longer kill and eat the children of his enemies, nor have unclean knowledge of his daughters. He has promised that he will remove the sodomites."

I said, "This was five hundred years ago?"

JoAnn looked at the paper. "The thing I just read, about killing children and the sodomites, it was written in 1568, a little over four hundred years ago."

After Tocayo hacked Salvador to death, the priest returned from Havana to discover that Tocayo had murdered fifteen principal men of neighboring villages and eaten their eyes. It was a belief of the Calusa that a man's permanent soul resides in the pupil of his eyes. The Calusa weren't cannibals, but Tocayo was. As Lopez de Velasco wrote, "They say that their idol eats human men's eyes."

Tocayo had made himself a human idol.

The priest found Tocayo and his captains holding a celebration and dancing with the heads of four chiefs, kicking their heads through the shell courtyards as if playing at sport.

Tocayo had also taken for himself the golden medallion— a *chaguala*—and the wooden totem, both considered sources of great power.

I leaned a little closer to JoAnn, listening carefully as she read, "'Fray Castillo believes that these two idols possess unholy authority. Now Tocayo guards them jealously and laughs when we ask to examine them. He tells us that Light is in one of the idols, Darkness is in the other. They are the source of all his strength and he will not part with them.

"'But he has kept his word on other matters. He now

kneels before the cross. He is serving Your Holiness as he promised. I know that Tocayo is not a tool of the Devil. He is a tool of the One True God.' "

JoAnn turned to me. "Dorothy found them both. The gold medallion and the wooden totem. When she was digging on the bank of that canal."

"How do you know they're the same artifacts? Maybe the Calusa had several."

"Tomlinson says they're the same ones."

"Ah."

"He seems pretty certain of it."

"I'm not surprised. Omniscience is one of his specialties."

One thing was clear, though: someone wanted those artifacts. Wanted them badly enough to risk several break-ins. Wanted them badly enough to dig up the grave of a long-dead child. Maybe wanted them badly enough to come after me. Because that was the night, a Friday night, the foggiest night of the year, when a sensitive and civilized dope surprised two intruders on his boardwalk.

Me, the sensitive and civilized dope.

The next morning, we were gone—on our way to Marco.

Seven

Marco Island is a community of block-and-stucco, landscaped lots, fairways and beach condos, everything laid out as symmetrically as a Midwestern community college. It illustrates the tidy Toledo-by-the-Sea approach to development that has become the template of modern Florida. The effect is all the more striking because Marco lies several miles deep into the confluence of a great saw grass and mangrove wilderness.

Until the mid-sixties, Marco was a fishing and clamming village. Enter three brothers, the Mackles, who decided to work a classic Florida finesse, but on a grand scale: presell lots to snow-weary northerners and use the cash to finance the infrastructure of an entire city; a city that had yet to be built.

For months, the Mackles ran ads in major newspapers touting a new golf and retirement resort in the Ten Thousand Islands. It was billed as a world-class facility even though no facilities existed. What did exist were artists' renderings and little diorama cities that real estate agents flogged at high-pressure sales "parties" that promised free trips to Florida.

The gambit worked. It's easy to push sunshine in The Great Gray North. They sold millions in raw property and used the profit to build precisely what they had promised, including a mazework of canals to create more "waterfront" lots.

The result? Marco was an environmentalist's nightmare, but a triumph of business ingenuity.

In recent years, development has stabilized and the community has found its own character and direction, though that was not easily seen as I summited the Marco bridge in my old pickup. From the peak of the bridge, the island spread away below: residential areas in computer-chip patterns, then a jagged fringe of high-rise condos on the beach.

I'd followed JoAnn down from Sanibel—not easy to do, because she was a fast, confident driver in her black Lexus. I had to keep my truck floored much of the time just to keep up. Prior to leaving, she'd told me she wasn't looking forward to the trip, and not just because of the funeral. "I come back like maybe every couple of years, and it's always the same," she said. "More houses, more building, more traffic."

I'd pointed out that the same could be said of Sanibel. The same, in fact, could be said of all Florida.

"I know, but it's different when it's the place where you grew up. That used to be a heck of a nice little island. Real friendly and simple. Piney wood houses along with the new stuccos, and still lots of barefoot kids. The monsters they got there now, they're like stamped from a mold. They say it's still Marco Island, but it's not. Not the way I remember it. What they did was, they built something over Marco but they kept the name."

I've listened to enough bitter fellow Floridians to know there is no sensible response to their lament nor to their rosy remembrances of the past. There are a couple of reasons. In a state so young that nearly everyone is only three or four generations removed from somewhere else, the birthright of "natives" is easily argued. Also, Floridians have chopped up, dredged and reconstituted their homeland as eagerly as the most thoughtless of outsiders. Or happily sold it to developers who did worse.

So I said nothing as I listened to her.

I'd driven because I was going to continue on down to Key Largo after the service. JoAnn was not. Also, my truck has a trailer hitch. If I was going to be on the Keys for a few days, I would need my boat. I told her it was because I wanted to hunt some big October bonefish.

Only partially true.

For me, being near water without a boat creates a sense of

confinement that approaches neurosis. Claustrophobia is a word that comes close to describing what I feel.

I followed her as she made a turn, and another. Then she pulled into a 7-Eleven. Got out of her car shaking her head and said, "Damn it all, Ford! There's so much new building been done, I'm not sure I can find the cemetery. I know it's off Bald Eagle, but it's such a little bitty thing. Let me run in and ask."

I sat in my truck, watching JoAnn through the convenience store window. Her face was framed by a Lotto decal and an ATM sign. She was standing at the counter, speaking to the cashier. I watched her nod and nod again. I watched her expression change as she looked outside toward me. Then she was crossing the parking lot, a wry smile on her face.

"Know what the clerk told me? She said she didn't think Marco had a cemetery 'cause everyone was boxed up and shipped back home. No one really stayed here. Isn't that hilarious?"

"You're kidding." I started the truck. "So next we stop at a gas station and ask directions. Or buy a map."

"We don't have to. When I looked out the window, guess what I saw? I knew we had to be close."

I looked where she was pointing and saw an American flag high in the breeze above a hedge of concrete buildings, a beige Church of God, a Citgo Station and more buildings beyond.

The cemetery was hidden back in there. Marco had squeezed up around it.

. . .

Tomlinson was weaving a little. He couldn't stand straight; had to brace himself against a tree for support as he told me, "We've got to look in the casket, man. I hate it. *Hate* it. For you, no prob-leem-oh. A man of science. No religious affiliations, zero politics, not much sensitivity that anyone's ever noticed. So it's no big deal for you. But me, it's a whole different gig. Know why?"

Tomlinson was drunk. Or high. Probably both. Easy enough to tell when I got close. The odor. "Tell me, old buddy."

"Reason is, you've never been trapped in the spirit world with a bunch of screaming ghost raiders. I have. So it's not like I'm eager to bend over a coffin, stand there with my nose open and risk those bastards climbing back into my brain. Seriously, man, the little devils consider LSD their own personal fucking ski trail. Keep in mind, this girl had a very ancient soul. There was lots and lots of karmic traffic."

We were standing side by side beneath two pine trees not far from Dorothy Copeland's open grave. They'd used a portable hydraulic sling to raise the casket, then screened it from view with a green tarp that was chin-high. The tiny cemetery wasn't much bigger than a baseball infield, so the canvas wall dominated the area. There were a few old headstones, bone-white, showing the decades, and a war memorial with a bench near a fountain and a flag.

I said, "Is that the funeral director over there?"

Tomlinson moaned softly, touched his forehead as if checking for a fever. "His name's Barry Caldwell, the one who looks like Lumpy on *Leave it to Beaver*. That's him. Did you hear what I said?"

"I heard. Demons up the nose. You don't have to bend over the coffin, no need for you to get near it. You've already told me what we're looking for. If it's there, it won't be hard to find."

"I'm not saying I *won't* look. I'm just saying that I've got to play this very safe. Wear a face mask, keep a little distance. I've made enough wallets for one lifetime."

"Um-huh. You spoke to Caldwell, the director?"

"He's a funeral rep, actually. Yeah, a pretty nice guy. He was going to hire a minister for what they call the 'committal service,' but once he found out I was an ordained Buddhist priest, he turned the whole thing over to me. With Della's permission, of course."

"Wise choice. Should be an interesting funeral."

"You betcha."

"Watch you don't stagger and fall into the hole."

"I can always count on you for encouragement, Doc. That's the kind of advice that actually helps."

Tomlinson looked the part. He was wearing billowing white pants and a shirt made out of some kind of linenlike material. It gave him an East Indian countenance except for his goatee and long hair, which was still in beaded dreadlocks.

"What about the cop? Did you speak with the cop?"

Through the trees, sitting on a marble bench beneath the flag, I could see Della Copeland hunched over a package of Kleenex, dabbing at her eyes as a man in a gray suit made notes. Standing nearby was her friend and coworker, Betty Lynn, a massively buxom blonde. Della was dressed in a black skirt and blouse. She looked smaller, more time-damaged than JoAnn had described her. When we'd shaken hands earlier, her eyes had the stricken, glazed look of a bomb victim. I doubted if she even heard my name.

"Nope, I avoid cops," Tomlinson said. "I leave all screw-heads and other uniformed types to you. Especially now, you wearing slacks and a black blazer. They'll open right up to Mr. America."

"Thanks so much. What about the other people? Any idea who they are?"

There were more than two dozen men and women standing individually and in groups, most of them using scattered pockets of shade to filter the heat. Mostly adults but a few college-age people, standing tight and dressed of a style. A very large gathering at a cemetery that had so few parking places I'd had to pull off and park on the side of the road.

Right now, I could look through the trees and see my boat strapped tight on its trailer. It was something nice to look at while waiting for the funeral to begin. Like certain fish, the skiff's lines were perfect and functional. It gave me pleasure.

Tomlinson said, "Curiosity seekers, most of them." His eyes began to pan, as if focusing for the first time. "Probably some real freaks scattered in there, too. Jesus. Witchcraft pretenders, some devil-worshipping vermin. Take your pick. Holy shit, check out the kid with the purple spiked hair! Pimply little heathen would chew through your chest to get to your heart."

There were four punker types, all dressed in black T-shirts, all with hair dyed in Easter egg shades. Lots of complicated body piercings, eyebrows and ears. Tomlinson had singled out the tallest male, a big sinewy guy with tattoos and something silver gleaming from his lip.

I said, "You've been smoking, haven't you? That crap you smuggled in from Belize. How many, six bales? The stuff that smells like mold from toadstools."

He sniffed his sleeve. "Dear God, it's that obvious?" Then he said, "Three bales. Not six. I'm prone to exaggerate when I'm sober."

I said, "What's obvious is the paranoia. You become extremely paranoid. But worse, it seems to scramble your judgment. Not a very healthy side effect, old buddy."

"You're serious."

"Oh yeah."

"Paranoia, well . . . if that's the only problem, rest easy, amigo. Paranoia and me, we've spent so many nights together, the fucker owes me rent. Some security damage, too. I've got Dr. Leary to thank for that."

"Then consider how it messes up your judgment."

"That's something to worry about."

"Yeah."

"If you say it's true, it must be. I know you wouldn't lie."

"I'm not."

He was pursing his lips, thinking about it. "Then I need to start cutting back a tad. That's what I should do. Use my supplies for research purposes only—I'm a scientist, you know."

"I'm aware of that."

He became contemplative. "What I may do is come up with some pleasant-tasting filtering device. Reduce the effects but not the enjoyment. I'm certain someone somewhere has the technology. One of my old classmates from Harvard, perhaps."

"What you better do is trot across the street, wash your face off and get some coffee. You don't sober up—and I mean fast—you're going to make an absolute ass of yourself."

"I will! Rest easy about that, old friend. I've dealt with this circumstance so many times in my life that my brain has adapted."

"Oh, I'm sure."

"I'm *very* serious." He placed a confidential shoulder against my arm before explaining. "I've developed what I think of as my 'Lifeguard Twin.' Imagine, if you will, a Tomlinson clone locked inside a tiny room in my brain. In an emergency situation, I open the door and the little fellow skips out and rescues my ass. Happens every single time I need him. It doesn't matter what a slobbering, pathetic wreck I've made of myself, he grabs the controls and takes charge."

"Fascinating."

"Oh, the little bastard's unbelievable! He speaks articulately through my mouth. He walks steadily on my legs. He's extremely courteous to law-enforcement types and attentive to attractive women. Unfortunately, the limped-dicked fool hasn't got the hang of intercourse, but we both have high hopes." Tomlinson leaned closer. "Personally, I think my Lifeguard Twin is further proof of evolution."

I said, "Uh-huh, no doubt," as I waved my hand back and forth in front of my nose. His breath smelled of rum and halothane gas and charred cannabis. Awful.

Halothane? Yes, no doubt. Smelled exactly like industrial insecticide.

"Damn it, Tomlinson, you don't learn. You've made some new little doctor friends down on the Keys. Didn't you? Medical types, hipster surgeons with canisters."

He sniffed the air primly. "People on Key Largo aren't like you, Marion. They know how to enjoy life. They're eager to share. Fun's a *good* thing, that's the way *they* think."

"You've got a funereal service to perform. You can barely walk."

"Don't chide me, please. You can see into my eyes but you can't see out of them. Lighten up. I feel shaky enough as it is."

"There's a 7-Eleven across the street. Get going. Wash your face and buy some coffee."

"I will, I will! In the meantime, though"—he used his chin to indicate the punk rockers—"don't turn your back on that evil little bastard."

Eight

The reason there were so many people was because, the day before, the Marco Island *Eagle* had run a front-page story about Dorothy and the artifacts she'd found, as well as a reprint of the story about her suicide. They'd used old file photographs. The Miami *Herald* had a shorter piece in its Florida section, too. There was also a reporter from the *National Enquirer* who'd been calling Della, wanting to do a story.

Della had refused.

Detective Gary Parrish told me this, as I stood with him and the funeral rep away from the waiting crowd.

Parrish had a wide, West African face, his head shaved clean; skin a lighter brown than his arms and neck. He had the look of a high school power forward who'd let things go, and the demeanor of someone who'd been at his job too long. It was a mixture of reserve and indifference. Sooner or later, all cops put up shields. Sometimes the shields are for protection, sometimes they are a device.

"Grave robbing in Miami, yeah, it happens a dozen times a year, maybe more," he said. "It's almost always the Santeria people, because they need artifacts. The people from down on the islands, all that voodoo shit. Skulls, a piece of bone for their ceremonies. It's like part of their culture, a religious thing. But on Marco? No one expected this."

The way they'd gotten into the grave was, they'd stolen a backhoe that had been parked beside the nearby church. The city was replacing a sewer line in the area. The backhoe had been there only a day or two. "It was one of those random deals," Parrish said. "The idiot workers left the key in the machine. Whoever stole the backhoe probably saw it when they walked by, said to themselves, 'Hey, lookee what we got here.' And right next to the cemetery."

The perpetrators, Parrish said, ran over several stones to get to Dorothy's grave, dug it open wide enough so they could drop down into the hole. "I don't think they expected to find the cement vault down there, though. Those vaults, it's a state law. You look at the cover? First, they use the backhoe to try and crack the thing open, then they got smart and just tilted it up and off."

I said, "All that noise, all these buildings around, and no one heard anything?"

"That's exactly why they got away with it. Everybody heard them. People saw their lights. A backhoe in a cemetery, what are you going to think? That they're digging a grave, getting ready for a funeral. Or maybe the city workers were at it late, trying to get the sewer line done. No one even called the station. When our deputy drove by, he was lucky to notice them. He told me if he'd heard a backhoe, he'd of gone right on by. Same thing: figured they was here working."

Then I listened as the funeral rep told us why he didn't think the casket had been opened. Caldwell looked like a construction worker, not an embalmer, yet he had a delicate tone and a soft voice. He used his stubby hands to talk, but in a way that people who take speech classes are taught to use their hands for effect.

"If they did get the casket open," he said, "they were careful, extremely careful, and they knew exactly what they were doing when they sealed it back. I say that because there are no crowbar marks on the casket that I could see. No marks where they tried to sledgehammer the thing open. Inside, nothing was disturbed. Nothing obvious, anyway. Wouldn't you expect vandals to do something like that? Bring a crowbar or an ax, I'm saying. If they really wanted to get inside."

I said, "You can't just lift the lid open?"

Caldwell's smile told me that I knew absolutely nothing about his industry. "Not exactly, Mr. Ford. I'll give you an example. Let's say that the deceased was in one of our top-of-the-line units. A Batesville, let's say. What you're dealing with is a unit made of eighteen-gauge steel. Heavy rubber gasket sealers inside and a cathodic bar on the bottom to stop electrolysis. A casket like that"—his smile broadened slightly—"you'd better bring a lot more than a crowbar to get it open. The only way to get it open is with a hex-key, specially designed, just like the lug nuts on a car tire sometimes require a special key."

"That's the kind of casket that Dorothy Copeland is in?"

"No, but the vandals couldn't have known that. Ms. Copeland is in a hardwood casket. Cherry wood, I think. Clients who . . . well, who are of limited means, often make that choice. It's a Marcellus, one of the best in the business, but it locks down with a pin and a heavy clasp."

"Is it possible to get it open?"

"Yes. If you know how it works, it's not difficult. But again, they couldn't have known."

"But if they did, is it possible that they could have opened it, then resealed it?"

"I suppose. But I think they'd have done the obvious thing and tired to pry it open."

I said, "If they were vandals, sure, a random act. But as Detective Parrish knows, Ms. Copeland has been the target of a series of burglaries over the last few months. It's possible someone knows exactly what they were after and they'll go to remarkable lengths to get it. Exhuming a grave in a city cemetery? That's risky behavior, wouldn't you agree?"

The plainclothes cop said, "So is murder, bank robbery, assault, the whole long list. You said you live on Sanibel? Lots of money up there, a nice safe little island. Marco, one of the safest communities in the state. Usually. Get away from the money places, though, there are way too many freaks. Understand what I'm saying? I deal with them every working day of my life. There ain't nothing risky to a crackhead. They'd bulldoze a church if they thought it would buy them some rock."

"Oh, I don't doubt there are bad people in the world," I said agreeably. "The kind of people you read about in the newspapers."

"Exactly," Parrish said, an expression of patience in the way he set his jaw. "The kind of criminals good citizens like you find folded on the doorstep every morning.

"Know what probably happened?" he added. "A rumor got started the little girl was buried with treasure. People love them stories about buried treasure. Probably got talked around the streets and some drunks or dopers noticed the backhoe and thought, What the hell, let's see what's in there."

Parrish's tone told me that he was taking me into his confidence, sharing some secrets.

"Could be," I said.

"Trust me. They come staggering by and go, 'Shit, let's get rich.'" He looked around for a moment. "That reminds me. Where'd your drunk hippie friend disappear to? The one in them weird robes."

"He's practicing his eulogy. He's kind of a perfectionist." Then I said, "You could be wrong, you know. Maybe it didn't happen that way at all."

The detective allowed me a pointed look of assessment. "Oh, really."

I chose my approach carefully. Proper attitude of respect; sufficient deference. I had suggestions to make, but no need to offend the investigating cop.

"It's possible the whole thing was carefully planned."

"All sorts of things are possible, Mr. Ford. I'm telling you the way it probably was."

"I realize that. I also realize that you're a lot more experienced at this sort of thing than I am. But know what might be interesting? Get a quick video of everyone here. Or anyone sitting off by themselves in a car, watching. I read somewhere that the sickos who light fires almost always try and find a private place to watch. That's how they get their kicks. Maybe it's the same with grave robbers. The people who did it? They might be in the area right now."

I received a stony look in return, and a very chilly, "There's an idea. Man, I learn so much on this job."

It's been my experience that most people in the emergency professions are good at what they do. They have to be, because there's so much depending on them. Parrish was behaving like one of the weak links. The type who used his shield as a power lever or an excuse. Or maybe he just no longer cared enough to invest the effort.

I got the same cold reaction when I said, "If I was serious about robbing a grave, know what I'd do? I'd do some research first. I'd check the city records and see what I could learn about how the girl was buried. The cemetery is maintained by the city, isn't it?"

Caldwell said, "But there wouldn't be anything in the files about the type of coffin. Whether it was steel or wood. That's where you're wrong."

"I wouldn't know that. The perpetrators wouldn't either, but it's a logical place to check. Then I'd go to the newspaper, ask to see the archives. I'd read everything I could about what happened here fifteen years ago. I'd try to find the name of the funeral home that handled the burial, maybe even call and ask them questions under some guise. Pretend to be a reporter doing a story. That could work."

Caldwell said, "We handled the funeral. I wasn't here at the time, but it was our shop."

I looked at Parrish. "See? An easy place to start. So then you take the video from here and start to match photos. The municipal building is bound to have a security camera. Maybe the newspaper, too. Even if they don't, you say to clerks, 'You get a visit recently from anyone you recognize on this video?' "

Parrish said, "Gee, there's another good idea."

It wasn't working, but I wasn't going to give up. "One more thing. These people seem determined to take what Dorothy found. So, I'd speak to an archaeologist and find out exactly where she was digging fifteen years ago. A golden medallion, a wooden totem, beads—they all have monetary value. Chances are, if they're really serious, they've done the research and are digging in the same area. Or have already dug there. Find one golden medallion, there might be more."

Parrish was done listening to it. His nostrils flared slightly as he said, "Very helpful suggestions, Mr. Ford. Really appreciate it, too. All I got to do is drop the twenty or so current cases I'm working on to bust some vandals. Of course, the cases I'm working on are crimes against real live people. Like, for instance, up 'round Golden Gate, we've had a string of sexual assaults on children. Real nasty ones. I've got three different disappearances, too. Three women, none associated with the other, just left home or work one day and never came back. Disappeared in a way that's got the feel of serial killer to them. I'm talkin' about a *real* freak. Someone doin' for a reason and *likes* it. Della Copeland's child, she's been dead, for what? Fifteen years. There's not much anyone can do for her."

I said, "Which means you're not going to do anything."

"I wish that's exactly what it meant, but it doesn't. What I should be doing is banging on doors right now, reading profiles. Doing serious work. Instead, I'm down here in rich people's land looking for vandals. Know why?" He looked past me to the road. "That there's why. You're lookin' at the reason. A man named Mr. Ivan Bauerstock."

I turned to see a black Humvee, doors open, men in dark suits ducking out. The oldest of them leaving the driver's seat was a very tall, gray-haired man with the bearing of someone used to giving orders and staring over the heads of lesser men while his orders were being carried out.

I watched three younger men wait for him. One of the three had a pumpkin-sized head and the body mass of a competitive weight lifter. I watched them listen to the older man intently, all eyes focused. Then they followed him toward us, into the cemetery.

"Ivan Bauerstock, one of the biggest men in Florida. Bauerstock as in Bauerstock Industries. Bauerstock as in cattle and citrus. Man, he got his own road construction business, condo projects, you name it. Now I hear he's heavy into computer software and the Internet, all that shit. You never heard of the man?"

I said, "I've heard of him. His companies, anyway. What's he have to do with this?"

" 'Cause he owns half of Marco, one thing. Another, his son and that dead girl used to be friends. Now Mr. Bauerstock wants his growed-up little boy to be a state senator. So they've come back to say goodbye. Show how much they care, with the press all around to see. Maybe get his son's picture in the paper saying how he's putting pressure on the sheriff's department to arrest the bad guys."

I said, "That sounds like more than a guess."

There was a cautionary edge to Parrish's voice, the black dialectic emphasized, as he replied, "No, that just a wild guess, man! I got nothin' better to do then sit around diss'in people can get me fired"—he snapped his fingers in my face—"that quick. Mr. Bauerstock, he the one friends with the President a few years back. Slept in the Lincoln Bedroom, flew Air Force One all the way to China or some damn place. You know how much cash something like that cost? So what the chances him callin' my boss and telling us exactly what he want done?

Him and the sheriff, it just a coincidence they in the same party, man."

I decided that maybe Parrish wasn't a weak link after all. "Someone as powerful as Bauerstock would order the sheriff to put his best man on the job."

Parrish touched a finger to his own chest in mock surprise. "Me? Aw-w-w-w, now I'm embarrassed. Thing is, Mr. Bauerstock's son, Teddy, he's actually a pretty good guy. Couple days ago, he shook my hand and listened to what I had to say about some stuff."

"That's what politicians do. Or so I hear."

Parrish was nodding. "I know, I know, but I got the feeling this one, he might be different. Seems to care about people, not just the ones with money. See that man with him? That's B. J. Buster; played linebacker for the Bucs but kept endin' up in jail, till Bauerstock hired him as his bodyguard."

"A politician with a heart of gold."

"Oh man, you wouldn't believe the people Mr. Bauerstock's hired to take care of his future President son. Just the way he sees it, too. Teddy, they say he's got that glow, the one you can't see till he's on the television screen. Excuse me, I mean *Theodore*. That the name they using now. *He* got the glow."

I wondered vaguely and bitterly if the linebacker knew the steroid freak who was in Mexico with Kathleen.

"So now Mr. Buster is a model citizen. All thanks to the man running for office."

Parrish chuckled. "I wouldn't trust B. J. Buster far as I could throw him. Once a con, always a con. Which Teddy

Bauerstock can't see and why the fool won't be getting my vote."

Nope, this was not a weak link. I said, "In that case, I'd like to start fresh. Here's what we do: first I apologize, then I explain why I'm here. I'm the friend of a friend. The little girl's mother needs some outside help. Which is why I pissed you off making suggestions."

Parrish's voice returned to normal as he said, "I feel bad for the woman, don't get me wrong. It was a hell of a nasty thing to do, dig her little girl up. But it's not a top priority. There's lots more serious crap goin' on out there. But know what?" He allowed me the slightest of smiles. "A couple of your ideas, they weren't that bad. You got pretty good instincts."

I said, "If you want any help, the private citizen type, contact Della. She'll know how to get in touch."

Caldwell had been listening, keeping up. "One thing Mr. Ford suggested, I can talk to our receptionist, see if anyone was asking about Miss Copeland."

"There you go," said Parrish. He turned to me. "You want to check out the casket, see what's missing? I don't think they got in there. I think our man scared 'em off. But you take a look and keep the mamma happy. Then we put that little girl back in the ground again."

Nine

I opened the top half of the coffin lid by myself, pressing its weight with both hands, while Tomlinson stood beside me, whispering some kind of rhythmic chant.

I'd removed my sports coat. We were both wearing white gauze masks.

There was an odor, not strong or offensive. It was as if an old trunk had been opened. Caldwell had already told me what to expect, explaining that the child had received a superb job of embalming. The casket was vault-dry, he said, and promised that I would be shocked at how little change there'd been in the body since burial.

"People not in the industry," he said, "don't realize how good we are at what we do. We're the best in the world, the best of all time. I guess the reason people don't know is obvious."

Yet, despite the briefing, I was not prepared for how near to life the girl appeared. Time had stopped for her. It was an unexpected and moving realization.

I'm not a demonstrative person. Tomlinson reminds me of that almost daily. I have spent enough time among the dead and dying to view both clinically. Yet, when I lifted the lid and looked down through glittering columns of dust and sunlight, I felt a jolt of emotion that caused my breathing to spasm.

I was looking into the face of a sleeping child. Dorothy Copeland didn't look like a teenager. Innocence dissipates years. She looked younger, ageless, without fear or flaw.

She wore a yellow dress with a collar of white lace. There was a thread of gold chain around her neck and a locket in the shape of a smiling full moon. Her hair was the color of Kansas wheat. It was fanned out halolike on the crepe pillow beneath her head. She wore white gloves with fingers interlaced, long and delicate as JoAnn had described them. It was as if the girl had dressed for church, but, instead, found a cozy meadow place to doze.

There was something about the delicate facial structure that was heart-wrenching. Our bodies are composed mostly of water. The water was gone from hers. The soft angularity of nose and chin was emphasized beneath skin that was white and fragile as parchment, yet her cheeks were blushed with embalmer's makeup like some China doll. The color added definition to lashes resting long over eyes that, it seemed, might flutter open in reaction to the offending sunlight. From what I heard, this was a tomboy girl who liked to explore and dig in the dirt. She'd been described as having an "extraordinary gift" for finding things. She'd been described as an old soul.

But this was also a child; a child who'd sometimes worn lace and crinoline. This was a child who, playing dress-up, had been forever frozen, as if caught asleep on a frosted field.

Seeing her produced in me sadness and a sense of loss far out of proportion to what I'd expected. I had not known this child. I'd never heard her voice. Now, though, I felt as if there were some inexplicable connection. She was here, right in front of me, yet she wasn't. It touched me in a way that squeezed the heart.

On Dorothy's right cheek was a splotch of pollen-colored mold. I was tempted to brush it away. Instead, I touched a gloved index finger to the collar of her dress. The lace disintegrated at my touch, revealing the area of skin beneath her chin. The scar there was a band of discoloration, gray on white.

Yes, there had been a rope. It had been knotted tightly enough around her neck to leave the skin forever marked. The scar was the residue of an unthinkable act, violence that was incongruous with the peaceful scene and angelic child before me.

Something horrible had imposed itself on this young life.

Why else would Dorothy Copeland hang herself?

I'd been so intent on visual data that all sound vanished.

Now, though, I became aware of a distant sobbing. I stepped back for a moment, listening.

"It's Della," Tomlinson said gently. "She's worried about what they've done to her little girl."

I looked into his face. The paranoid druggie had vanished, purged not by coffee, but out of regard for the circumstances. Here was the man I liked and respected. His expression was one of haunted sadness.

I indicated the necklace. "There's the locket, just like Della told us. I don't think they got the coffin open. They probably would've taken it."

"Perhaps. But that's not what they were after."

I said, "Then let's find out."

I lifted Dorothy's hands very gently. They had the weight of air. Beneath her white gloves was a flat wooden carving that was as large as both her palms together. There was also a small Bible, white cover, Dorothy's name imprinted in gold.

Della had told Tomlinson that she'd slipped the Bible and the carving into her daughter's casket just before they'd buried her. Said she did it privately, when no one was look-ing, because the Bible and the wooden carving were the only things that had given Dorothy comfort during the nightmares that preceded her suicide.

During the worst of it, Dorothy had slept with both, clutching them to her chest.

She slept with them still.

Without disturbing the Bible, I removed the carving with my left hand and held it up to the light. It was heavy for its

size, black as oiled mahogany or iron wood. It had the shape
of certain badges. At what seemed to be the top of the carving
was a cross. Centered on the cross were concentric circles. At
the middle, there were square holes. Beneath the holes were
inverted droplet shapes. Teardrops? At the bottom were half
rectangles within progressively larger half rectangles.

"These designs are similar to the ones you drew for
JoAnn. Was it from photographs or were you just guessing?"

Tomlinson hesitated for a moment, his blue eyes locked
on the carving. "I've seen photos. The designs are the same as
on the gold medallion. They're symbols, very powerful symbols. Take a look at the back. There should be two crescent
moons."

I turned and studied the back of the carving, saying, "They
didn't get to her." Meaning the grave robbers.

"That'll make Della feel better. A little, anyway."

"We need a small sack or a cloth. I want it wrapped."

"You're going to leave the Bible?"

"The people who did this have no interest in stealing a
Bible."

"We walk out of here with a sack, they'll know we found
something. The fact that it's wrapped will tell them it's personal or valuable." Tomlinson leaned a little closer to me before he added, "They're here, you know. The ones who dug
her up."

I said, "I know."

I looked at the girl once more, her pale face in repose. The
moon-shaped locket drew my attention. I took it between

thumb and forefinger, touched the clasp and the locket opened. Staring out at me was an older Dorothy Copeland, this one with blue eyes and very much alive. There was a strange intensity to those eyes. They did not seem to stare into a camera, they seemed to look directly into me. Her expression was confident, knowing, yet touchingly wistful, as if she longed for something.

What?

There are certain adolescents, usually female, who possess wisdom far in advance of age or explanation. That wisdom fades quickly when reproductive hormones kick in, but it is there for a while and the few who possess it seem to carry it like a weight.

That wisdom and the weight of it were in the face of the girl who looked out from the locket. Her eyes were in mine, sharing both with me.

"Keep it, Marion. She'd like you to have it."

I was so captivated by the photograph, I'd momentarily forgotten that Tomlinson was still beside me. His voice was a startling intrusion.

I said, "Keep what?"

"The locket. Dorothy would be pleased if you took it and kept it near. Della won't mind."

I turned to him. "What're you talking about? You didn't know this girl, let alone what would please her."

He was looking down into the casket. Very softly, he said, "No. But maybe you did. Maybe you knew her. I sensed the possibility. It didn't become real until just now. Seeing her, seeing your reaction."

"My reaction—? I have no idea . . . look, I never met this child."

"Maybe not. But I think you have."

"Impossible. Fifteen years ago, I was . . ." I had to think for a moment. "Fifteen years ago, I was in Central America. Nicaragua, Panama, all around. There was a war going on. Far away from Marco Island."

"Not in this lifetime. I didn't mean that."

Finally, I understood. I said, "Oh, please. Don't start."

"You two . . . the energy is unmistakable. That's what I meant. Different *samsaras*. Different incarnations. You don't feel it?"

I hesitated for a moment before I answered, "No. No, I don't. I don't feel anything."

"Are you certain? It's . . . *there*. The connective energy, like a switch being thrown. Or a circuit that's just been completed." After a few seconds, both of us looking at her, he added, "It must have been very, very powerful. You two as a couple, I mean. To have lasted through this many transitions."

The man was maddening. "I don't know what you're talking about. Knock it off."

"Look at her, Marion. Look at her and tell me you can't feel it. You and Dorothy. This time around, you only missed by a decade or so. You both keep trying to find each other and you're getting closer."

Ridiculous. Even so, I concentrated on the child's sleeping face and then the photograph, those wistful eyes staring out. Was there something familiar? Something far away, on the distant fringe of memory, but always and forever important?

No . . . of course not. Yet, it was difficult to explain my feelings of loss and the powerful sadness that was now in me.

"Let her be, Tomlinson. Enough of your talk."

"Had she lived, it would have been the ideal time. The perfect age for you to meet. Again. Someone took her from you, Marion. Took her too soon."

My head snapped around, and he saw in my eyes that he'd gone too far. "Go find something to wrap the carving," I said. "A shirt, a shopping bag, I don't care. Let people see what you're doing. Make a show of it. Act secretive, that'll be sure to get their attention. And tell Della that no one's bothered her child."

"You're not going to even consider what I'm saying."

"When you stop talking nonsense, I'll give consideration."

"I've never had such a strong sense of the inevitable. Now it's up to you." He was chewing at one of his Rasta braids, an old nervous habit. "I have a feeling they keep hurting her over and over. For how many lifetimes? This may be your only chance, Doc. Out of all the incarnations, it may be the only time you can stop them."

"No more! Get moving!"

As he left, he said, "The locket. You should keep the locket."

When he was gone, I touched Dorothy's folded hands lightly, a farewell gesture.

I looked at her sleeping face one last time. Then I closed and bolted the heavy lid.

Tomlinson was standing at the head of the casket, people gathered in a semicircle before him, heads bowed slightly. Della was seated next to Betty Lynn, leaning her weight against JoAnn, who had an arm around her, all three of them weeping but listening as Tomlinson spoke articulately and with sincerity. The man had a genius for knowing what gave people comfort and peace of mind.

I stood behind him and slightly to his right, memorizing the faces of those in attendance. Ivan Bauerstock stood at the front, bracketed by his men. Silver-haired, aloof, hands folded, long fingers moving as if attempting to scurry away on their own. He had an air of impatience and superiority, gray suit cut perfectly, face angular, square-jawed like a model for expensive clothing.

To his right was Teddy, the son running for the state senate—my guess, anyway. Similar genetics. Well over six feet tall but broader in the shoulders, a linebacker size to him, but a quarterback's cleft chin. A more expressive face, listening to Tomlinson's words, showing pain, nodding his understanding and interest. Black hair combed back TV anchorman–style, razor-cut, blow-dried to form, flawless. His face reminded me of someone, some actor, or maybe a politician who was often on television. The nose was distinctive, but I couldn't match the face with the name. Not surprising. I don't own a television.

I watched the would-be state senator's expression flex with attention as Tomlinson said, "Dorothy had a kindred relationship with the people who built mounds on this island. An archaeologist said she had a great gift for finding things. But she didn't find things; she was called to them. The people who built the mounds spoke to her. It is fitting that she go back to be among them."

He took up a book, saying, "In 1568, Father Juan Rogel, a missionary to the Calusa people, wrote, 'The King of these islands told me that each person has three souls. One is in the pupil of the eye. Another is in our shadow. The last is our reflection in a calm pool of water. When a person dies, two of the souls leave the body. But the third soul, the truest soul, lives in the pupil of our eye and remains in the body forever."

The four punk rockers stood at the back of the circle, off by themselves. Two guys, two chubby girls with bad posture, their body piercings gleaming like surgical staples. I guessed the guys to be in their early twenties, the girls younger, maybe still in their teens. All of them with an attitude, hanging with their leader, the tall, knobby guy who had a dragon tattooed on his forearm. The other male, shorter but much thicker, had what looked to be the tail of a snake winding up his bicep; the four of them whispering among themselves as Tomlinson spoke, which I found irritating as hell.

The others there were pretty easily labeled. Several newspaper types, all female. One late forties and very fat—from the *Enquirer,* judging by her brightly flowered look-at-me caftan and floppy straw hat. Two in their early twenties, serious expressions, journalism school aloofness. A photographer, male, late twenties. A cameraman from a local TV station and a female reporter who kept checking her makeup; she carried lipstick and hairspray in a little pouch.

Two men, however, were not so easily assessed. One was massive, with florid cheeks and nose, a beer drinker's paunch, deep into his forties. He wore shorts and a T-shirt, as if this were a recreational event, part of the Marco Island tour.

The other stood off by himself in the shade listening. Abe Lincoln face, black Navaho hair, dark eyes, wrists protruding from a cheap dress shirt that was too small, baggy pants belted around his waist. He had the shrunken look of a whiskey alcoholic, a pack of Marlboros showing through breast pocket, his hair greased back.

I moved slowly toward Detective Parrish as Tomlinson finished, saying, "What better proof of God and immortality than Dorothy's great genius? Than all the fallen Calusa who spoke to her? Their truest soul, the soul that lives in the pupil of their eyes, will be comforted by her return."

After a prayer and an appropriate silence, I spoke in a low voice to Detective Parrish, "Who's the man in the white shirt? The skinny guy."

Parrish was standing, arms folded. He was wearing Ray-Bans now that the service was over. He said, "You didn't already find out your ownself? I'm surprised."

"It's what I'm doing now," I said. "A smart cop is the logical place to start, right?"

He pursed his lips, smiling. "The skinny man, he's the girl's father, the one run off and left them. Ms. Copeland, she asked me not to let him near her, wouldn't speak a word to him. Said he didn't care 'bout the girl when she was alive, why bother now she's dead? I took him aside and told him stay away, and he just said, 'Fine, fine,' like he didn't have much fight left in him anymore. Said his name is Darton."

I'd watched Darton Copeland stop and say something into the ear of Ivan Bauerstock. Watched Bauerstock turn as if Copeland didn't exist, then walk away from the smaller man.

Now Darton Copeland was crossing the street toward the 7-Eleven, a scarecrow figure, diminished in size by distance.

"How about the guy with the red face? He looks like he just got off a cruise ship."

"Man with the belly? No, he's local. Got that hard-ass, I'm-a-tax-payer attitude. Wouldn't tell me nothing. Gave me the Negro cop look, like why waste his time? So I asked around and his name is Rossi, has a construction company on the island. Apparently got some money. Guess he just came for the show. Next you're going to ask me about the freaky kids, the ones with green and purple hair. Why they here?"

I nodded.

Parrish was looking at them, taking in how they reacted to his stare. "Some coincidence, huh? how I already checked what you think needs to be checked."

"Like you're a mind reader."

"Uh-huh. What the tall one told me was, the one with the thing in his lip. Like a silver horseshoe? He told me they read about the girl in the paper, how cool it was she could find things, things that was lost. Like maybe she had psychic powers or was a witch or something, so they were curious. Decided to come and watch the psychic girl get buried, that's what he told me. Only they're kind of disappointed they didn't get to see her body when the casket was open. They said that was pretty much a bummer—the short fat girl, she told me that. 'We're kind of, you know, bummed 'cause we waste all this time and, you know, don't even get to look inside.' Know what the fat girl asked me? 'Is she like a skeleton now or just rotted?' "

I said, "Indignant because they'd been left out, that was her attitude? They couldn't even shut up during the service."

Parrish allowed a confidential chuckle. "Oh yeah, man. These kids today, everybody owes them something, huh? Makes me want to move to my cabin in Colorado, go up there and wait for the end to come. You white people, you're bad enough. But it's gotten so I don't even like my own kind no more."

Ten

One of the women I'd guessed to be a newspaper reporter stopped us in the little parking lot, saying, "Excuse me,
Mrs. Copeland, I'm with Everglades University, Museum of
Natural History. Any chance we can sit down and talk about
your daughter, how she did what she did? At your convenience, of course."

Long minutes before, we'd had to wait while Della was
comforted by Teddy Bauerstock, Ivan's politician son, the two
of them embracing, swaying back and forth, while she
sobbed, "You were the only one who was kind to her, treated
her like she wasn't strange. It's so sweet of you, Teddy, to

even remember. I thought you forgot about us years ago," as he patted her back, tears in his own eyes, camera shutters making their scissors sound.

We had to wait a little longer as he spoke to reporters, his arm around Della's shoulder, a protective posture. "Dorothy was my friend. No . . . she was more like my little sister. I didn't know her well. We didn't spend a lot of time together, but enough to become close. Her brilliance made her seem different, and we all know how cruel kids can be to those who are a little different. More than once I had to step in and tell the local bullies to back off, leave her alone."

That caused Della to smile as she dabbed at her eyes.

He wasn't finished.

"As some of you know, my family's beach house is on the east point of the island, near Indian Hill. There're a lot of mounds on our acreage. Dorothy liked to walk up there by herself and just sit. Sit there and look out over Barfield Bay. That's what I'm going to do right now. Before Dad and I head back to the ranch, I'm going to sit on one of those old Indian mounds and think about Dorothy, and what's happened to this great state of ours. Think about what a sad thing it is that thieves and bullies can do what they want to innocent people when there's no one there to protect them."

Bauerstock had the ability to grit his teeth and flex his jaw muscles in a way that suggested resolve. He flexed jaw muscles now as he added, "It's time we put a stop to this sort of thing. Dorothy had a lot to teach us. I think she's teaching us still."

Which got more tears from Della, Ivan Bauerstock standing in the background, nodding at the way his son was handling himself, and no wonder: Teddy Bauerstock was very, very good. A compelling voice, lots of eye contact, forceful in the right places but also a self-deprecating way of smiling that suggested boyishness over a core of strength.

Earlier, I'd watched him shake Tomlinson's hand, speaking animatedly as Tomlinson nodded a solemn understanding. Same with the journalists, one by one. Got them off alone, face-to-face, slightly closer than the thirty-three inches of comfort space that behaviorists say we require.

But me, he'd dismissed with a frank glance of assessment: I am a person without politics, and he was able to read that. There was no way I could help him, so I was an unproductive investment in time.

I'd stared back into Teddy Bauerstock's congenial face with its congenial smile and I saw eyes that were as expressionless as holes in a small-bore rifle. I had seen eyes like his once before.

Where?

The man had a future in Washington. No doubt about that.

Now this woman from Everglades University wanted attention, which I found irksome. I'd had enough of cemeteries and crowds. I was eager to get on the road, change back into canvas shorts and T-shirt, put my boat in the water as soon as possible and feel wind in my face.

But no, we had to stop again. And this woman wasn't even a reporter.

Talking to a reporter, at least, was something that I planned to do willingly. . . .

Her name was Nora Chung, an Amerasian, probably half Vietnamese with some Indian in her, too, though I'd already misjudged her once and was reluctant to make any more assumptions.

The card she handed us said she was assistant director of anthropology, and a Ph.D. Impressive for a woman who looked just a couple of years out of her teens. Tall with broad shoulders—maybe a competitive swimmer at one time. Very long legs in beige dress slacks; a lean upper body, thin and bony beneath a dark blouse with pearl buttons; wire-rimmed glasses over sloe eyes and an Anglo nose; hair cut rice-bowl style, advertising her ethnicity.

Della Copeland had the voice of a veteran waitress, deepened and slowed by smoky bars and sore feet. She took a cigarette from her friend Betty Lynn and lit it now, letting her breath out slowly as if she'd been wanting to do it for a while; making the feeling last. Then she looked at the anthropologist through a haze of blue, saying, "We already talked to a bunch of archaeologists. Back when my Dorothy was still with us. We talked to a couple people they sent down from Tallahassee. I don't know what else I can tell you."

The younger woman said, "I've read the transcripts, the interviews with Dorothy, but there are some other things I'd like to ask. Not now, though. It's not a good time, and I sincerely don't want to impose."

Della's eyes were red from crying. She was probably short-tempered, too, from the heat and a week of emotional abrasion. "What I suppose you really want is to find out what valuable things might have been buried with my little girl. Something nice for your museum. You get me off and make nice to me, hoping I'll say, 'Here, take it for free.' That's what Dorothy and me used to do. Gave it away. We gave it all away, not a penny for ourselves."

The anthropologist stayed cool, nodding her empathy. "That's in the records, too. Your generosity. I'm not going to pretend I wouldn't love to see anything your daughter found. But later, when you've rested. Can I call you? Thing is, I don't have your number."

Della made a sound of exasperation and opened her purse to find a pen and paper. "You scientific types," she said, "you never get tired of asking."

A couple of people had stopped close enough to listen: two other women I assumed were journalists, including the one in the caftan who now had a little camera in one hand while she waved for attention with the other, calling, "Mrs. Copeland? Mrs. Copeland! The thing the gentleman's holding"—she pointed to me—"why's it wrapped in a handkerchief?"

Della took a deep drag on her cigarette as she handed her number to the anthropologist, dark eyes focusing. "'Cause maybe what my friend's got there is private. Maybe something just between my little girl and me. Which means it's no-body's business but my own, lady, and sure 'nuff none of yours."

The woman's voice had a bellows quality that I have come to associate with a predisposition to hysteria, neutered cats and astrology. "Your friend took something from your daughter's casket. Is that what you're telling us?"

"Lady, what I'm telling you is, it's none of your affair."

Speaking more firmly, letting everyone hear her reporter's voice, she said, "Please don't be that way. Why the secrecy? I believe your daughter actually possessed real psychic powers. I want to write about her for one of the biggest papers in the nation. I'm psychic myself. It's what I *do*."

"You're a psychic?"

"That's right."

"Then why bother asking questions? Read my mind, get your own answers. Maybe you'll see a real butt-whipping, you look hard enough."

Caftan-woman's reply was an insincere smile that was a parody of patience. "I'm not the enemy, I'm your friend, Mrs. Copeland. It was the golden medallion, wasn't it? That's what you hid in Dorothy's coffin."

"My daughter's coffin is none of your business, lady!"

"You're upset, I can feel it. But people have a right to know. No matter what you think, readers have rights." Caftan waved the little camera. "How about letting me take just a quick picture? Maybe you holding the medallion and stand-ing by your dear daughter's casket."

I was aware of a soft growling sound, a feral-like purring, and realized it was coming from Della who had begun to move slowly toward the woman in the caftan.

Time for someone to step in and take charge.

I touched Della's elbow, gave it a meaningful squeeze. It stopped her. I waited for a moment before I put my lips to her ear and whispered, "Trust me, trust what I'm going to do," before I said to everyone close enough to hear: "This lady has a pretty good point. Ms. Copeland is understandably upset, but we have no desire to be secretive. Della? Do you mind if I show them?"

"I think the fat tramp better watch her mouth, is what I think."

I chuckled as if she were joking. "Then I have your permission."

"Whatever you want. But me, I've said all I'm going to say."

I became a public speaker for the little group and others still coming from the cemetery who lingered to listen. Teddy Bauerstock and his father were pulling away in the black Humvee, but the rockers were still there. So was the man in the Hawaiian shirt.

I told them, "The late Dorothy Copeland found many artifacts. You think you've read about all of them? Believe me, you haven't, not even close. Ms. Copeland still has a number of items in storage. But the artifact that Dorothy treasured most was this"—I took the handkerchief away, held the wooden totem up briefly, then handed it to Tomlinson before anyone had a chance to snap my photograph—"a very valuable carving which we will be taking back to Ms. Copeland's home in Key Largo." I turned to Della. "What marina will we be staying at? In case the reporters need to contact us."

Her expression described puzzlement. Did I really want them to know? I nodded that, yes, I wanted them to know. "At the Mandalay," she said slowly. "Mandalay Marina and Tiki Bar. Little place on the ocean side."

"At the Mandalay Marina," I repeated. "We don't know what the symbols on the carving mean. You'll have to ask an archaeologist about that. All Ms. Copeland knows is that Dorothy treasured it. Even slept with it at night. It gave her great comfort. Which is why Ms. Copeland placed it in her daughter's hands fifteen years ago.

"We don't want there to be a third burial. That's the reason I'm speaking to you now. We don't want Dorothy disturbed again. There's nothing else to find, and we want it known publicly. We're asking whoever did this, please leave the girl in peace."

I told them that was the end of the statement, but caftan-woman pressed questions on me. Then a couple of legitimate journalists—they'd put a lot of distance between themselves and her—began to ask questions, too.

I answered them all politely.

Made sure to mention the Mandalay Marina, Key Largo, several times. It troubled me that I'd never seen the place, didn't know the layout. I had no idea what the security problems would be, or the ambush potential, and I wouldn't know until I got there and did my own quiet survey.

It didn't matter. I wanted it in print. I wanted anyone with a personal interest to know where they could find the totem. I wanted them to know where they could find me.

Not that I had some fatal intent, no. What the thieves had done so far constituted small-time theft and a monstrous indifference to the feelings of others.

Yet, there are some acts that transcend legalities.

I wanted to confront them. I wanted to bait them, isolate them and give them a very serious scare before telephoning Detective Parrish, saying to him, "Guess who wants to confess to you. . . ."

They maybe didn't belong in jail, but they sure as hell belonged in court. Or a psych ward. . . .

As I spoke to the reporters, I became aware of anthropologist Nora Chung's expression of distaste. Perhaps even disgust. Her standing there on the periphery, hands in pockets, sullen-faced, listening.

Was the expression a reaction to me?

Yes. Not much doubt about it, judging from the way she turned away, shaking her head.

She made it even clearer a few minutes later. As I was accompanying Della, JoAnn, Betty Lynn and Tomlinson to the parking lot, she caught up to us, saying, "Hey, look, I'm sorry to intrude again, and my timing's rotten, but I have to respond to what you just did back there. That little press conference you just held." Disapproval was in her voice; some anger, too.

I stopped. "Oh?"

"Yes. I'm not blaming you, Mrs. Copeland, don't misunderstand. But what this gentleman did, showing a very rare artifact to a bunch of reporters, letting them take pictures. Then implying that Dorothy found it along with lots of other valuable artifacts in the mounds demonstrates a complete lack of . . . well, let's just say that I don't think you appreciate the kind of damage you'll cause when newspapers run that story."

Listening to Teddy Bauerstock's slick act, then dealing with caftan-woman had depleted my reserve of patience. Also, the inexplicable sadness I felt had metamorphosed into a sort of vengeful anger. Anyone who violates a defenseless young woman deserves punishment, right?

Right.

So I was already focused, on attack mode, and in no mood for criticism from a self-righteous twenty-year-old. I said, "You're quite correct, Ms. Chung. Your timing's rotten. Check back when your judgment improves," and moved past her.

She started to speak, but, instead, reached, grabbed and held my wrist. Her intent was to stop me, so I stopped. Then I turned my head very, very slowly and stared at her until she removed it. It didn't take long.

Reacting to my expression, she stammered, "I'm . . . I'm sorry. I am very sorry. I shouldn't have done that."

"Yeah. You certainly should not have done that. Take my advice: don't ever try it again." I resumed walking.

"At least listen to what I have to say!"

I hesitated, then stopped once more, and motioned for

Della, JoAnn and Betty Lynn to walk ahead. Tomlinson shrugged and stood quietly beside me, him with the carving in his bony hands, me holding the keys to my truck.

"Okay. Talk. We'll listen while you explain to Dr. Tomlinson and myself about our complete lack of knowledge. That's what you were going to say, isn't it? And our lack of understanding."

I think it's silly for Ph.D.'s and the skippers of small boats to affect titles in public places. But this seemed a rare and appropriate occasion, and I watched it set her back a bit. It leached some of the anger from her voice.

She said, "I apologize for making assumptions. I don't know who you are, and I shouldn't judge."

"Like I told you: we all make mistakes."

"It's just that I'm so passionate about the subject."

"So explain to us how passion excuses rudeness."

She had the nervous habit of combing fingers through hair so short it didn't need combing. A way of gaining a few seconds to think. Her eyes, I noticed for the first time, were a lucent shade of amber. Striking enough to suggest contact lenses, but there was no telltale demarcation between lens and iris. A pleasant-looking woman; part jock, part academian.

She was not the type to remain defensive and apologetic for long.

"I can tell you from personal experience," she said, "that every idiot with a boat and shovel is going to find a local mound and start digging if they read about that totem. It's bad enough when developers do it. At least some of them give us time to do quick-and-dirty survey digs before they start pouring asphalt. I get so upset because there's not much left to save."

When I didn't reply, she took a deep breath, let it out. "Know what the saddest thing is? Dorothy didn't find anything in the mounds. Know why? Because there's *nothing* to find. Nothing except lots of shell, bits of fish bones, traces of pollen, tiny little pottery shards. Things that, mapped in context, can tell us a lot about how the water level's changed, about the weather, about if there really is global warming, about what the Calusa ate to survive.

"It's all worthless to a treasure hunter, but that's what they'll be destroying with their picks and shovels. They'll be out there digging up history, ruining more mounds."

"All because of me," I said. "That's quite a burden."

"Um-huh, I'm sure. I recognize sarcasm when I hear it."

"Then I'll try to be a little more subtle next time. Out of respect."

She turned to Tomlinson. "Judging from the eulogy, you, at least, are an intelligent, sensitive man."

"Oh, yes, I am. You are a superb judge of character, young lady. I am both those things."

Chung had an endearing smile when she chose to use it. "Then you, at least, can appreciate what I'm saying."

Tomlinson gave an open-palmed it's-out-of-my-control gesture. "I do, I certainly do. But my friend here tends to be the proactive one. Don't let his lack of sensitivity fool you. He's equally impersonal and obsessive. So I just kind of sit back and watch."

"So I see."

"Everything he does, though, there's a reason. Just like gravity. He can put on quite a show."

Looking at me, she said, "I don't doubt it."

It was possible that Nora Chung had information that might be useful to me. . . .

I told her I had a question—if she'd finished lecturing us.

She sighed, frustrated by my lack of remorse. "Yes. End of lecture."

"Okay, the question is this: from what I see, the mounds on Marco are already covered with houses. So why're you worried? What's left to ruin?"

"You're right. There's not much left here. But Dorothy didn't make her discoveries on Marco."

JoAnn had already told me that. I wanted to know the exact spot so I could check to see if it'd had recent visitors.

"Really? Then where?"

Her voice was no longer flexible and expressive. It became a flat bureaucratic barrier. "I'm sorry, I'm not at liberty to give out that information."

"Can't or won't?"

"Let's say both so there's nothing to argue about."

"Ms. Chung, if you want Della Copeland to grant you an interview, you're going to have to be willing to do a small favor or two for her friends."

"Meaning you."

"Exactly right."

"At the site we're discussing, Dorothy Copeland found . . . I can't remember all that she found, but I have the list in my car. Something like twenty significant wooden carvings, the gold medallion, the totem Dr. Tomlinson is holding, plus smaller things. Tell the truth, do you think it would be wise for us to release the dig site to the public?"

I said, "For one thing, I'm not the public. For another, if artifact hunters risked digging in a city cemetery, do you think they'd hesitate to destroy an archaeological site? You can bet they did the research and found out where Dorothy was. Maybe not the exact place. But close enough."

I watched her put a determined chin on her fist and mull it over, weighing the possibilities.

"It's possible, I guess."

"No, it's close to being a certainty. When's the last time you visited that island?"

She shook her head. "I've been working in the Bahamas and Haiti; they just transferred me back to the states two weeks ago. Because of my promotion."

"You've never been there?"

"Well . . . no. Not yet. But I've been through the files. I've studied the photographs. And I have plans to go. Soon."

I nodded, enjoying her discomfort. "Don't you think you have a professional obligation to find out if looters are tearing the place apart?"

"I plan to!"

"Then take me along. Not for artifacts. I want to find the

people who violated Dorothy's grave. If they're out there, they maybe left something behind that will tell me who they are. Will you show me?"

She'd taken a step or two back, as if trying to create some space between herself and my sudden offer. "I can give it some thought. Tomorrow . . . no, tomorrow's Sunday. Monday I can check with my boss, give Fort Myers a call and ask—"

"Nope. I want to go today. Now."

She was shaking her head, grimacing at my persistence. "Look, mister. I don't even know your name. Besides, I can't take you today. I don't have a boat."

Tomlinson interrupted. "Ms. Chung, you mind some advice from an intelligent, sensitive man? When choosing between two evils, always pick the one you've never tried. It keeps things interesting."

"Well . . . I guess it wouldn't hurt. . . ."

I said, "My name's Ford." Then I pointed to the street where my truck was parked. "We've got a boat."

Eleven

It was a small island just a quarter mile across the bay from Marco, maybe a hundred acres counting mangroves, with a nice little stretch of beach backed by a high tree canopy, vines and shadows.

Seen from the water, the mounds were a distinctive elevation, humpbacked like a turtle, with a dome of gumbo limbo trees above the mangrove hedge.

The gumbo leaves were parrot-green, amber branches showing through the foliage.

To Nora Chung, I said, "This is better than driving, isn't it?"

I was at the wheel of my skiff. She was beside me. Without much enthusiasm, she said, "I'll let you know when we're safely back on land."

That would be awhile.

When it comes to moving boats and cars, logistics are never easy. After the funeral, we'd stood in the parking lot discussing who'd drive what to where, and who would wait for whom until I said to Della, "You three drive to Key Largo, don't worry about me. I'll run the boat across Florida Bay. Either way, land or water, it's about the same distance. I might even get there before you do."

Florida Bay is the waterspace which separates mainland Florida from the Keys; a tricky series of banks and twisting channels through water that is seldom more than waist deep. It was a nice day for crossing. Slick out there on the water. As if the Gulf was lifting and falling beneath a sheet of pliofilm.

I stood there listening to them sort it out, looking through the trees. There was Dorothy's casket. It appeared smaller in the filtered light, a distinctive shape; it reminded me of a box that had been abandoned in an open field.

Two city employees were erecting the canvas screen again, waiting for the funeral party to leave so they could finish their day's work.

I noted that Della took pains not to turn her head in the direction of the cemetery.

First things first, Betty Lynn said. Was the anthropologist willing to guide me to Dorothy's dig site in exchange for an interview with Della?

Chung was reluctant, but agreed.

In that case, there was a way to get all the cars to Key Largo without anyone having to wait. Tomlinson would drive my truck, Della would drive her own car, and Betty Lynn would drive Nora's little Honda Accord. That way, Nora could travel to Key Largo by water with me, ask Della all the questions she wanted, then drive back at her convenience.

Which seemed to make the anthropologist uneasy.

"You don't have to worry a thing about Doc," Della reassured her. "A friend of mine's told me about him for years. He's just a big ol' puppy dog. Wouldn't hurt a fly."

"I don't know. . . . What about boating experience?" Asking JoAnn, Tomlinson, everyone but me.

"I get out when I can," I told her.

"Unless you know your way across Florida Bay, I don't think I should go. I hear those waters are very dangerous."

"They can be. I haven't made the run in years."

She didn't find that very reassuring. "I'd feel better if you went along, Dr. Tomlinson." Making it clear that she didn't want to be alone with me, either.

Lately, I seemed to be having that effect on women.

"I am always at Marion's side," Tomlinson replied. "Sometimes spiritually. Sometimes with the beer. Either way, it doesn't make a lot of difference. He's the one who runs the boat."

The anthropologist said, "Marion?" increasingly dubious.

We found a public boat ramp on 951, across the bridge and just north of the Marco Yacht and Sailing Club. Using our cars as shields, I changed into blue cargo shorts and a favorite old khaki shirt that had been sun-bleached gray. The woman stepped away from her car, wearing olive drab pants and shirt with button-down bellows pockets, sleeve tabs and epaulets, basic military issue BDUs, battle dress uniform.

"Shopping for clothes at an Army-Navy surplus store," I said. "Is that a new college fad?"

She replied, "Army ROTC has never been much of a fad," as she helped me shove my skiff off the trailer, then swung herself aboard, showing she knew a thing or two about boats.

Once we put a couple of miles of water behind us, she began to relax a little. The antagonistic tone vanished and she talked more freely. It is one of the effects of a small boat. A small boat reduces personal space while increasing interdependence, so it is impossible to maintain a formal relationship.

Well, not impossible. But rare and unlikely.

I handed her the chart book and she flipped pages until she found Marco and the Ten Thousand Islands. Without being asked, she'd assumed the role of navigator, which was fine with me. She seemed confident. Asked me the right questions about moon phase and draft. I complimented her and apologized for my own gruff behavior.

"Crowds and funerals rank right up there as my least favorite things," I told her.

"Crowds, yeah, I know just what you're saying. A rock concert or something like that? Forget it. Because of all the people bumping into each other, talking when they're supposed to be quiet. My gosh, I can't tolerate it, so I don't go."

She used expressions like that: My gosh, gee whiz, holy cow, I'll be darned. Midwestern, probably small town or the farm.

"So what do you do for recreation?"

"Movies. I absolutely love movies. The place I grew up, out there in the cornfields, there wasn't much else to do but read and watch the VCR. I love those action movies with all the suspense. Car chases, explosions. Escape from all that boredom, I guess. You know the ones I'm talking about?"

I'd heard of the actors she named, but hadn't watched their movies.

She said, "I bet you like the arty foreign films. The kind with subtitles that everyone pretends to understand but no one really does. Why're you smiling?"

"I've never been accused of being arty."

"Then what about the old action films? *To Have and Have Not,* Bogie and Bacall. *In Harms Way*–the Duke. Man, one of my favorites."

"*The Searchers?*" I said.

"I loved that movie!"

We talked about films for a while before I asked her what else she did for recreation.

"I get into boats with total strangers. Let them shanghai me to God knows where."

Which was a way of letting me know that she was willing to make peace.

I listened to her tell me that my chart book was at least a

couple of years old. The way she could tell was, the place we were headed was an island named Swamp Angel Ways— swamp angel being a common cracker euphemism for mos- quitoes, "ways" indicating the place where sailing boats were hauled out on rails and scraped clean.

The days of winching sailboats ashore were long gone. The mosquitoes, though, Nora had been told, were still terri- ble. Even so, certain local chambers-of-commerce types had battled to have the island's name changed. Anticipating de- velopment, a mosquito eradication program and perhaps even a bridge, newer charts were showing the island as Cayo de Marco.

"See what I mean?" she said, speaking not much louder than normal. No reason for her to. I was running at a com- fortable cruising speed with a very quiet engine. "People don't care about history. Worse, they have no respect for it. Some of these greedy jerks would rename the moon if they thought it would increase their cash flow. Moon? That's an offensive word, right? Like teenagers sticking their bare butts in the air. So give it a new name and make it marketable. Call it Satellite de Lunar."

It seemed to please her that I smiled.

Chung had been born and raised outside Davenport, Iowa, a little place called Eldridge. She'd applied to the Uni- versity of Florida on a lark with a friend, never really expected to come south, but the academic scholarship that Gainesville had made available was so enticing she'd accepted. That plus the ROTC scholarship made school practically free. But she'd dropped the ROTC program after a year because she was offered a work-study package through the Everglades University's new Museum of Natural History.

"So much for my career in the Army. That's one thing I could tell about you right off. You're not the military type."

I said, "Oh?"

"I'm right, aren't I?"

"It's amazing you can tell."

"That's what I figured. It's a hobby of mine, looking at people, trying to figure out who they are, what they do. You can tell a lot about someone if you pay close attention."

"No kidding. Give me an example."

"There's the obvious stuff like rings and watches and necklaces. But if someone doesn't wear jewelry—like you?—then you just have to read the person. From the way you handle yourself, I can tell that you're perceptive. The way you take things in, snipping little bits and pieces of what you see and filing it away. But not in an aggressive way. More the studious type. Like maybe a professor at a small college. Laid-back, passive except for the occasional zinger or two. The kind who has stacks of books laying around; always losing your glasses."

I said, "You've been talking to my friends behind my back."

I told her maybe it was because of what I did for a living.

"A marine biologist?"

That seemed to please her, too.

Her father was George Temple, a Yavapi Apache mix,

who'd served with the 82nd Airborne in Vietnam. After returning home, he'd wired his wife-to-be money for a plane ticket and helped her get a visa out of Bangkok just before the fall of Saigon. Nora was born more than a decade later, less than two years before her parents divorced. Thus the maternal last name.

"Quite a coincidence, me, a transplanted Iowa girl, ending up down here in the land of coral." She gave me a knowing look. "Don't worry. I'm not suggesting there's some great significance to it or anything."

I sat at the wheel; made no reply.

"What I mean is, I don't believe in things like that. The pseudo-sciences. I don't believe in numerology, phrenology or providence. None of that."

I said, "See? We do have something in common."

"Amazing, huh? Numerology, that's the new thing. Go to a bar, at least one guy comes up and wants to add the letters in my name. It's a come-on, I know, but they really seem to take it seriously. Which is why I didn't much care for the guys I met in college."

I asked, "Oh, what kind of men did she like?" Just making conversation, but I saw in her expression that I had crossed a line. I was being a little too personal, so I wasn't surprised that she quickly changed the subject.

We'd run through Big Marco Pass into the open Gulf. We ran along the beach looking at all the tourists roasting in the sun, high-rise condos behind them. Lots of jet skis and a couple of inboards pulling parasails. Summer scent of coconut oil,

Coppertone and burgers. Pool bars seemed to be doing a booming business for hurricane season. The Marco Island Hotel had a big buffet going on, reggae band playing for several dozen men and women wearing name tags as they mingled around the pool. We were that close.

Then we cut north into Caxambas Pass; followed it inland through No Wake Zones where ranch-style houses, Spray-Creted white, sat in rows on irrigated lawns fronted by seawalls.

"That must be it," Chung said, meaning Swamp Angel Ways. She was matching the chart to the mangrove maze ahead and off to the right.

I could see the dome of gumbo limbos that are always indicative of mounds.

"Does the chart show any water?"

"There's a little cove this side, a little cove on the east side. Not much water in either one, so it doesn't much matter."

It mattered to me.

I wanted to take a look at both coves before wading ashore. Make certain someone wasn't already there.

It comes from old habit. I don't like surprises.

The mound islands of Florida's Gulf coast have a distinctive odor, a mixture of decomposing wood, skunk leaf and lime, dampened by rain and photosynthetic density, incubated by white shells that absorb sunlight then radiate heat.

I'd chosen the cove on the eastern side, shielded from the boat traffic of Barfield Bay. I poled my skiff in through the shallows, anchored off the stern and tied the bow to the limb of a black mangrove.

"Gosh almighty, do you hear them coming?"

I didn't know what she meant at first, but then I did. It was an electronic hum, like a wave of miniature bombers approaching.

Mosquitoes. A pewter cloud of them above the tree canopy.

Then they were on us, glittering mobiles orbiting around our heads, creating a cobweb feeling on nose and ears, collecting on my bare forearms and legs as if I'd been doused with black pepper.

"We should have brought some bug spray!"

I said, "You ever wear a bug jacket?"

"A what?"

From beneath the console, I took two Ziploc bags. In each was a hooded jacket made of wide cotton mesh, not unlike fish netting. I'd saturated the mesh with citronella oil; kept the jackets in bags so the oil wouldn't evaporate.

Nora opened one of the bags and made a face. "Smells like crushed-up orange rinds. Or really cheap perfume. You come home with this stuff all over you, what do the ladies say?"

I was buttoning my jacket. The mosquitoes continued their satellite pattern around my face, but didn't land. I told her, "Lately, they haven't been saying too much."

Nora told me, "Fifteen years ago, back when the Tallahassee group surveyed the island, this looters' pit was already here. Same as most of the ones we've already passed, too.

They took pictures; made a little map. The archaeologists from back then, they kept good notes."

There were dozens of looter pits. They reminded me of bomb craters, but were actually holes dug by men sweating over their shovels, miserable in the heat but determined to find treasure. What they'd found was what they created—a hole in which to throw their beer cans when they'd finally given up.

She was standing in one of the pits now. It was a square-sided trench that was chin-deep, the walls a mosaic of shells: whelks, and conchs and fist-sized tulips. Big shells that were bleached as white as the little grave markers back on Marco.

The entire island was like that, surface and substructure. Shells everywhere you walked. The shells had a resonance when weight was applied, hard and hollow, calcium carbonate grinding, so it was like walking on bone.

Now Nora was standing in one of the holes, studying the layers of shell. She had a sheath of papers in her hand and was comparing the old survey notes and diagrams to patterns of the shell wall.

"You see the sequence of sedimentation? The different layers, I'm talking about. See where there's a stratum of shell, then a layer of organic material beneath it, then another stratum of shell? It shows how the sea level's changed. This low stratum, I think it's related to the Holocene rise in sea level."

I was standing on the edge of the hole, looking through the trees, seeing nothing but jungle, glancing at her every minute or two to show she had my attention. "You lost me."

"I was talking about the Holocene. That's . . . well, it describes a period of time. The Pleistocene, the Holocene? They were right on the boundary of the Ice Age. It was toward the end of the Pleistocene that glaciers lowered the sea enough to create a land bridge between Siberia and Alaska. You see signs of it in this shell wall. That was fifteen, maybe twenty, thousand years ago."

"Which is when humans first came to North America."

"That's what most people believe; they migrated across and worked their way from north to south. But there's another theory."

I said, "I hope you're not talking about visitors from space."

Her expression told me she wasn't going to dignify that with a reply.

She had her notebook out, writing with the stub of a pencil as she said, "Some believe that a separate group of people came to the Americas at about the same time as the Siberian crossing, but a different way. That a small, advanced tribe island-hopped across the Pacific and worked their way north. They became the Inca, the Maya and the Aztec. All brilliant, all very violent, with similar religious ceremonies. A much different people than the woodland and western Indians. Some weirdos think the Calusa were a part of that group."

"All pyramid builders."

"Uh-huh. Not necessarily that they came from across the Pacific, but that they worked their way up from the Bahamas, moving south to north."

I told her I'd heard rumors of that before. I'd also heard that the Calusa had traded with the Maya.

"That's not what I'm saying. There may have been some occasional contact between the two groups. A thousand years ago, some restless kid gets in a canoe, starts paddling the coast and ends up in the land of stone pyramids. Or vice versa, ends up in the land of shell pyramids. Sure. That could've happened. But a few visits don't constitute a relationship."

I was looking down into the hole, when she pulled what looked to be a flat brown rock from the wall and studied it closely for several seconds. "I wouldn't have touched this, by the way, if the looters hadn't already made such a mess."

"What is it?"

"Pottery. You can see one side is black from being fired. Pottery's not my specialty, but it looks like it could be from the Glades Plain Period, or maybe Glades Tooled. There's not enough to say. It would date back a thousand years, maybe more. Here"—she handed the pottery to me—"the last person to touch that probably believed exactly what Dr. Tomlinson said. That she had three souls. That inanimate objects absorb energy. That's why, when she was done with this pot, she intentionally broke it to free her own spirit. These mounds are littered with pottery."

I was still looking at the shard. It was reddish-brown with a hint of a rim. "You and Tomlinson will have lots and lots in common."

"Oh boy, there's that tone again. Okay, most people think, hey, that's stupid. Objects don't have a spirit—bowls and rocks, metal and things. But stop to think about Saint Christopher medals and crosses, Rosary beads, Stars of David. Those are the obvious ones. They're not just symbols. People believe they have power. Tattoos and piercings? Same thing. The Nike swoosh mark—check out the ghetto gangs. Power objects."

"Animism." .

"Yes, animism, you bet. It's the most consistent connection between religions."

She took the potsherd and fitted it back into the shell wall exactly where she'd found it. "Connective religions, that's my specialty. I also happen to be one of those people who believes that the Calusa came from the Bahamas. Maybe South America. There's not a bit of artifactual evidence, but I think we'll find it."

"So you're one of the kooks."

For the first time, I was favored with her endearing smile. "Actually, I said weirdos. Yep, I am a weirdo. A hundred-percent weirdo. I believe that ten thousand years ago, people were just as motivated to roam and explore and pass along their personal religion as people are today. Isn't that crazy?"

"Quite the radical."

She began to fight her way through the brush again. "That's what my professors always thought."

"Then how'd you end up assistant director of a museum so young? What are you twenty-two, twenty-three?"

She wagged her eyebrows as if she were being tricky. "Until there's proof, I keep my weirdo opinions to myself."

Twelve

Did you hear a boat?" I'd stopped on the crest of a high mound, my head tilted, listening.

She stopped ahead of me; waited for a moment in silence. "I can hear boats out on the Gulf. That's all." She pulled a bandanna out of her pocket and wiped her face. "Some view, huh?"

I touched an index finger to my lips. I could hear the buzz of cicadas . . . the ascending whistle of ospreys . . . the thoracic rhythm of a pile driver burying condo footings on Marco. I thought sure I'd heard an outboard, but it was gone now.

"Maybe it was a boat coming out of Barfield Bay."

Through limbs and vines, we could see the bay glittering

Formica-like in noon sunlight. Beyond, on Marco Island, were rows of houses, then a high hill topped with trees. Indian Hill. What else could it be? I wondered if Teddy Bauerstock really was up there on the mounds looking out. I wondered if he really was thinking about Dorothy.

The thought keyed an unexpected mental portrait that was as dazzling as a camera strobe.

When an image has been deeply imbedded in the brain, our neurotransmitters can become potent, high-resolution cathodes. For a moment, Dorothy was gazing into my eyes once more. It was a familiar and knowing look. Her face was as pale as a mushroom. Dark pupils within her blue eyes burrowed into mine.

"We're almost there. Her dig site."

Nora didn't use a name. As if she knew Dorothy was in my thoughts.

I followed her across the mound.

On a couple of the mounds were bathtub-sized cisterns sunken into the shell. American settlers had built them to catch and store fresh water.

There were raccoon skeletons in one of the cisterns. From the second, a rat the size of a dachshund flushed ahead of us while a red-shouldered hawk screamed overhead.

There were key lime trees flowered with ivory-yellow fruit; an avocado tree, a knarled grove of sour oranges, papaya on delicate, tuberous trunks, and a huge tamarind tree, too.

Survival food in a difficult land.

"Dorothy understood what all of these idiot treasure

hunters never seem to realize. There are hundreds of stories about pirates burying treasure in this mound or that mound, and they are all absolute bull crap. There were no pirates in this area. Ever. You want to say to these dopes, 'Hey, dumbo, these islands weren't even *on* the trade routes, so what were the pirates going to steal? Oysters? Use your darn brain!"

I smiled at her indignation. The woman had a temper.

"Something else I think Dorothy understood was that the Calusa feared their dead. The more powerful the person, the more dangerous the spirit. The Calusa, to protect themselves from the dead, used water as a barrier."

I said, "You mean they floated the bodies out on funeral rafts?"

"No. What they did was . . . well, first you need to know that spirits can't cross water. That's an old, old belief. So they built moats around the burial areas. Back in archaic times, they actually buried individuals under water. Staked the bodies down or buried them in a low area and flooded it. There are water burials at Little Salt Spring near Sarasota; lots of places. You ever hear of the Windover site in Brevard? Same underwater burial system.

"Anyway, when it comes to power people, water's the key. People they feared, it made sense to bury them in water. Keep all those evil qualities from escaping. That's what I think, anyway. Which is one reason there's nothing to find in the mounds."

I mentioned that Tomlinson had me read something about a chief named Tocayo.

"Oh yeah, Tocayo was one of the really bad ones. According to the Jesuits, anyway. Tocayo lived right where we're standing now, or maybe Marco, we're not sure."

"You trust those accounts?"

"From the missionaries? Absolutely not. They were biased and self-serving hypocrites who were cruel as heck. But it's all we've got. What they wrote about Tocayo, though, is pretty consistent and comes from more than one source. For starters, they say that he made a sport of raping his own daughters; seemed to prefer sodomy. He cannibalized children because they were so tender. Columbus, on his second voyage, described how the Caribs would castrate boys because they tasted better when they got older. Tocayo supposedly did the same thing; that's why I think he was a Carib."

Nora had stopped at the base of the mound. She was peering down into the gloom of a mangrove swamp, black muck and shadows, comparing what she saw with the xeroxed map she carried. She said, "Here we are."

Meaning Dorothy's dig site.

"It all looks the same to me."

"Yeah. What we have to find is a real small area. What used to be a water court, but the shape is tough to see because of the mangroves. Even says in the notes that it's hard to find. What happened was, back when the state and developers drained the Everglades, it emptied some of the ancient lakes. The Calusa wouldn't have liked that. Expose the water burials, let all those evil spirits loose."

We'd gone so quickly from sunlight to shadow, that my

eyes were having difficulty adjusting. I saw what looked to be a shallow creek bed, black muck spiked with mangrove roots. Lots of low brush and vines and some kind of fern growing up. There were shell inclines on each side: the basework of more mounds.

The creek bed looked exactly like a dozen other mucky areas we'd crossed, and Nora voiced the same question that was in my mind: "How could Dorothy have *known?* Out of all the places on this island, how could she have possibly known to dig here?"

I remembered Tomlinson saying, *She didn't find things. Artifacts called to her. . . .*

Which made as little sense as the proposition that a teenage girl had found this place at random.

As we maneuvered through mangroves around the base of the mound, Nora stopped so abruptly that I nearly banged into her from behind. Heard her say, "Oh my God. Oh my God! You were right."

I said, "About what?" But then I saw what she meant.

Treasure hunters had found the place, too.

Thirteen

With all the equipment the looters had ferried out, the site looked more like a small construction area. It looked as if it were being cleared and plumbed for a sewage system and parking garage in preparation for condos.

Nora was moving from pit to pit, shaking her head. "These kind of people, they have no respect. It's ruined. They have absolutely destroyed the entire site."

Yes, they had.

This was a high-tech operation. A lot of time and expensive equipage had been invested.

There was a golf cart–sized backhoe with a metal cage

over the driver's seat and controls. The machine was painted blue on white with "Nokonia MX" in big black letters on the side. There were a couple of shovels propped against it.

The backhoe had been used to dig a hole as large as the foundation of an apartment complex. They'd squared it off sloppily and dug down to sea level. The bottom was black muck, and water had seeped in, creating puddles.

Beside the pit was a troughlike flume made of plywood and aluminum. The flume was elevated shoulder-high at one end, was terminated by a screen sieve at the lower end. Near the high end of the flume was a stocky Honda generator and a portable pump with a fire department–sized hose running from it.

It is an old process; the same miners once used it to find gold: dump a bunch of mud in a sluice, jet some water, then watch the screen where the heaviest material separates naturally from the sludge.

It was an obvious and effective little operation. Use the backhoe to load the flume. Use the pump to hose the mud down the gutter. Use the shovels to clear the residual sludge while someone searched the filtering screen for artifacts.

"Know what I think we should do?" I could tell she was furious. Her movements had quickened; she couldn't stand still.

I said, "This sort of thing's against the law, correct?"

She was pacing now, looking at the generator, looking at the little backhoe. "Goddamn right it's against the law! A thing called the National Antiquities Act!"

Profanity. The first time I'd heard her use it. I could tell she was unaccustomed to forming the words. They came out awkwardly; each syllable enunciated with the precision of a novice attempting to speak a foreign language.

"The goddamn son-of-a-bitches! They're treating history like it's . . . like it's a piece of crappy junkyard!"

I took pains not to show that I was amused.

"Calm down, take a few slow breaths."

"It makes me want to vomit what they're doing here!"

"I know. I don't blame you. But there's something about this that doesn't make any sense at all."

"Goddamn right it doesn't make any sense."

"Now wait. Listen to what I'm saying. I'm talking about all this equipment. Think about it. I expected to find signs of fresh digging, sure, but nothing like this. Someone's going to risk all this equipment to find a few artifacts? To get this gear out here, they had to use a barge. People would have seen them bring it ashore. We're only a quarter mile from Marco. Sound travels over water. People would *hear* them. In other words, this is more like a public operation. I think they've probably got permits."

"It's *illegal,* I'm telling you. I don't care if they used a helicopter to chopper it out. You can't intentionally destroy an entire . . ." She stopped for a moment. "Jesus, you doubt what they're doing out here? Look at *this* goddamn stuff. You know what this is?" She kicked the side of a five-gallon can. I had to stoop to read the label. *Carbowax.*

"This chemical, it's what we use to preserve wooden arti-facts found in mud. We call it PEG for short, polyethelene something. I can't remember the rest of it. It prevents the wood cells from collapsing as they dry." She tested the lid of the can. "At least it hasn't been opened. Maybe they haven't had a reason to use it."

"The totem I took from Dorothy. That's why it was so new-looking, it'd been treated?"

"No, the totem's different. It was never touched. What she found is so darn rare. The wood it's made from, it's harder than most metals. Lignum vitae wood, you heard of it? It's so hard and heavy, it won't even float. Who knows how they carved it. Oh . . . God, look at this."

She had knelt near the sluice screen over a pile of what ap-peared to be shells and calcified wood. As I got closer, I could see that I was mistaken.

"These are bones. *Human* bones. Thrown away like trash because it's not what they're looking for. It's not gold. It's not something the son-of-a-bitches can sell."

I watched her touch the bones with a care that approached reverence: a piece of mandible, molars worn flat, presumably from chewing food in this sandy environment. A length of fe-mur scarred with a black fissure: a leg that had broken and healed badly. There were cranial chunks the size of coconut shell, though no intact skulls. There were bones from fingers and feet and scattered rib cages, all dumped in a pile.

The size of some of the bones was distinctive.

I said, "These are the remains of more than one person. The pelvis, the narrow opening, that's an adult male. A pretty big guy. But there're also two, maybe three children."

She was touching the bones one by one, trying to put them into some kind of order. The indifference with which they'd been thrown into a heap seemed to offend her. "That's not normal. It's not common. They could've done something like that, but they would've needed a reason."

"For adults and children to be buried in the same grave?"

"They did it for royalty. Children to serve them in the afterlife. But underwater? A water burial, that's what's not common. Maybe if the guy who died was really powerful and his people feared him, it might make sense. They kill his children and bury them all together. They want to get rid of the whole line forever. I'm just guessing. There's nothing we've found to back me up on this. We'd have to do DNA to make sure." She'd stopped to inspect something. "Oh, shit, look at this—"

What she was holding looked like a chunk of skull, but she told me it was actually something she called a *Zemi;* a little god all the way from the Bahamas. Then she added, "You know what these bastards may have found here? They may have stumbled onto the evil guy himself. I think they've dug up Tocayo."

I wasn't amused now.

She didn't say anything for awhile, but kept digging through the mud with her fingers. "That's what makes me so damn mad. If there's a connection between the Caribs and the Calusa, it's not going to be something obvious. There's not going to be a sign that reads, 'Look here!' It's going to be little bits and pieces tied together. Exactly the kind of subtle stuff these jerks stomp on and destroy. They're a type, they really are. It's like they got a sneaky gene."

It took me a moment before I realized she was back on the subject of looters again.

"They've got contempt for everybody and everything but themselves. Bastards like that are ruining our chances of connecting the travel routes. Out of pure selfishness, too." She took up the potsherd again and studied it for a long moment, stuffed it into her pocket. "Goddamn them. *Goddamn* them all to hell." She looked at me, looked at the excavating equipment. "You know what I'm going to do?"

Some of the color had drained from her face. She was that angry.

I said, "Nope. I know what you should do. Get on that cell phone of yours, call your colleagues at the museum and tell them you've got an emergency situation, get down here. Have them notify the sheriff's department, maybe send a fax. Put it on a formal basis to make certain they light a fire under the right people."

She had an odd expression. It reminded me of a petulant child, the way her lips were pursed, but it was more than that. There was a quality of cold fury. "Oh, that's exactly what I'm going to do. You can bet on that, Marion. But first, I'm going to show them what it's like to be violated. That pile of bones, it used to be a person. A person who lived and breathed, not something to be treated like garbage."

An adult male with children who'd been buried beneath water—I didn't remind her of the implications of that.

I said, "Exactly why we need to get the law involved. Detective Parrish, he'd be the guy. The people who did this are the same ones who used the backhoe on Dorothy. Count on it."

She said, "There you go. All the more reason to give them a taste of their own medicine."

I watched her step carefully over the pile of bones. Watched her take one of the shovels and walk to the front of the backhoe. Then watched her swing hard from the heels and bash out a front headlight. She got a new grip on the shovel, swung just as hard and broke the second one, too.

The vacuum explosion of glass spooked birds in the high tree canopy. Caused them to shriek and chatter as they took flight.

She took a step back, as if savoring her handiwork. "What do you think?"

"I think that was bad judgment. I think it was a very unfortunate thing to do."

"Really."

"Yeah. There's a chance you just tipped them off. They'll shut down the operation, which means the cops won't be able to catch them in the act."

"I didn't think about that. But it's too late now, that's what you're saying?"

"I think they'll notice a couple of smashed headlights."

"In that case, I might as well keep going. As long as I shut the assholes down, why not do it right?" Without waiting for a reply, she walked to the generator and started hammering at it with the shovel. It took her awhile, but the cowling finally flew into pieces.

By now she was breathing heavily; sweating, too, but she had a nice little smile on her face. "All through high school, I played fast pitch softball. Number three hitter. Can you tell?"

"Oh, it shows, it shows. Pretty nice stroke, yeah. I still think you're making a big mistake."

"Know something, Marion? You actually seem almost human when you smile."

I'd never met a woman I'd so immediately disliked, but who, in the space of a few hours, had completely transformed my opinion. I liked her quirky sense of humor and her fierceness. Tomlinson had once described a woman I loved as an "extreme person." Nora reminded me of that. Style and lots of spirit.

"Something about kooks, you people make me smile."

"Weirdo. You keep getting it wrong. I said weirdo." She dropped the shovel and backed away from what was left of the generator. "So tell me something. Are you going to just stand there like a big goof or are you going to help me tear that trough thing apart?"

"Flume. That's what it's called."

"See? The bookish type. You know what it's called, but do you have the balls to help?"

Someone was coming. . . .

We'd been at the dig site for half an hour or so when I

heard the distant garble of voices and rhythmic snap of branch that told me people were approaching; walking and talking loudly, which suggested that they didn't know we were on the island. They seemed confident they were alone; were used to having the place all to themselves.

No telling why they hadn't heard the crash of metal and wood as we destroyed their equipment. Probably because they were making so much noise themselves.

Coming at us from the west, the cove closest to Marco, which is why they hadn't seen my boat. They seemed to be traveling along what may have been a path, because they were moving a lot faster than Nora and I'd been able to navigate the island. Probably the path created to transport the equipment. Moving so fast they were almost on us before we had time to react.

When I heard them, I cupped my fingers around Nora's bony arm, pulled her close to me and said, "We've got company. Probably the looters."

She'd heard them in the same instant. Her amber eyes had widened and become rounder, the characteristic reaction of fear as her brain tried to gather sensory data. It is a primitive response, signaled from deep beneath the cerebral cortex, an atavistic reaction. The brain seeks a quick answer so that it may make an ancient, ancient decision: Should we fight? Should we take flight?

Our revulsion for snakes is stored in the same dark little crevice. Right there next to our panicked reaction to lightning and our dread of murky water.

I whispered. "Stand your ground. Stay behind me."

She said, "You sure? Boy, are they gonna be pissed off!"

"Oh, I think that's an understatement. Furious is what they'll be."

"Then let's get the hell *out* of here."

"You want someone chasing you through this jungle? That's what'll happen. They take one look at this mess, they'll be hunting us. Panic's contagious. And what if they have a gun?"

The voices were closer now. Adult voices; at least two males.

Nora laced her arm under mine and pulled herself close. "Damn it, Ford, I don't think this is smart! But I'll tell you one thing"—she released my arm, began to search around in the brush, then stood, finally, holding a chunk of button-wood—"I'm not going to let them give me any crap. Not the bastards who did this."

I released a long, deep breath; told myself to stay calm, don't react to her anger, because I'd have enough to deal with in a minute or two.

What I would have preferred to do was hide in the brush; do some first-hand surveillance. Watch them to make certain they were the ones who'd been digging at this site. Listen while they went about their work; maybe discover what they'd found, if anything, what they hoped to find. Also, maybe find out what cemeteries they'd tried to rob lately.

Let them incriminate themselves while we stayed back in the shadows, taking it all in.

I looked at the mess that, minutes before, had been an efficient, high-tech dig site. The flume and the generator were in pieces. No way the pump would still work with all the sand Nora had jammed into its fuel tank. Same with the backhoe. Lots and lots of expensive damage, with air still hissing out of industrial tires, telling anyone with an ounce of sense that the person who'd slit those tires was still on the island, very close by.

I said, "At least you didn't set their machinery on fire."

Nora was holding the club like a bat, looking in the direction of the approaching voices. "Uh-huh, that's the one bad thing about not bringing cigarettes. You never have a lighter when you need one."

Fourteen

When the punk rockers came crashing down the path into the clearing, I stood facing them, wearing a big smile. I said in a loud, cheery, voice, "Well, well. Look who just stepped into our trap. You boys have some explaining to do!" Acting very friendly but vexed, like a school principal unhappy with their behavior.

I wasn't certain it was the punkers at first. There were two males, no doubt about that, but they wore mosquito head nets and long sleeves. It gave them an entirely different look: forty-year-old beekeepers or butterfly collectors on expedition. They could have been that.

But when they stopped, surprised to find us standing there, it allowed me a moment to observe the knobby hands of the leader; it was the tall guy with the dragon tattoo. Yep, and the distinctive body width of his slouching partner suggested he was the kid with the snake crawling up his arm.

When categorizing strangers, the brain differentiates by that which is most obvious: Female/male, black/white, Dragon/Snake.

The chubby girls weren't with them?

Yes . . . but only one. She came stumbling down through the brush, fanning at the haze of mosquitoes around her head net and making a woo-woo-woo wailing sound that I initially thought was sobbing, but translated after a few seconds of listening: "You two . . . hey, you two! Bastards went off and left me—!" But then she saw me and said very quickly, "Oh, shit!" and froze as if she was playing that old kid's game, statue.

Her abrupt silence accentuated the hushed stares of the two men who'd stopped a few yards from me. We stood there listening to the birds and insect whine and steady *thud-a-thud-a-thud* of construction over on Marco.

Dragon was closest; Snake a follower's pace or two behind. The girl now pulling in closer, using Snake as a shield. Dragon was the spokesman as well.

"What'd you just say mister? I must'a not heard you right."

I repeated myself, remaining cheerful but adding a condescending note, letting them know who was in charge.

Dragon had an unexpectedly deep voice, the hint of a

New Jersey accent, and his words were accompanied by a mysterious metallic clicking noise. It took me a moment to realize that, along with the horseshoe in his lip, he had something skewered through his tongue. A silver bead, it appeared to be. It kept hitting his teeth, which created the clicking. Tough to see through the netting.

"Trap? I got no idea what you're talking about, man. We don't know nothing 'bout no trap. This machinery here, that what you mean? We never seen this stuff before—" He stopped, saw the wreckage for the first time and it really hit a nerve. An expression of shock crossed his face, and his chest started heaving.

"Holy shit, the whole fucking place is wrecked, man!"

I stood smiling, saying nothing.

"Jesus Christ! Who did this? Did you people do this?"

I said, "Do *what?*" Still cheery, but virtuous, too.

"Who the hell . . . hey, do you know how much that equipment's worth, mister? Fucking backhoe alone is like fifty, sixty grand. Fucking pump, the generator—goddamn it, I bought that myself—" He caught himself just in time, and stood there, visibly trying to regain control.

I said mildly, "I thought you'd never seen the equipment before."

Snake was peeking out to see; so was the girl. "Jesus Christ, Tony, your dad's gonna shit when he sees what happened to his gear."

"Shut the fuck up, Derrick!"

So the spokesman, Tony, was Dragon. Derrick was Snake.

Very gradually, I had been moving toward them, trying to force eye contact. In return, I'd been receiving all the comforting signs of submission that are similar in primates and pack animals. Tony would not return my glare. He kept his head down when listening; looked beyond me and to the side when speaking. For each step I moved toward him, he scooched back a foot or two.

I didn't have a very clear plan of what I wanted to do, but I knew if I could bully their leader, the followers wouldn't be a problem. They certainly recognized me from the funeral. Already, they'd identified me as someone in authority. I couldn't say I was a cop. Lie about being a cop and, no matter what, you're going to court along with the bad guys. But if I could reinforce the impression of unquestionable authority, I might be able to leverage them into giving me information. If I got real lucky, I could maybe con them into following me to Marco for a meeting with Detective Parrish.

Dr. Ford, did you tell the accused that you were an officer of the law?

Absolutely not.

This deposition is being taken under oath.

I'm aware of that. I have no idea why those three people followed my orders. They must'a jumped to the wrong conclusion.

That was the best I could hope for. It was a stretch, but what other options did I have?

I said to Tony, "Know what I think you boys ought to do? First thing is, take off those nets. Makes you look like someone tied a bag over your head. Like the old joke about being so ugly?" I watched them slouch in sullen protest before I barked, "Get 'em off NOW!"

They jumped a little; ripped the nets off and tossed them on the ground as if they were throwing down weapons.

Derrick's hair was longish, dyed an iridescent maroon. Tony had the spiked purple hair; the kid Tomlinson had said would chew through a man's chest to get to his heart. Both of them had lots and lots of body piercings, ears, eyebrows, lips. Tony had a nose ring, too, brass with a turquoise setting.

Had he been wearing the nose ring at the funeral? No. It was the sort of thing impossible not to notice. Maybe he removed it for formal occasions. Such a thoughtful kid.

"Girls, too. Lose the head net, sweetie. We want a good look at your face before we start asking questions, then haul your butts into jail. Grave robbing. A charge like that, you're gonna spend a year or so behind bars—unless you cooperate."

"Grave robbing?" The girl pulled the net off, showing her flushed cheeks, eyebrows and ears slotted with rings, already sobbing. Her voice had the same irritating whine that it had when she was angry. "I didn't rob no graves, mister, I don't got nothin' to do with what these guys did. I haven't done nothin' wrong, I swear to Jesus, honest. They're like, 'Hey, Tisha, let's go for a boat ride. We'll show you this cool island.' And I'm like, 'Why not, I got nothin' better to do.' So, yeah, I go with them on the boat, but I don't got a damn thing to do with diggin' shit up. That's all their idea."

I'm like, they're like—Tomlinson says the uneducated must now speak in the third-person present tense because their only reality is a television screen or a computer screen. Their brains can convert images but not ideas.

I said, "Really, Tisha? You're just an innocent bystander."

"Yeah, really. You got to believe me. But already, you're like, hey, I'm guilty just being here, but I'm not, so please don't put me in jail, mister. I'm not even eighteen yet; I still got to finish high school, so please don't take me in."

I've known worthless teenagers who grew to be first-rate adults. As of now, though, this was a sad and unattractive little girl who was on the fast track to an empty future.

Time once again for my bemused smile. "You weren't helping them dig? Then how'd you know they were looking for something?"

"Shut your fucking mouth, Tisha! Both of you, shut up, don't say another word!" Tony was losing it: knees wagging as if he needed to urinate; fingers snapping; tongue moving, wetting his lower lip as if to cover the lip ring while showing the silver stud in his tongue. He seemed to be on sensory overload, and probably for good reason. Daddy's equipment had been ruined and, very soon, he'd have to ask Daddy to bail him out of jail. Or so he thought.

Push any living thing into a corner, get too close, and sooner or later it will fight.

It was time for me to back off just a tad, return them to their comfort zone.

Unfortunately, I didn't get the chance.

Tony was still talking. "What's your point, mister? You wanna arrest us, arrest us. But I'm tellin' ya right now, lotta important people know my dad and he's gonna go fucking ape shit when he finds out what you did to his equipment. So you're in trouble, too, dude. I don't care if you're a cop or not; you had no right to ruin all that expensive shit."

Nora had remained an effective background prop, stern and official-looking in her military BDUs. Arms folded, staring at them through blue mirrored sunglasses, she did a good job of playing my loyal backup. But then Tony looked at her and said, "Hey, if you two are cops, where's your guns? And how 'bout you show us some identification."

Nora said, "We've got guns, dumbass. Don't you worry about that."

"Yeah? Where?"

"We keep them locked on the patrol boat."

I watched the expression in Tony's face change very, very slowly. Cartoons use a lightbulb to illustrate sudden understanding. I saw a light appear in Tony's eyes. He was a big lanky guy with ropy muscles, not used to being bullied. "Really? Cops who leave their guns behind. Know what, lady? I think you're full of shit."

Now he was considering me, considering the odds; gauging what his best move would be. The women canceled each other. But there were two of him and only one of me. It put a thin smile on his face. He actually seemed to swell up as he stood a little straighter. Then he made direct, glaring eye contact and I listened to him say, "Then fuck you, dude. Some asshole with glasses and GI Jane. You two wrecked my dad's gear. Then you stand there like hot shits, giving us orders?" He gave a little chuckle of relief. "Some people, they are like so fucking stupid. Seriously. Couple of hicks, I think that's what we got here."

Now he was moving slowly to my right. He glanced over his shoulder at Derrick, communicating something.

Derrick seemed to understand instinctively and began to move slowly to our left.

Like elements of submissive behavior, aggressive behavior is just as telling. This slow dividing of pack members and changing of angles was typical. They were moving into attack formation.

I took a step back, shielding Nora. I said to her softly, "From now on, just follow my lead."

She still didn't get it. "What's that supposed to mean? These people have no right to accuse us. After what they've done?"

Tony had one of the shovels in his hands now, looking at it, testing the heft of it.

I said to her, "You watch too many movies."

The best approach in any conflict is find a way to win without fighting. I tried. I offered Tony and his little friends logical, conciliatory options, even implying we'd pay for the damage, Nora and me backing away a little bit at a time, until he said, "Fuck you, four-eyes. Mister big shot back at the chick's grave. So look at you now, big shot. Begging."

When he mentioned "grave," something happened.

It was the word, or maybe his flippant tone, I'm not sure which, but hearing it changed something in me. It brought the pale image of a sleeping girl into my mind once more. That powerful image was accompanied by a low-pitched roaring in my ears. The sound is not unknown to me. It was an occasional visitor from a dark, dark room.

I said softly to Tony, very softly, feeling the words of a stranger flow out with my breath: "Begging? I'm *begging?*"

"Yeah, dude. You can't hear yourself? Then you must be deaf, man."

I have my own rule when it comes to dealing with more than one attacker, and it has nothing to do with deception. The rule is simple: do your damnedest to eliminate the weakest attackers first.

Do it quickly, brutally, and you will not have to deal with that attacker ever again. It allows you to give full attention to the man who can do you the most harm.

I watched Tony lift the shovel in both hands and rest it on his shoulder as he walked slowly toward us. He had a nasty little smile on his face; he looked like some freaky laborer on his way to work.

By moving in opposite directions, they'd reached an angle of separation where I had to face Tony or I had to face Derrick. I knew that the man at my back would be the first to charge, so I faced Tony. He was still coming toward us, but now I was paying less attention to what I saw than what I heard.

Derrick, a big, doughy man, was behind me. I listened to his careful steps. He'd gotten into some of that black muck. I could hear it sucking at his boots.

Good, he'd be a little less agile. He didn't look particularly agile to begin with. Probably in his early twenties, but lots of baby fat.

"What's the matter there, dude? Don't want to beg no more? Big ol' nerd like you, you ought to be on your knees right now."

I gave Tony a very different kind of smile. "It's those pretty earrings of yours. I don't know whether to beg or flirt."

I half expected Tony to come lunging, but he wasn't taking any chances. Momentarily, his eyes bulged. Nothing more. He was probably waiting for the same thing I was anticipating—Derrick to make his move.

Derrick was back there now, clumping along, trying to work up his courage. At least, I hoped he was. I kept waiting and waiting as Tony drew closer.

Tony was about three shovel-lengths away, but moving more slowly. Yep, he wasn't going to do a damn thing until Derrick attacked.

There are active cowards and passive cowards. Neither are decisive. They almost always need a visual stimulant to act.

I decided to give Derrick an opening he couldn't refuse.

Nora was to my right. She was still holding her dumb little club, a fierce expression on her face. Not at all like the chubby girl who now stood watching from the perimeter. I could hear her siren voice yelling, "Kill 'em, you guys! Beat the shit out of 'em. Kick that mouthy bitch!"

Desperation has a tone and so does fear. I tried to imitate both when I said loudly, "Okay, okay, enough. We don't want any trouble, we quit, we give up. We'll do whatever you want us to do."

Nora rebuked me with a swift turn of the head, eyes furious with disappointment. "*What?* Don't speak for me, buster."

Now I held my hands up in the most primitive gesture of surrender: palms face-high and turned outward. "I mean it. We'll do anything you want. Just please tell that girl to shut up about killing us because there's no reason for anyone to get hurt," which is when I heard the brush crash behind me as Derrick came charging from behind . . .

I didn't want Nora within reach of Tony's shovel, so I swung her hard to my left, catapulting her toward the blustering Tisha. I ducked as I threw her, allowing the momentum to carry me around so that my eyes were belt-high as Derrick plowed toward me.

He'd found a club. I'd expected him to have something. It was wood, about the width of a broom handle but not as long.

When he swung at me, he gave a grunt of effort, put all his considerable weight into it, which threw him off-balance. I leaned away from the club; even so, I took a bruising shot against the ribs. It nearly knocked the wind out of me; created a whistling noise in my lungs, but I locked my elbow down when he hit me and caught the club under my arm. At the same time, I drove up hard and hit him in the crotch with a full right fist. I put all my weight and the strength of my thighs into it, so it drove him a couple of feet into the air.

I heard him scream as his legs collapsed beneath him, but I didn't let him fall. I caught him under the throat with my left hand, forcing him to stand.

I held him there like a fresh shield, me behind him, looking at Tony, who was marching toward me, shovel held overhead like a workman with a sledgehammer who was about to drive a stake into very hard ground.

I stuck my thumb into Derrick's right ear, dug my fingers hard in behind it. I had a pretty good grip on the thing.

People don't realize how tenuously the human ear is attached to the head. I gave Derrick a painful demonstration. Early white settlers who were scalped by Indians but managed to survive described the terrible, deafening sound their skin made when it was ripped away from the bone.

I suspect Derrick's ear made a similar sound as I tore it away from his temple. I didn't pull it completely off. No. But I broke the skin and popped enough tissue to send a message: it was mine if I wanted it.

The sound of Derrick's scream froze Tony in midstride, shovel overhead.

I locked my eyes into Tony's as I spoke into Derrick's ruined ear, "Leave. If you come back, I'll make you eat this. You'll be listening to music through your asshole. Nod if you understand."

Derrick moved his head up and down carefully.

Still holding the guy by the throat, I pushed him toward the mangroves. I didn't bother to look at him as he scrambled off into the bushes. Then I stooped and picked up the limb he'd dropped. I stared into Tony's troubled face and grinned. The color of his cheeks had changed. They were splotched with white.

"Look, mister. Maybe you were right. Maybe we can talk this over. You pay for what you did to my dad's shit, sure, fair enough. Just like you offered."

I was still grinning, walking toward him, the broom-thick stick in my hand. Said, "That offer was for a limited time only."

Fifteen

A long time ago, in a different hemisphere, they made us take martial arts instruction. One of the weeklong evolutions was an introduction to *kendo* and *kenjutsu*, Japanese stick fighting and sword fighting, two very serious disciplines.

The martial arts were useful in that they taught pressure points and power points—unexpected places on the body where it is painful or dangerous as hell to hit or get hit. To this day, I cannot see a man wearing an open-collared shirt without looking at the third button down and thinking *solar plexus*.

They drove us hard, drilled us so incessantly that we learned to react without thinking.

Some of it stuck. Most of it did not.

I took away from those evolutions two memorable lessons. I learned that, nine times out of ten, a mediocre wrestler can beat a martial arts "expert" senseless, because all fights, if they last beyond the first series of blows, end up on the ground. The second important lesson I learned is that I have absolutely no talent as a swordsman or stick fighter. Zero. My peripheral eyesight is not good to begin with, and I'm at a marked disadvantage if I lose my glasses.

But even a talentless stick fighter such as myself knew more about it than Tony.

As I walked toward him, I noticed that he shortened his grip on the shovel. Unknowingly, he'd just told me something very important. He'd gone from a defensive posture to an attack posture.

Had he recovered from his fright? Seemed so. He looked not just ready to fight but eager. Lots of nervous movement. Probably because his chubby girlfriend was still watching, urging him on, yelling, "Kill 'im, Tony! See what he did to Derrick? Knock his head off, man!"

I approached him carefully. He was big enough, plus he had that look of fast-twitch quickness. A more compelling reason was that Tomlinson's paranoid assessment was probably accurate: the kid had the pinched manner of someone who enjoyed cruelty. It is a hyena furtiveness; a snap-at-the-heels, eat-them-when-they're-down demeanor that is subtle but unmistakable.

If Tony got me on the ground, he wouldn't stop. That was

my guess. He'd damage me and enjoy it. Maybe even kill me if he allowed it to go too far. He would probably enjoy that, too. What I had to do was find a way to hurt him badly enough so he'd no longer pose a threat to me and Nora.

At least, that's what I told myself. When emotion takes control, when the roaring comes into my ears, it is difficult to say what is true and what is justification for my behavior.

I listened to him say, "Dude, let's drop the sticks. You got the balls for that? Just you and me, using our hands."

I stopped as if considering. Let him see me relax for a moment, which is when he swung the shovel hard at my face.

It was not a surprise.

I ducked under the shovel, moving to my left, and used the tree limb to hammer him hard just above the pelvis, kidney high. The limb Derrick had chosen had a sapling springiness to it. The spring added a whipping effect. Wood hitting flesh made a hollow sound like bamboo smashing a pumpkin.

Tony moaned, dropped to one knee—then tried to cut my legs out from under me when I took a step closer. "Fucker, you *hurt* me."

"Put down the shovel, I'll stop."

"Sure—after I knock your head off!" He lunged at me as he got to his feet; took a series of wild cuts, driving me toward the mangroves. I backed away, sucking my stomach in, feeling the wind off the blade, he was that close. He had a split grip; the rhythm was consistent. When I got the timing down, I anticipated his backswing and smashed his right hand, then his left elbow, with a kayaklike stroke.

He dropped the shovel, moaning.

I took one step toward him, and put much of my weight behind a golf stroke that caught him just above the knee. His scream was a terrible thing to hear, and he fell to the ground in a fetal position.

"Stop it! You're going to kill him!" Tisha had gone from cheerleader to protector.

No, I wasn't going to kill him. But I was going to get some information out of him.

To Nora, I said, "I'm really getting tired of her noise."

I liked her quick reaction. She seemed to know instantly what I wanted her to do—stay between the hysterical girl and myself. I didn't want to be put in the position of having to fight her off.

She gave Tisha a warning look. "I'm getting kind of sick of her myself."

Just like that, Tisha became very, very quiet.

Tony wasn't being cooperative. He was hurt and furious and he had a very nasty mouth. His attitude was as foul as his language. I was getting sick of both. Now I nudged him with the stick and said, "You need to answer my questions, little man, or I'm going to get mad. You don't want me to get mad, do you?"

He told me to go do something to myself—a physical impossibility.

He was still on the ground. I was standing over him. I said, "Did I mention that was your last warning?"

"Get away from me, asshole!"

"See? A perfect example. You don't seem to have any concern for my feelings." I knelt, put a knee in his side, slapped him twice in the face when he tried to fight me off, then I reached and got a good grip on his earrings, left hand and right hand. They became very effective steering devices. I turned his head until he was facing the ground, neck bent upward, toward me.

"That hurts, damn it!"

"I bet it does. But know what's gonna hurt worse? From now on, every time you don't answer a question, I'm going to rip a pretty little ring out of your nasty little head. First one that goes is that nose ring. *That's* going to hurt."

"Ford."

I turned to see Nora's quizzical, worried expression—I wasn't really going to torture the man, was I? I gave her the slightest nod in answer. It changed her face; changed the way she looked at me.

I said, "Okay, let's try it again: tell me why you dug up Dorothy Copeland."

"I didn't!"

I changed my grip on his head so fast that I had the nose ring in my fist before he could react. I gave it a sharp tug, hard enough for him to feel it, but not hard enough to rip it away.

"Shit!"

"I don't think you heard the question: Why'd you open her grave?"

"Honest, I didn't! I swear to Christ I didn't! I don't know who did, either. Some sicko, man, but it wasn't us."

"Then why were you at the funeral? And don't give me that crap about nothing better to do."

"To see what was in the coffin. People on the island knew there was something buried with her. That was always the story. I grew up hearing it, man, and I wanted to see for myself. Derrick and the two chicks, they were just tagging along."

"You have no idea who did it?"

"Not a clue. Honest to God. Yeah, we've been digging out here, but we haven't found shit. Some bones, that's all. Some pottery. But digging up the girl's grave, no way, man. I had absolutely nothing to do with that."

"Your dad's such a nice guy, he loaned you all this expensive equipment. He must be big on hobbies."

"When he sees what you did to his shit, you're going to find out how big my dad is, asshole!"

"There's that mouth of yours again." I twisted the nose ring until he made a squeaking noise. "Sneaking onto an island, digging up an important archaeological site. I hope you're nicer to the cop who arrests you."

"We ain't sneaking, man. We don't got to sneak. My dad's general contractor for the dude who owns the whole fucking island, man. They're gonna start clearing and building in a couple of months anyway. What we done here, shit, this ain't nothing compared with what my old man's gonna do when he gets the rest of his permits."

I said, "See how easy it is? I ask a question, you give me an answer." I released the nose ring. "Who does your dad work for?"

His eyes were watering; he had the sniffles, too. "The old man who was at the funeral today. The rich dude, Ivan Bauerstock."

Tony was Tony Rossi, son of Frank Rossi, the big man with the florid face and the T-shirt I'd seen at the funeral. He'd been working for Bauerstock for nearly fifteen years, according to his son, and both men had a passion for Indian artifacts.

"It's like their thing, you know? They collect the shit, trade it back and forth. It's what they got in common. Mr. Bauerstock, he's into all kinds of stuff. Artifacts, that's just one of the things. So when they get a construction deal going, and it's at a place that might have something to find, they make it a point to get in a little early. Dig and sift; no big deal. Which is my whole point, man. You think we're gonna get arrested? Shit, dude, you're the one who's gonna get arrested. My dad's boss *owns* the fucking place."

I thought I was going to have to restrain Nora when he said that. I waited patiently while she lectured him. I saw at least one point hit home—"We'll have Ivan Bauerstock arrested and make you testify!"—before I asked him a few more questions. We were both standing now; me leaning on my stave, him limping around when he moved, nursing an elbow that had already swollen to the size of a baseball. Whenever he balked at a question, all I had to do was take the stave in both hands. It kept him talking.

It wasn't unusual for his dad to pay him and some of his

buddies to do that hard, hot labor. He'd been doing it off and on for years. The difference this time was, his dad had been so insistent that they put in a lot of hours and make a very, very careful search. Tony was vague about what he hoped they'd uncover.

"Stuff like the girl found, that's what my old man said. I'd seen those pictures a thousand times. Wooden masks, Spanish beads. That thing you took out of the girl's coffin, they'd love to have that, man. They're big on carvings or anything made of gold. Something major, Mr. Bauerstock is gonna pay me a big bonus. Two thousand bucks cash plus a thousand each for my friends."

"Plus he was paying you to dig."

"Hell yes, he was paying us. Lot more than I'd make at Wendy's."

I asked him, "Does that make any sense to you? To pay so much for a carving?"

"A rich man doesn't have to make sense. He just has to be rich. Know what you might try, dude? When my old man figures out where you're hiding and comes to beat your ass, you might try offering him that carving in trade. Get yourself off the hook."

Before I turned him loose, I told Tony his old man wouldn't have to look hard. I'd be on Key Largo.

We were nearly to the long bar off Lostman's River before Nora spoke. We'd ridden all that way in silence, past Panther Key and Jack Daniels and Pavilion Key; the Ten

Thousand Islands off to our left, mangroves so dense that they absorbed sunlight; they seemed to create a dark dome beneath the bright blue October sky. I saw only two other skiffs the whole way, plus a sailboat on the far horizon probably outward bound from Key West or the Dry Tortugas. The two of us sat side by side but alone, as silent and remote, it seemed, as the dark islands touched one after another by my skiff's trailing wake.

Violence releases a potent chemical cocktail into the muscles and the brain. The aftereffects can be a little like a hangover. It produced a gloom in us both. I had drifted so deeply into my own thoughts that I actually jumped a little when she spoke.

"Ford? You really *would* have done it. Why's it so hard for me to believe that?"

It took me a moment to understand the question. "The rings, you mean."

"Yes. You'd have torn them out to make him talk. You really would've."

I thought about lying, then decided to hell with it. "Probably. A couple of them, at least, just to let him know I was serious. Until he convinced me that he wasn't the one who dug up Dorothy, it seemed like the thing to do."

"It was so . . . brutal."

"He wasn't all that nice to me, if you think about it."

She touched her fingers to my arm, a signal of some type. "I wasn't criticizing you. It was an observation. I've never seen anything like that. The whole scene keeps going through my mind over and over. Wasn't that girl awful?"

I nodded.

She touched my arm again and looked at me. "Some puppy dog. Della called you that. You're no puppy dog."

We cut in close to the beach at Cape Sable where mangroves grow a hundred feet high, then ran Tin Can Channel past Flamingo. Had I been alone, I might have stopped and placed a wild flower on a little marker that commemorates the passing of someone who was once very near and dear. Instead, I accelerated over a shoaling bottom, feeling the skiff gather buoyancy as the bottom pressure created lift.

Doing an easy fifty, we flew through the narrow cut at Dump Keys, then past Samphire Key where the water changed from gray to iridescent green over a coral bottom that showed a blur of sea fans and sponges. To the east was Key Largo. The big micro tower there punctured a cumulous cloud that was feeding on exhaust fumes and asphalt thermals.

The water continued to clear until it had the density of bright air. The eye told the brain that to fall from the skiff meant a drop of ten or twenty feet. I waited until I found a perfect basin of clear water, then backed the throttle and switched off the key.

"Why are you stopping?"

"Water like this, I've got to swim. The starboard locker, beneath all the ice, you'll find bottles of beer. There are a couple of Cuban sandwiches, too. Help yourself. All I've got is underwear, so turn the other way if you want."

"My God! Look at your side."

I had my shirt off. I looked where she was pointing and

saw a tubular bruise where Derrick had hit me. A very serious hematoma that appeared as if it might still be bleeding.
The bruise was black in the middle, green and red at the
edges.

"If he'd hit you in the head, he'd have killed you."

I said, "I don't doubt it," and dived in, feeling the clean-
ness of water cover me. I swam out another twenty yards, letting my muscles stretch, my hands feeling the weight of water,
and then I dived to the bottom once again. I surfaced to see
Nora standing on the casting deck, ready to dive. She'd stripped
down to bra and panties; a tall, flat-chested woman with ribs
showing beneath dark skin. Bony hips and very long, smooth
legs with a firm muscularity.

It was a nice image: dark, lean woman, lucent water,
green horizon. Seeing her brought some light back into me
and brightened my thoughts.

She did a pretty good dive, had a very nice, long-distance
stroke.

Back in the boat, her black hair dripping, unselfconscious
about her body showing through wet bra and bikini panties,
she said to me, "I know what you mean. Water like this, you've
got to get in."

Sixteen

Speaking from inside the little tiki bar at Mandalay Marina, Della hung up the phone as she said, "That was him. That was Teddy. He'll be here around sunset and answer all your questions. You just wait. He's a sweetheart."

Tomlinson and I were standing outside on the tile floor beneath ceiling fans and a blue-and-white waterproof canopy that provided shade for a half-dozen picnic tables. Behind us was the marina basin: a row of docks and sun-bleached fiberglass hulls, *No Más,* moored bow-out at the last slip, twenty or more sailboats afloat in the anchorage a few hundred yards off the rock jetty.

My pretty yellow Maverick was tied in the charter slip next to the bar.

On the other side of the basin, on white coral rock, were a few palm trees and a row of trailers. Della lived in the beige Holiday Rambler with the screened porch, the tiki torches, the shrimp net curtains and the Conch Republic sticker on the front door. She'd made it a homey place with aloe plants on the porch and candles in the windows.

Mandalay was really a fish camp and bar. All the regulars had nicknames: Conch Jerry, Queenie, Little John, Donald Duck, Lucky John. Twenty or thirty people called the place home or used it as a second home. They'd work on their boats barefooted on the coral, or sit at the bar drinking beer in their *Mandalite* T-shirts.

Everyone there called themselves *Mandalites,* as if they were a separate tribe. It reminded me a little bit of Dinkin's Bay, only the architecture was Tropical Transitory, had a more Keysy feel.

Keysy is a word you hear a lot down there.

It was Sunday afternoon. Nora Chung had been very busy on the phone. Sunday or not, she'd tracked down the director of her museum and several of the museum's most powerful board members. She'd told them it was imperative that they get together on a conference call and decide whether or not they should issue a formal complaint to Ivan Bauerstock and his son, the candidate. The result was a telegram which read: *We insist that you immediately cease the illegal destruction of burial sites on Cayo de Marco and we intend to hold a press conference on this matter if you refuse.*

To Nora, I'd said, "They still have telegrams?"

"Yep, and this one will stop the bastards in their tracks. If we hold a press conference, tell reporters about the big man's hobby, his son can say goodbye to the state senate. He's aware of that, which means he'll be ready to jump through hoops. You know the only thing I'm uncomfortable about? I *like* Ted Bauerstock. Just from the little bit I talked with him. I hate to drag him into this because of something his dad's doing."

Nora was now upstairs in the Mandalay's two-bedroom rental apartment making more phone calls. I had a few calls to make myself. I wanted to speak with Detective Parrish, see if he'd found out anything new or if maybe he'd received a complaint from a couple of punk rockers about a big man with glasses attacking them. I also wanted to speak to the funeral rep, Caldwell.

But Sunday wasn't the day to do it. I'd actually forgotten what day it was until I walked downstairs to the outdoor tiki bar to find locals already gathering there, popping beers while a man in a dark suit preached a sermon. The Church of Hawk's Channel, the outdoor service was called, with a congregation composed of live-aboards and ocean wanderers. It was maybe the only church in America where men and women could drink a Budweiser, watch the sunrise and pray. Keysy, real Keysy.

Key Largo—one small planet in a solar system of islands all connected by orbiting blue water.

Now Tomlinson lifted my wrist so that he could see my watch. "Yep, just like I thought. Beer time. Della? I'll have a Hatuey, and my politically insensitive friend will have a Coors."

Della handed out two bottles already mounted in Styrofoam coolie cups. She was wearing a pink tank top and cutoff jean shorts and had a hawk's feather in her hair. All the waitresses dressed like that.

"He said he'd be here sooner, but he's bringing the boat up from Marathon."

She was still talking about Ted Bauerstock. She was smiling, the first time I'd seen her smile since I'd met her. With her narrow chin and black hair, she reminded me of a country-western singer. She had the underfed look of coal mines and sawgrass. "You know how politicians used to go by train and make what they called 'whistle-stops'? Teddy, he's doing the same thing by boat. He started in Key West and he's gonna work his way up the coast. Stops at marinas, talks to the fishermen, the *real* people, then meets with reporters. He said he was actually thinking about dumping the whole plan and have his boat taken out of the water. But he's so upset about what you say his daddy's doing, he's on his way right now."

I said, "The marina stops aren't getting enough publicity?"

"No, they're going just fine. It's not that at all. Haven't you listened to the weather this morning? There's another couple tropical storms forming. One's down off South America someplace, the other's off Africa. Weather people say they probably won't head this way, but they could. Teddy, he's bringing the boat anyway."

Since there is only one road that links the Florida Keys—Highway A1A—and since the road effectively divides the Atlantic from Florida Bay, all directions are given in relationship to the mile marker nearest the destination and to the body of water it sides. Mandalay Marina, Tiki Bar & Restaurant (*rental apartments available,* according to the plywood sign out front) was on the ocean side at mile marker 97.5, meaning it was ninety-seven and a half miles from Key West, the geographical and social equivalent of Florida's Ground Zero.

The Mandalay was next door to *Road Hog Harley Service,* both businesses squeezed in between two trailer parks off 2nd Avenue, which intersected Marina Street near Calusa Campground and Shell World, two miles south of the Kmart Plaza on A1A.

I knew about the Kmart because Tomlinson and I drove there in my truck. I carried the wooden totem with me in a black canvas briefcase. Everywhere I went, the totem went.

I carried the thing around Kmart, where I bought duct tape, electrical tape, clothesline, a spool of cheap six-pound-test fishing line and a small cassette tape recorder plus several tapes.

I had fishing gear on my skiff, but I didn't want to waste it. This cheap line wasn't going to be used for fishing.

Tomlinson gave me a very odd look when I picked up the package of clothesline. I am fussy about the kind of line I buy for my boats, and he knows it.

"Planning on doing some laundry, are we?" he asked wryly. When I didn't reply, he said, "Oh Lordy, you've got that look. That if-I-told-you-I'd-have-to-staple-your-tongue-look. Alcohol. I need alcohol!"

His way of reminding me what he'd already mentioned a half-dozen times: he was in a mood to go barhopping. "We need to get out, trade a few lies and meet the locals. Absorb some local color. Maybe absorb a few *mojitos* while we're at it. Frankly, my friend, I'm tired of the company of the same familiar women."

I said that was fine with me, but first I wanted to stop at the police station, introduce myself and try to set them straight on Della Copeland. She wasn't crazy. She was having real problems and they needed to keep an eye on her. But give it a few days. Couch it so they'd wait until I was gone.

The woman cop at the desk told me I'd have to stop back, the man I needed to see wasn't there.

"It's Sunday," she said. "In the Keys, not much gets done on Sundays."

Tomlinson said, "When you drift off like that, the way your eyes lose focus, I can tell you're thinking of her." Meaning Dorothy.

"Enough, enough," I said. "You're wrong, as usual."

Actually, he was right. The girl's image would flash like a camera strobe, then vanish.

We'd stopped and had a drink at Sharkey's, talked to some of the local dive masters; heard about how good the reef-diving had been, and how they sure hoped that big blow off South America didn't keep coming because it'd been a hell of a season up to then.

I saw a satellite picture of the storm on the TV above the bar: a red swirling shape at latitude 15.4, longitude 83.4, which put it south of Cuba. It had been out there building for a week, sitting over many thousands of acres of super-heated water. It had already reached wind speeds of sixty knots, which meant it was still a tropical storm, not yet a hurricane. Florida dodges a half-dozen or more a year. This was only the third, and it was huge: it blotted out a massive patch of water between open ocean and Jamaica.

Mostly, we sat around and talked about our own home, Dinkin's Bay. We did a lot of laughing. I sometimes forget how insightful and witty Tomlinson really is.

We stopped at Snappers and I stood on the dock, studying schooling tarpon while Tomlinson pounded drinks and entertained the waitresses behind the bar. At the Caribbean Club—the old Key Largo Hotel from the movie—I knew it was time to get him home when I overheard him tell the girlfriend of a Harley rider, "Know what scares me most about reincarnation? That I won't be hung as good next time around. The Buddha said not to grasp, life is so transitory, but damn it, some things a man gets *used* to grasping!"

Now we were back at the Mandalay, sitting outside beneath raw wood beams and ceiling fans, looking across the water at deserted Ronrico Key and Mosquito Bank Channel beyond.

Della was sitting with a Bud Light within easy reach, the three of us off by ourselves, while the two other waitresses, Betty Lynn and Salina, took care of the busy bar. It was the first chance we'd had to sit down and talk since my arrival. Della'd apologized earlier, saying, "I'm sorry I haven't had a chance to answer your questions, sugar, but I've got to cook and wait tables till Salina shows up at four."

She told me that when I'd asked her about the gold medallion. Nope, she didn't have it. Told me that I'd have to wait to hear how she lost it. "That's a long, sad story."

Now Della took a sip of her beer and said, "You're gonna call me an idiot, everyone does. Because of what I did. The way I gave the medallion away."

I said, "Idiots don't have women like JoAnn Smallwood for friends. There's no need to be ashamed of anything. Not in front of us. We're on your side."

She reached across the table and patted my hand, "That girl, she's like a little sister to me. She's absolutely wild about you, hon. Thinks the sun rises over your head. Only she says you two can't never be more than friends. I guess I'd have to move to Sanibel and live at that weird little marina of yours for me to understand that."

Della had the easy familiarity of the longtime waitress. Called everyone "babe" or "sugar" or "hon."

"JoAnn described the medallion as being very beautiful."

"Oh, it was. It truly was. Kind of took your breath away looking at it, the way it glittered and shined. Got to feeling hot in your hands if you held it too long."

Tomlinson hadn't heard that before, I could tell. "You actually felt heat?"

"No, probably not. I'm sure it was just my imagination, but Dorothy, she said the same thing. She found it. She was real proud she found it. But she didn't like it much. She didn't spend a lot of time touching it or looking at it. Not like some of the other things she found."

Della nodded at the black briefcase that lay on the picnic table near me. "She loved that thing there. She'd sit on her bed looking at it, tracing the designs with her fingers. Told me she loved the way the wood felt, so smooth and old."

As Tomlinson asked, "Did she ever tell you what the designs meant?" Nora Chung walked toward us, smiling, then touched her hand to my back as she took a seat beside me. She was already listening; didn't say a word.

"Dorothy's ideas about the designs were completely different than what the archaeologists said. She said . . . well, here, let me show you—" Della unzipped the briefcase, took out the wooden totem and pointed to the face of it. "See these circles within circles? Dorothy said that's the way the clouds look at night during a bad hurricane, only she called it something else, an Indian word. She knew lots of Indian words. She said those people were terrified of hurricanes; they were the most dangerous things in their lives. These teardrop shapes? These are really raindrops, only they're inverted because they want to send the storm back to the sky. It's like a charm against hurricanes, understand?"

It seemed reasonable, but I said nothing. Much of religion is a reply to fear.

Della said, "The cross, it's not like a Christianity thing, but it represents all that's good. These doors within doors, they're like the doors to heaven where those big storms come from. Plus they also represent something else, some ancient place. I can't quite remember where she said it was, but it was a place that had stone pyramids." Della turned the totem toward me. "From that angle, see how the doors resemble one of those squarish pyramids you see in the *Geographic*?"

It was true. They reminded me of the entrance to the Temple of the Jaguar at Tikal in Guatemala.

Now Della turned the totem over. "On the back, the gold medallion had the same thing, these crescent moons. Dorothy said they represented endless hope. She called them Tortugas moons, just like she called a nice balmy breeze a Tortugas wind. Living on Marco, both were from that direction, the southwest.

"Then there's these two square holes, side by side. If I hold it up, see how they're black? Dorothy said they're like the pupils of God's own eyes. That's what the Indians believed, that our souls are in the pupils of our eyes—but wait, you already said the exact same thing at the funeral." Now she put her hand on Tomlinson's arm; gave it a squeeze. "I know I already told you, but you did a real good job. I loved what you said. It was a lot better than the first sermon the preacher gave over her."

Della finished her beer and stood. "I don't know how Dorothy learned all that she did, or knew all that she knew. In ways, she was like a stranger. But I loved her more than my own life. You folks ready for another round? I'll get it."

I watched her walk away, a woman accustomed to pain. It happens sometimes: a parent and child so dissimilar that it seems one could not be related to the other. I saw nothing of Della in what I imagined the girl, Dorothy, to be.

Tomlinson nudged me and said, "You're doing it again. Drifting away."

.   .   .

The person who'd found Dorothy's body was Ted Bauer-stock.

I sat a little straighter when Della told us that; sat listening very carefully. It was a couple hours or so before sunset, the westward light already illuminating reflective markers out on the channel.

Across the water, mangroves on Ronrico Key were black; the hulls of anchored boats were a lucent white.

"Mr. Bauerstock and Teddy, they were out hiking on their property. Indian Hills was right behind where we lived at the time, and they found her on the highest mound. She had her favorite dress on, the one I buried her in. She had a rope around her neck, hanging from a branch so low that her feet still touched the ground."

Della stopped for a moment to regain control of her emotions. Took a drink of her beer, lit a cigarette. Her hands were shaking. "That's why I think she was experimenting with unconsciousness. Haven't you heard of kids doing that? Shut their air off until they hallucinate or have visions. She was having such terrible dreams by that time—and always about that damn medallion—I think she was just looking for some relief. Didn't leave a note, didn't tell me goodbye. Dorothy would of never left me like that. She was too kind, too loving."

"What did Ted and Ivan Bauerstock do when they found her?"

"They did the best they could, I guess. She was still warm. She hadn't been gone long. Him and Teddy both did mouth-to-mouth. But no use. I know it was real hard on both of 'em. They both knew Dorothy because she spent so much time poking around their Indian mounds. She always had permission, anytime she wanted. They knew about her gift. Everybody on Marco knew. Teddy was one of the few who didn't make fun of her or talk about how weird she was." Della smiled, eyes glazed with introspection. "He was quite a bit older, four or five years. But I think Dorothy had a kind of crush on him. Her first crush, and I think Teddy knew it."

"You and the Bauerstock family, you've remained close ever since?"

Della shook her head. "Finding her upset Teddy so bad that he left Marco right afterwards. Went off to some expensive boarding school. The place they sent him was more like a monastery, very strict—there was just a story about him in the *Herald*. It had him saying how it improved his life, going to such a strict school. Lord knows, he could have turned out bad instead of being such a good, successful man. His mama died when he was real young, and his daddy, he's such a rich, busy man he didn't have much time for kids or dirt-poor neighbors like me. I thought Teddy'd forgotten all about us until he called just a couple days ago, asking if there was anything he could do to help. He read about Dorothy in the papers."

I touched the wooden totem. "Did you ever tell Ted or anyone else about this? Where you'd put it."

"I don't think I ever saw Ted Bauerstock again until yesterday. I may have told some other people. I can't remember. The months after Dorothy's death are a blur. There's a lot of it I don't remember. I remember despising that damn gold medallion. It's what killed my little girl. I believe it to this day. It's got all those good, godly signs on it, but it's not good. It's like the fallen angel, that's what I think.

"One night, when I was 'bout half crazy, I damn near threw the thing into the ocean. There was a big rainstorm going on; lots of lightning. I stood there on the beach at Marco, holding the medallion up at the sky, hoping God would strike me dead and put me out of my misery. Throwing it into the ocean, it seemed like the right thing to do at the time. But I didn't. What I did made even less sense than that. At least throwin' it into the water would've been just between God and me." Della's thin laughter was very old, very tired, but it still had a spark of life and amusement. "Us country women, we never seem to miss a chance to show how dumb and trustin' we can be."

What Della did was give the medallion away.

A month after Dorothy's funeral, a man had contacted Della at the chickee bar in Goodland where she worked. He'd just moved down with hopes of getting into the construction business, he said, but collecting Indian artifacts—pot hunting, he called it—was his hobby. He was from New Jersey, had a wife and kid, and he seemed trustworthy.

He told Della that he'd met Dorothy and had actually helped steer her toward the water court on Swamp Angel Ways. He'd known it was a likely spot because of his more mature knowledge, but he was happy to let the young girl take the credit because publicity meant nothing to him.

"I should'a knowed right then he was lying. Dorothy didn't

need no help from Yankee trash like that. The guy made it sound like he'd been so much help to Dorothy, but always staying in the background, that he could make a claim on the medallion if he wanted."

I'd guessed the man's name before Della said it: Frank Rossi.

Fifteen years and forty pounds ago, though, he'd been a very convincing fellow. Della described him as a big talker, loud voice, very dominant.

That made sense. Obnoxious fathers tend to raise obnoxious sons.

Rossi finally worked the conversation around to psychic powers. He had none, but he knew a woman from Immokalee who did. He'd attended one of her seances and was very impressed. She was like a gypsy woman, only she wasn't a gypsy, and had amazing powers. Why not contact the woman, ask her to hold a seance and see if they could speak to Dorothy from the grave?

A parent who has lost a child will do anything on just the chance of meeting with that child one more time.

Della said yes. Sat at a table in candlelight, her and Rossi and a dumpy old woman, who smelled like a drunk. She listened to the woman ask questions as if speaking to Dorothy's ghost. The table shook and rattled and Dorothy's "ghost" rapped on the table in reply.

"I knew it was either her or Rossi knocking on that table. I had the sickest feeling in my stomach because I wanted so bad for it to be Dorothy. To kiss her sweet face one last time,

to tell her I loved her. I pretended to believe for the same reason we all do—because I *wanted* to believe.

"When the woman asked Dorothy if I should keep the
medallion or give it away because it was cursed, I knew what
the answer was going to be. But know what?" Della swirled
the beer in her bottle, looking at its amber sparkle. "That
was the only time I felt Dorothy really was in the room. I
could feel her there. She really didn't want me to have it. I
could almost hear her say, 'Don't keep it!'

"So I gave it away. Gave it to him, Frank Rossi. Made him
real happy. We'd gone to my little place to get it, just the two
of us alone, and he went out to his car to get a bottle of wine.
He said why not have a couple glasses, help us relax after
dealing with the spirit world. But I know he went to the car to
hide the medallion so's I couldn't change my mind."

Della looked from me to Tomlinson to Nora, the sad, bemused expression still on her face. "Know what Frank Rossi
said to me yesterday at the funeral? Same thing he said to me
after strippin' me out of my clothes that night and forcing me
to bed years ago. After getting me fallin'-down drunk the
night of the seance. He didn't say nothin'. Not a goddamn
word. Just turned his back and walked away."

Seventeen

Just before sunset, Ted Bauerstock brought his 36-Hinckley cruiser through some invisible cut west of Ronrico Key, running at speed through water I would have guessed was way too shallow for a boat that size. He had to be doing at least thirty knots, throwing a wake as streamlined as the Hinckley itself, one of the most beautiful yachts in the world.

Tomlinson and I stood beneath a thatched chickee at the end of the boat basin, watching. Tomlinson, who followed yachting magazines, said, "That's their new hull, they call it a Picnic Boat. It's got a water-jet propulsion system, only draws eighteen inches. Base price is over three hundred grand."

"A half-million-dollar picnic boat?"

"Yeah, when you add a few options. But think of all the money you save not going to restaurants."

Nora came up beside us. We'd been in the bar listening to Bauerstock talk to Della on the VHF radio. He told her he was only ten minutes out, could she have a pot of fresh coffee ready for him and his two-man crew? Maybe some sandwiches to go, too. They didn't have a lot of time to spare. He had to scoot back across Florida Bay for a fund-raiser in Naples the next afternoon.

Now Nora stood, hands on hips, watching the yacht with obvious admiration. "Is that thing gorgeous, or what?"

It was, too, with its flared hull of midnight blue, its water-line trimmed with apple red and its white lobsterman cabin.

Her expression of admiration didn't change much when Teddy Bauerstock appeared on the aft deck after backing the boat in smartly and tying off. He wore a white pressed guay-bera shirt, a Latin touch, plus khaki slacks and white boat shoes. He had the wind-blown look of someone who'd gone to a good fraternity, owned more than one tuxedo but who could also tell a joke or two. He swung down on the dock wearing a big smile, combing fingers through his black hair, and singled out Della right away. He went to her, hugged her like he might have hugged his mother, then saw Nora. He hes-itated, looking from Tomlinson to me, then swept up Nora, too, lifting her feet briefly off the ground. He said to her, but loud enough for everyone to hear, "Sorry, but I couldn't help myself. You've got the most beautiful eyes!"

Then he was done with her, moving down the dock shaking hands, his left arm thrown over Della's shoulder, leaving his crew to tend the boat. There was a tiny man, thin-haired, dressed in white—the actual skipper of the boat, I guessed. B. J. Buster, with his pumpkin-sized head, was coiling a line on the stern, wearing a black T-shirt stretched over his shoulders and biceps, bunched up at his skinny waist. In golden letters, the T-shirt read: "Bauerstock for Senate."

On the stern of the boat, in much larger golden letters, was the yacht's name: *Namesake*

Key Marco

Tomlinson was kneeling, trying to see the boat's underside. There had to be a state-of-the-art jet system down there. Some kind of tunnel hull with no propeller. To me, he said, "The man knows how to make an entrance, you have to give him that. I like his style."

I watched Nora using her long legs, hurrying to stay close to Della and Bauerstock. "Everyone does, apparently."

Buster had moved across the aft deck and was looking down on Tomlinson. "Hey . . . you there. Get yourself away from the back'a this here boat."

Tomlinson glanced up. "I was trying to see the stern drive. The mechanics of it. How it works."

"I don't know nothin' 'bout no stern drive. But you get your ass away. Hear?"

As Tomlinson and I walked toward the bar, I said, "I suppose you like his bodyguard, too."

He shrugged, not upset. "No, but I understand the philosophy. It's easier to be a genuinely humane person if you can afford to hire your own personal son-of-a-bitch."

Theodore Bauerstock was sitting across the picnic table from Nora, Tomlinson and me. He was sandwiched between Della and Conch Jerry, one of the locals.

No telling why Conch Jerry was sitting in. He floated around from table to table, listening, hearing, but not saying much. The Mandalay was that kind of place.

On the table before him, Bauerstock had a nonalcoholic beer and a laptop computer, the screen opened to our side of the table. Attached to the top of the screen was a dime-sized micro-camera with a cord that was linked to a satellite cell phone, its antenna blossomed round like a metallic daisy.

As Bauerstock pieced together the components, he told us that his boat had a fully integrated electronic computer system, everything—Global Positioning System, weather satellites, telephone and single sideband radio, satellite Internet and World Wide Web, plus a special mobile Doppler radar system mounted forward on the cabin roof right next to the aircraft-rated spotlights.

"I've been watching the satellite shots and the Doppler. The storm's . . . well, here, I'll show you." His fingers made a plastic sound on the laptop, and, a moment later, we could see the swirling red shape of the tropical storm, just like on the TV back at Sharkey's Bar. "Okay . . . what do we have here? The storm's moved north and west a few tenths of a degree, wind speed at a steady sixty." He looked up. "That's good for us. It's moving offshore, away from land. Got lots and lots of rain in there. Big bastard, though, isn't it? It's got to be a hundred miles wide, maybe more. The eye's already clearly defined. Let's see how deep the eye is." He touched more keys, and we could see a cross section of the storm; the picture transmitted carrying an explanatory line at the bottom: *"Graphic based upon NOAA 41-C Aerial Photo."* He gave a low whistle. "She's already thirty thousand feet deep. Do you folks know how a Doppler radar system works?"

Before he could continue, Tomlinson said, "It's named after an Austrian physicist, the Doppler effect. It's like when we hear a train or a plane, the pitch of the sound is higher as the object comes toward us. Then the pitch drops as it passes and moves away. The radar calculates wind speed and precipitation by measuring the distance between sound waves. At least, that's what I've read."

Bauerstock was smiling at him. "I defer to the more informed man. What I know is far more basic, but here I am trying to explain it. You like computers? Modern gadgets?"

"Nope. I keep spilling stuff on them. But I find symmetry interesting. Think about it: we use our eyes and ears to measure speed and distance. Built-in Doppler. We've all got it, but few of us make an effort to get in touch with our own gifts."

Now Bauerstock was laughing; he really seemed to be enjoying Tomlinson. He was enjoying Nora, too, judging from all the eye contact, the private winks. To Della, he said, "This is a very intelligent man. You have good taste in friends."

"Tommy-San? Oh, he's been a blessing to me. Been here

just over a week, and he already draws a lot of water at the Mandalay."

He returned his attention to Tomlinson, gesturing to the computer. "You want to give her a test drive? It's the fastest portable system around. My family's in the business, so I get first crack at all the new toys."

"Normally, sure, I'd love to. Fast computers and fast women, huh? But, hey, I need to be honest: I'm a little too drunk to be trusted with anything breakable. Been overserving myself all day."

More laughter. "Then let me show you. If you like computers, modern technology, you're going to love this." He punched the keyboard again. There was a dial tone, the sound of electronic digits, then a warble. Now, instead of the tropical storm on the computer screen, we could see the face and upper body of an older man, thick silver hair combed back.

It was Ivan Bauerstock.

He was wearing a dark sports coat, sitting in a red leather chair, books, plaques and mounted cattle horns on the wall behind him, looking at us; looking into his own computer screen, I realized, apparently seeing a wide-angle shot of the Mandalay, because first thing he did was smile a formal smile and say, "Good evening! You've got quite a crowd there with you, Theodore!"

"Before noon tomorrow," Ivan Bauerstock said, "I will issue a formal, written apology to the Everglades Museum of Natural History, its employees and board of directors. The fact that employees of mine are robbing Indian burials on company property is absolutely intolerable, and rest assured that I have put a stop to that for now and all time. Teddy? Can you think of anything in our family's history that's been as embarrassing as this?"

Bauerstock was standing while the rest of us sat, everyone staring at the laptop's small screen. "Dad, I truly can't. When Ms. Copeland contacted me and told me what her friends had found on Cayo de Marco, I was shocked. What upset me the most was that the young man—Tony Rossi?— that Tony Rossi implied he was working under direct orders from you to plunder that site. I knew right away that couldn't be true."

I spoke for the first time. "Rossi didn't imply that he was under your direct orders, Mr. Bauerstock. He said it very plainly. That you and his father, Frank Rossi, were enthusiastic artifact collectors."

I was surprised that Bauerstock already knew exactly who I was. "Dr. Ford, it's my understanding that Frank Rossi's son was under extreme duress when he spoke to you. Coercion so . . . well, let's be frank. Methods so brutal that there's been some talk of charging you with assault, perhaps even attempted murder. The boy's in the hospital, you know. Ruptured spleen." He paused for a moment, letting it sit there. "Personally, I think it would be unfortunate if law enforcement gets involved. We're all reasonable people with similar goals. We all want to protect the history of this great state. I'd prefer to drop the whole matter. Under the circumstances, Dr.

Ford, don't you think it's possible that you misunderstood what the young man said?"

"I didn't misunderstand him, Mr. Bauerstock. The kid said you'd been robbing sites for years."

"Marion!" Nora's voice was surprisingly sharp. "Mr. Bauerstock is trying to help. Let's not argue with him."

"Thank you very much, Dr. Chung. Theodore has already spoken to me of your intellect and your professionalism—"

Ted was laughing, showing himself to be an eager peacemaker. "I told you about her eyes, too, dad. They're amber, the color of a cat's eyes."

Nora blushed, pleased by the compliment, but Ivan Bauerstock clearly didn't see the humor. "Theodore, if I might continue? Along with the written apology, I will also deed over fifteen acres of Cayo de Marco for the museum's ongoing archaeological studies. Finally, this afternoon, I told our attorneys to begin the legal groundwork to establish a scholarship fund in the name of Dorothy Copeland. She was a delightful young woman and deserves to be remembered for the contributions she made to archaeology. Would that please you, Mrs. Copeland?"

Della was dabbing at her eyes. "I think it's wonderful, Mr. Bauerstock, and I think your son is wonderful. If there's anything I can do to help you or your family, please just let me know."

The fixed, formal smile appeared on his face once more. "As a matter of fact, there is, Della. Make sure that son of mine goes straight to our boat and shoves off for Marco. I don't like the way those storms are shaping up out there in the Caribbean. And get him all the Key Largo votes you can. We *need* Theodore Bauerstock in the Senate."

"May I speak to you privately, Dr. Ford?" Ted Bauerstock was talking, being respectful and very serious. It got me another sharp look from Nora—why was I such a troublemaker?—and an abstracted, drunken shrug from Tomlinson.

As Bauerstock and I stood to leave the tiki bar, Conch Jerry, who hadn't spoken a word all evening, said to him, "How'd you get that cut on your hand?"

Bauerstock stopped, momentarily surprised. "This?" I hadn't noticed the flesh-colored surgical tape angling from the palm of his left hand to his wrist. "I'm a klutz, that's how I got it. Slipped and fell on the dock yesterday. Almost went into the water." His expression said, *I'm a dope.*

Conch Jerry said, "Really?" then got up and walked away, carrying his beer.

Now Bauerstock and I were standing side by side at the marina basin, close enough to *No Más* that I could smell the incense that Tomlinson was burning below, patchouli, his favorite. Bauerstock was looking past his yacht toward Ronrico Key. The island was glazed with gold in the sunset light.

In a low voice, he said, "May I speak to you confidentially, Dr. Ford?"

"Please don't. Not if it concerns any of my friends."

He chuckled, resigned but amused. "You really are a straight shooter, aren't you? And you don't believe my father."

"No. No, I don't believe your father."

"Would you be surprised if I told you that I don't believe him either?"

I turned to look at him. "If you're trying to get my attention, you've succeeded."

"My father is the most ruthless person I've ever met. He's built his great financial empire on the bodies of men who chose ethics over survival. I don't mean that he's actually murdered anyone—not that I'd put it past him. But he's only interested in people who can help him, people he can use or manipulate."

I said, "Why are you telling me this?"

"The truth? It's got to be confidential."

"As long as it concerns just you or your father, fine. The only caveat is Tomlinson. We tend to bounce things off one another. But privately."

"I don't blame you, he's a brilliant man. Rhodes scholar, the Sorbonne, threw it all away to pursue his own philosophical interests. You know, of course, that he was involved with a political terrorist group that was responsible for the deaths of at least nine people. Two of them Chicago policemen. Yes . . . I see by your expression that you do know about your friend Tomlinson."

I looked at him for a moment, then motioned him away from *No Más*. When we were at the end of the jetty, I said, "That was nearly fifteen years ago. No charges were ever formally brought against him—"

"I wasn't speaking badly of the man, I admire him—"

"I wasn't finished, Ted. Let's drop the gamesmanship.

You speak of Tomlinson, but what you're really telling me is that you have people to do your homework for you. That you have avenues of information not available to the average citizen. You found all this out in, what? a little more than twenty-four hours."

"This is the computer age. If you carry enough political weight and can press the right buttons, there's instant information available on everyone. Including you, Dr. Ford."

He said more with his intonation than his words.

"Don't believe everything you read in government files."

"With you, it's just the opposite. My guess is, your life is more accurately described by the blank pages. By what my staff didn't find in government computer banks."

I said, "You still haven't answered my question. Why are we having this conversation?"

"Did you see the expression on my father's face when you called him a liar? I've seen that expression before. He won't tolerate that kind of disrespect from anyone. Period. Believe me, you're on his shit list. You will pay for humiliating him like that."

"Is that a threat?"

"Dr. Ford, I'm being as sincere as I can be. It's a warning. My father scares the hell out of me. He should scare you, too. You want a couple of for-instances? You've secured a very dubious federal lease on a stilt house off Sanibel with the help of some of your old colleagues. You work for Mote Marine, which depends on state and federal agencies for permits. That expression Della used, 'He draws a lot of water.' I liked that.

Honestly, Dr. Ford, my father draws a massive amount of water in Tallahassee and Washington. If you cross him, everything you have is at risk. Your house, your association with Mote, everything. And there is also the very real possibility that he could arrange for your secret past to become public record. Think the international courts would take an interest in prosecuting you?"

"I have no idea what you're talking about."

"Of course you don't."

I said, "We're being honest? Okay, then tell me this: You think your father could've had anything to do with exhuming Dorothy Copeland?"

I thought he'd be offended by the question. He wasn't. "No. Not directly, anyway. Not that the indecency of it would bother him, but the risk is greater than the potential for gain. That's how he makes decisions. More likely, it was . . ." He paused for a moment, waited for one of the locals to check his boat lines, then walk away. "It was probably one of his flunkies. Steal the totem, then sell it to my dad, that was probably the plan. If someone knew he wanted it, they'd try to get it for him. All dad would have to do is mention the thing in casual conversation, and his staff would get the wheels turning. He owns so many people in this state. You have no idea. To an average guy, the totem would be well worth the risk. A year's salary, dad would pay that without blinking an eye."

I said, "But why? It can't be worth one-tenth of that on the market."

"Actually, you're wrong, Dr. Ford. Auction it at Sotheby's

or Christies, or—what's the famous auction house in New Mexico?—auction it at any of those places and it would sell for close to six figures. I just read that pre-Columbian arrowheads in fine condition sell for more than $1,000 each. In a global economy with the population booming, rare collectibles are far more valuable worldwide than gold. That totem"—he looked frankly at the black briefcase I continued to carry—"is worth a bundle. But see, that's not the reason my father wants it. It's not the monetary value."

"Then what?"

"This is the part that needs to remain confidential. If you repeat it to anyone, I'll swear you're lying."

Once I'd nodded, he continued.

"I know a side of my father that the public will never see or even suspect. He's obsessive to the point of—how did a psychiatrist once put it to me?—he's prone to manic fixation, that's the phrase. The same psychiatrist told me that his obsessions were also key to his success. It's true of many great men. Most people let up, back off or come to an ethical crossroads their conscience won't allow them to cross. Not men like my father. Ever. That's how they get so rich.

"Something else about him, he's just as obsessive about his ideology. Let's face it, nearly all of us are superstitious to a degree, but some of his beliefs have become fixated. We used to have this Colombian maid, Bella, who called herself a *bruha,* meaning a Santería witch. She'd laugh like it was a joke, but she meant it. Bella raised me until father sent me away to boarding school. Bella was very beautiful. She was his mistress for years."

I noticed that Bauerstock stuttered momentarily as he said *mistress;* an emotional stumble that made me think of Jeth Nicholes back at Dinkin's Bay.

"Bella had a powerful hold on Dad. I think it was through Bella that he began to believe that certain objects made him stronger. If he wore them or touched them or placed them under his bed. Our estate is on the Indian mounds at Marco. We've got more mounds at our ranch east of there in the Everglades. Dad and Bella, most of their . . . well, let's just say private encounters occurred on those mounds." Bauerstock smiled an uneasy, reflective smile that bordered on embarrassment. "I was a kid, but I wasn't dumb. And I sure as hell wasn't deaf. The point being, Dad's manic fixation is with the Indians who lived on those mounds. They controlled Florida for thousands of years. He *wanted* to one day control Florida. He was a poor orphan kid who had to fight for everything, and he wanted to end up on top.

"My dad worked his ass off, but he was also fantastically lucky. *Unbelievably* lucky. Always made just the right connections, always bought and sold at the perfect time. With Bella's help, he came to believe that certain artifacts taken from those mounds were the source of his good fortune. That much of his power came from them. When I was younger, it was just kind of a hobby. He'd even joke about it, like, 'Well, I've got a new artifact so I should make an extra hundred grand in the negotiation.' And he *would*. Year after year those things worked for him, until it became an absolute fixation. Tomlinson's eulogy so exactly described how he feels about the mounds that dad was actually spooked. That's why we left in such a hurry. As badly as he wanted to see that totem, we couldn't stay."

"He doesn't seem like a man easily spooked."

"He's not. Not normally. But wait—I'm not finished. My father's delusion has gotten to the point where he genuinely believes that he has a spiritual connection with a certain Calusa war chief. I won't bore you with the specifics, but their most powerful chief carried that totem. That's why Dad wants it."

"A man named Tocayo carried the totem and wore the gold medallion."

Bauerstock's expression changed slightly; a look of evaluation. "Yes, I think that's the name. Tocayo. Look at photographs of my father. You will never see him wear an open-collared shirt. It's because he always had the gold medallion around his neck."

"He got it from Frank Rossi?"

"Della told you the story, I guess. The medallion played a role in Rossi and dad's business relationship, that's all I know. Another example of dad's fixation? At the ranch, we have what the Spanish call a *cenote*. A *cenote* is a—"

"I know what a *cenote* is, Ted."

Florida has many *cenotes,* though they are known by the more popular name of springs: Crystal River, Weekie Wachee, Silver Springs. All are deep water holes formed when the limestone surface collapses over an underground river. Fresh water floats atop a saltwater passageway to the sea. They are very clear and deep, often with sides as sheer as the inside of a volcano. *Cenote* is a Maya word. I'd swam and dived dozens of them in Florida and Central America.

Bauerstock said, "He's come to believe that our *cenote* has restorative powers. He swims there every single day he can. When he travels, he takes bottles of the water with him. Maybe you already know this, but it's not legend, it's fact that Ponce de León came to Florida looking for what he called *El Río de Jordan* in his ship's log, the River of Life. That was an Indian prophecy he'd heard in Cuba. See the connection?"

Of course I could understand it. I had an uncle who'd once believed in the same thing.

"I can see why someone would convince themselves it's true," I said.

"He has. But what I'm getting at is, more than three months ago—the twenty-first of June, I'll never forget the day—Dad went for his swim, and he lost the medallion. Jesus Christ, to him it was like the end of the world. He hasn't been the same man since. His world hasn't been the same since, either."

I said, "The chain broke?"

"No, he was fanatical about the chain. You can imagine. Somehow the medallion broke. He doesn't know how. It went fluttering down into deep water with my dad swimming like crazy after it." Bauerstock laughed softly. "It's actually kind of pathetic if you try and picture it. No one knows how deep that lake is. He hired a professional cave diver to search. It went on for months, but the diver gave up at three hundred feet.

He found some interesting bones from mastodons and giant sloths, but no medallion. Unfortunately, Dad pushed him a little too hard and the diver was killed. Went down and never came back."

"One diver? He was diving alone in a spring? No diver, particularly an experienced cave diver, dives alone."

"I'm not sure why, but that's exactly what happened. Maybe the poor guy wanted to keep the reward all to himself. Not that it was much of a bonus. It wasn't. Dad offered the guy five thousand dollars plus his regular pay if he found it. The medallion was worth at least twenty times that. The diver's body never surfaced."

"Was it on the news?"

"No. But it will be. It's only a matter of time. My dad paid off the family, but it'll get out. Since he lost the medallion, Dad's had a surprising number of business failures. In the last twelve weeks, in fact, it's not an exaggeration to say he's lost at least thirty percent of his wealth—many millions of dollars. You beating a confession out of Tony Rossi was the latest of many setbacks. Frankly, I've had some setbacks myself in my race for the state senate."

"Oh?"

"You can look it up, so I might as well tell you. I've been falling in the polls. Turns out, my newest opponent is the son of one of dad's oldest enemies. One's as unscrupulous as the other. This guy hired two prostitutes to claim I tried to force myself on them. Sexually. Complete bullshit, but that's what politics has come to. To Dad, I'm just an extension of his business interests. He's lost the medallion and now my Senate race is going to hell along with everything else. That's the way he sees it. He wants to reverse the momentum. He believes the totem might do that."

"What if Della doesn't want to sell it?"

"Oh, he'll get the totem, count on it. That's why I've called you aside, Dr. Ford. He'll buy it from Della or use Dorothy's scholarship fund to leverage it out of her. Or he'll have someone steal it. That's why I'm talking to you now. It's not for you or for Della, even though I'm fond of her. It's for Dorothy. She really was something special. I didn't know her well, but she had a quality about her that was . . . well, I guess angelic is the only word that fits. She seemed too good for this world. I don't want to see her mother get hurt."

I ignored the strange urge to ask him more questions about Dorothy. What did her voice sound like? Did she have a favorite expression? An interest in natural history? It was irksome that he'd actually spent time with her, but I hadn't. Instead, I said, "You're an unwilling pawn, just trying to help."

He stiffened slightly. "I don't care for your tone and I don't need your sarcasm. This may come as a big shock, Ford, but I really am going into politics to try and do some good. My father has spent his life hurting people and destroying lives, living a completely selfish existence. You'll read this, too, so I might as well tell you: I spent my teenage years in a privately run cloister, fighting to overcome the emotional damage my father did when I was young. This was in North Dakota. Can you imagine a Florida kid being sent there? But

I made it. I came out with my sanity and the conviction to live a constructive life."

When I offered no expression of empathy, the indignation faded. "You're not interested in my personal history, nor my politics. I knew that the first moment I laid eyes on you. But you're a rational man, so let me give you a condensed version of why we need strong people in political office with good motives. Shrink the earth's population to a village of precisely a hundred people, and here are the ratios. There would be fifty-seven Asians, twenty-one Europeans, seven South Americans, nine Africans and eight from the U.S. Seventy of those people would be non-Christian, eighty would live below the poverty level and half the world's wealth would be in the hands of only six people, all citizens of the United States. And only two of those hundred people would own a computer."

I said, "Meaning there are dark days coming for a pampered nation."

"Unless we get very tough, quick. Yes." He held his hand out to me. I didn't want to take it. It is a common social quandary. Finally, I shook his hand as he said, "I'll tell Dad you're counseling Della on what to do with the totem. I suspect he'll go easier on you if she decides to sell. I made her an offer. She'll speak to you about it."

As he walked away, I told him, "Breaking the lease on my house, I can see why you'd do that. But this's got nothing to do with Mote Marine. They're doing great things for this state."

Over his shoulder, Bauerstock said, "You think my father gives a damn?"

Eighteen

Tomlinson was talking. "Know what I think I'll do? I think I'll cut my hair, buy some decent clothes, trim my nails and move to Pittsburgh. I hear it's a lovely city. They have a surprisingly good baseball team and a great manager. Watching the Pirates at Three Rivers. That would become my hobby. I'll send my sweet little daughter postcards and knickknacks."

I said, "Oh?"

It was nearly midnight. The wind had freshened, gusting hot, then cool, followed by long moments of calm. Somewhere in the darkness, far out to sea, hot-air thermals were ricocheting skyward, absorbing tons of water vapor and beginning a slow, counterclockwise momentum.

I was sitting in my skiff, wrapping tape onto a length of electrical conduit I'd found. Tomlinson was standing near me on the seawall. I'd loaned him my stout Loomis bait-casting rod with a fine old ABU reel that is loaded with twenty-pound test. I carry it for stopping big-shouldered fish around docks and mangroves. My fly rods are for sport. This bruiser was for putting food on the table.

Tomlinson had tied on a very large lure called a Bomber. It was studded with gang hooks, all very sharp. When it hit the water, it sounded heavy as a brick. He was casting out onto the black water, then reeling it back slowly, very slowly.

Behind us, there were still a few people on stools inside the tiki bar, but the music had stopped. Beside the bar was a flat-roofed, two-story stucco building rimmed with a balcony. It was an upstairs-and-downstairs rental duplex. In the lemon lights of the marina, the building's green paint had turned gray, and the sliding glass doors of the upstairs apartment were illuminated. Nora was still awake up there, her silhouette moving across the scrim of living room light, maybe talking on the phone.

The woman spent a lot of time on the phone.

"When I get to Pittsburgh, I think I'll buy a two-bedroom house in the suburbs—never know when a babe might want to sleep over. Yes, and get a nice desk job. County government, perhaps, something secure. Good money, good benefits. A meat-and-potatoes kind of job. I'll buy life insurance. I'll file my taxes quarterly. Perhaps marry a God-fearing Christian with multipersonalities. That way I could come home to a different woman every night. Whoops. Holy *shit!*"

I heard a tremendous thrashing out on the water, then a whistling noise as the Bomber came zooming past my ear and landed in the coral rock by a coconut palm.

I'd thrown my hands up—way too late—and now I sighed and returned to my wrapping. "You get a tarpon on like that, Tomlinson, you've got to bow when it jumps or it'll throw the plug back at warp speed. You're going to get one of us killed. That thing only missed me by a couple of feet."

"Sorry, sorry." He was stripping out the tangle, retrieving the lure. "Big bastards out there in the dark. Absolutely fucking ferocious. If tarpon grew teeth, I wouldn't go anywhere *near* the water. What I want is a nice snapper. Something tasty for lunch. Perhaps invite Della. They ought to be hitting on this falling barometer." He began to cast again. "Where was I?"

"Pittsburgh."

"Ah, exactly. I've come to regret this pirate's life of ours, Marion. A life of excess and immorality. A man can only take so much sunshine and water, plus the constant party-party-party that Florida requires. I fear that chemicals are starting to take their toll. Reptiles have been visiting me in my dreams. I need to steel myself or rent a U-Haul."   ·

"Um-huh. Tomlinson? Are you sleeping with Della?"

He stopped reeling for a moment. "Of course I'm sleeping with Della. The poor woman needed comforting. I'm just what the doctor ordered."

"Then you know that Ted Bauerstock made her an offer on the totem."

The totem was still in the black bag, beside me on the boat.

"I know, she told me. More money than she makes in two years. I told her to keep the totem for a while. Absorb some of its goodness, some of its power, then sell. But Ted wants it right away. She's thinking it over." He was silent for a moment, then: "You had a long, private talk with the man."

"Yeah."

Tomlinson's laughter was oddly nervous. I'd never heard him make such a sound of discomfort before. "Know what he said to me? He said his father read somewhere, some deep government file someplace, that I was involved with a left-wing terrorist organization that killed nine people. His father warned him about me. This was like twenty years ago. The killings, I mean."

"An obvious attempt to leverage you. A ridiculous charge."

Tomlinson looked at me for a moment, then began to cast again. "That's what I told him. Exactly my reaction. I like Ted. I like him a lot. I think his father is one evil son-of-a-bitch, but Ted's trying to make up for it. You don't like him, though, do you, Doc?"

"Nope. I'm not sure why. He says all the right things in just the right way. Politically, he's got great radar. This afternoon, he told me exactly what he knew I wanted to hear. But it's like . . . he sees everyone else as a stage prop for his own life. Objects to be manipulated. That's the impression I get.

He's too careful; had way too much practice at being smooth. No, I don't like him. I don't like Ted Bauerstock."

He sighed. "You're wrong. Trust me on this one, amigo. Trust my instincts. I think Ted's a good man."

I'd finished taping the length of electrical conduit. Now it was an effective sap, and I smacked it into my hand. It made a satisfying *thwap*.

I said, "Really? I agree that he's very charming, but when he talks about his father? I think he might be describing himself."

I awoke in a freezing sweat on the couch of the upstairs apartment, dreaming that I'd stepped into some slow-motion booby trap in a faraway jungle, and that a rope was pulling me up into the trees . . .

I sat upright, groggy at first, then all senses at alert.

Something had yanked at my ankle. Now it yanked again.

It was fishing line.

There were fifteen metal steps leading to our apartment, the only conventional entrance. I'd taken the weak, six-pound test line I'd bought at Kmart and tied it shin-high across the first step and one of the middle steps. From those lines, I ran a single piece up the wall, through a space between the window air conditioner and the window seal, then across the carpet to the couch.

It was a very simple, very effective early-warning system. The line was so sheer that it was easily broken; it wouldn't trip a person traveling the stairs, nor would they notice it. But it was strong enough to wake me.

I popped the line from around my ankle and stood. Glanced at the door to the bedroom where Nora was asleep. It was closed.

I was wearing gray boxer underwear. I slipped my boating loafers on and moved quietly to the sliding glass doors that I'd intentionally left unlocked.

The glass doors looked out over the marina basin and a balcony that circled the second floor. The steps were on the opposite side by the road and parking lot. I went through the doorway onto the balcony and circled to my right. Below, the marina was asleep. I was at eye level with the masts of sailboats. I could see *No Más* out there, a ghostly white. Could see the porch light of Della's trailer.

I stopped at the first corner and peeked around. Nothing. Stopped at the second corner and peeked around, expecting to see someone futzing with the door, trying to break in. Nothing.

Who the hell had hit the trip wire?

I retraced my steps just in case my late-night visitor had gone around the other side of the balcony. No one there; still no one at the door . . . but there *was* someone coming up the stairs now: a tall, lean shape moving quietly in the dim light. Maybe he'd forgotten something. Had to go back to his car, and was coming up the steps for a second time. That would explain the lapse in time.

I pressed close to the stucco. As I did, I realized I'd left the sap I'd made on the floor by the couch.

Damn it.

I had no choice, now, but to go after him empty-handed.

I waited . . . waited until he was at the door and hunched over fiddling with the knob. That's when I swung around the corner, driving hard with my legs, planning to smash him into the wall, then overpower him . . .

. . . heard a woman scream "FORD!" and looked up just in time to see Nora's terrified face a microsecond before I crushed her. I twisted hard to my right, hit the railing at full stride, somersaulted over the rail, fell feet-first ten feet or so and landed in a sea grape tree at the edge of the parking lot.

"Jesus Christ, Ford, is that you?"

I didn't want to answer, but I had no choice. "Yes, it's me, Nora. Out for a stroll, were you?"

"Okay, so now that I know about your little alarm system, no more going outside at night to sneak a cigarette from my car."

"You said you don't smoke."

"On Swamp Angel? Not having a lighter, I said that's what I get for not smoking. And I don't. I don't smoke normally. I smoke occasionally. But I got out there and thought, nope, this time I've quit for good. So I didn't have one."

I was still in my underwear, lying on her bed while she used a washcloth and pan of soapy water to clean out a scattergun variety of puncture wounds and abrasions. She'd insisted; had led me by the hand into her bedroom—but not before I'd tied new fishing line and snaked it past the air conditioner, resetting the trip line. When I was back on the couch, I'd attach it to my ankle once again.

And I *would* get back to the couch, even though she was being attentive beyond expectations. I have no interest in casual encounters.

"My God, that bruise on your side looks awful." She touched her fingers to my rib cage, tenderly, then got up, went out the door and came back with a plastic sack full of ice. She was wearing a gray T-shirt that read *Eldridge Softball.* Pearl-white panties, too, which turned her long legs nearly black. Now she combed fingers through her rice-bowl hair and used the pillow to brace the ice against my side.

Ted Bauerstock was right. Through those wire-rimmed glasses, she had extraordinary eyes. As she leaned over me, I could look through the clear corneas into the optic disks. Her irises were a mahogany shade of amber. The amber was three-dimensional with wine traces, flecked with gold. Her pupils were big as a cat's in the soft light, black and flawless.

By moving my head slightly, I could also take churlish advantage and see down her T-shirt—the flat muscularity of stomach, flat breasts with dark aureole rings around elongated nipples, a hint of tan line. Not much. She apparently liked to spend time outside.

"Know what you reminded me of? You know that old Cary Grant movie, the one he goes running around looking for this jaguar that's escaped? *Bringing Up Baby,* that's it."

She had the washcloth again, warm water-sopped, and she was moving her fingers through my chest hair, cleaning the scrapes. To get a better angle, she scooched farther onto the bed; had one foot on the mattress, leg bent, so I could see her pearl panties; the swell of pudenda and outlined curl of hair.

"The reason Cary Grant is chasing the jaguar is, a dog stole this very important dinosaur bone and—how'd it go?—I think they were worried the jaguar ate the dog and, heck, I can't remember, but it was hilarious." She stopped rubbing my chest with the cloth for a moment, as if she'd noticed something. Her eyes slowly widened, then she stood up fast. "Marion! You've got the wrong idea about this!"

Hastily, I pulled the blanket over my hips; felt like an idiot. "Nora, I'm very sorry. I had no idea . . . I mean, I didn't realize what was happening . . . don't think for a moment . . . I didn't even *touch* you."

Now she was laughing. "Don't worry about it. I'm flattered, but no more sponge baths for you, mister." Her laughter faded; she stood there staring at me in her T-shirt. "Know something, Ford. I thought you were one of the biggest jerks I'd ever met. And a bookworm. I don't think I've ever misread someone so badly in my life. Now it turns out I like you. Something else?" She waited for a few beats, looking at me before she added, "You are a very attractive guy. I didn't even realize it at first, now I do. But I'm real slow about this sort of thing. Physical contact, I mean. So it's probably good I'm leaving in the morning."

That was the first I'd heard it. "Oh?"

"Yeah. I'm driving up to Ted's ranch tomorrow, but I'm not supposed to say anything because he's had a lot of bad press lately about him and women he's dated, so he's trying to play it cool. Keep it private. Not that it's a date," she added quickly, "because it isn't. He wants to talk about the museum, how he can help and the scholarship fund they're going to set up in Dorothy's name."

"A business trip," I said.

"Exactly. To surprise him? I think I'll take Della along. That way I can interview her on the drive up. No interruptions. But later this week, or maybe next week, give me a call, we'll get together and do something. Fish, hang out, explore some islands. Whatever you want."

I leaned and gave her a kiss on the forehead before walking to the living room. "I'd like that."

Early in the morning, with the first gray dust contrails of light filtering through curtains, I awoke to find Nora kneeling beside me. I felt her kiss my cheek, then touch her lips to mine. Heard her say, "Move over, big guy."

I looked and saw that she was naked. Felt her bony rib cage as she slid in close; felt the heat of her nipples through my chest hair as I cupped her in my arm; felt her fingers trace my stomach and spread the elastic band of my shorts, searching. She kissed me hard when her fingers found me, and she whispered, "It's officially later this week."

I said, "I told myself I wouldn't let this happen."

She said, "Was that earlier this week or later?"

"I can't remember. It's hard to think because of what you're doing."

"Really? Then break off that damn fishing line."

Nineteen

On Monday at noon, the fourth of October, the director of the National Hurricane Center at Miami announced that the third tropical storm of the season had now officially reached hurricane strength, with winds exceeding the required seventy-five miles an hour. Off Jamaica, in fact, one gust was measured at 103 miles per hour by the British Volunteer Observation Fleet, which made it a Category Two hurricane on the Safir-Simpson scale.

They named it Hurricane Charles. It had a regal sound.

I was standing at the bar drinking a Diet Coke, watching television with Tomlinson and a dozen others, when the announcement was made. I heard a man and two women sitting at the bar exchange the standard remark common to some Floridians when a hurricane is mentioned. "We're due for a big one. I've been saying it all along."

Many do say it, usually with a perverse wistfulness. My own dread of hurricanes is compounded by all the dopes who'll say, "I told you so!" after it does happen. And it will. It most certainly will.

Tomlinson was drinking a bottle of Hatuey in a coolie cup, standing there in his cutoffs and leather sandals, wearing a black silk Hawaiian shirt with a hula girl on the back framed by pink frangipani blossoms. He'd caught a big mangrove snapper the night before and it was now roasting in his little gas oven aboard *No Más*. It made a nice aroma when you stood on the dock near his boat.

There was still a silver smear of scales on his shorts.

After breakfast, we'd said goodbye to Nora and Della; gave them sterile, impersonal kisses on the cheek, each of us keeping our private business private. I went for a long run through the backstreets off A1A, then spent the morning making phone calls from the apartment. Checked with Janet Mueller, whom I'd asked to take care of my fish tanks. My fish were doing fine, except I was running low on food for my sharks. Before I could stop myself, I told her to talk with Jeth. He'd cast-net some mullet.

Decided what the hell, maybe it would at least get them back on friendly terms.

I left a message for Detective Parrish and another for

Dieter Rasmussen, the big cheerful German at Dinkin's Bay, who was also a retired Munich psychopharmacologist. I wanted to speak with him because I was troubled by a simple realization: everyone liked, admired and trusted Ted Bauerstock except for me. Was it possible that there are people so practiced and devious that they can fool all but a very, very few? Or was it because I found his looks, his wealth and his charisma intimidating? Perhaps I was being unfair and judgmental, the typical alpha male, as Nora had once called me.

Other people I tried to reach were involved with government service. One was Bernie Yager, a computer genius.

Ivan and Ted Bauerstock weren't the only ones who had access to classified files.

Unfortunately, a woman who didn't give her name left a message for me at the bar: Bernie was on vacation, wouldn't be back for three weeks.

Now, this news of the hurricane meant that I couldn't spend much more time on the Keys. Depending on which way Charles went, I might have to get back to Sanibel in two days, maybe three at the most, to button up my stilt house. If it looked like it really was going to get bad, I'd have to release all my fish. Let them fend for themselves—not a pleasant option.

According to the cheerful weather guy, NOAA had sent its 41-C four-engine prop plane into the eye of Charles to measure pressure gradients, wind speed and temperatures at various altitudes. All data was fed into the onboard computer, then transmitted to the weather center in Miami where it would continue to be analyzed, along with high- and low-pressure profiles in all directions, with temperature ridges and wind patterns factored that might alter the storm's path.

A hurricane is not unlike a bead of electricity. It follows the path of least resistance. High-pressure areas, pressure ridges, cold fronts and opposing winds are all objects of resistance.

Over the night, Hurricane Charles had shifted direction. It was now moving west, gobbling water and pockets of low pressure, already blotting out the eastern tip of Cuba as it moved toward the Florida Straits and the Gulf of Mexico, traveling at the speed of a dependable ocean freighter.

Tomlinson said to me, "You hear it? The waves."

The wind had continued to freshen; was now blowing a steady fifteen with gusts to twenty. I looked at small white caps breaking over the rock jetty. "What about the waves?"

"The rhythm, the pattern. It's changed, can't you hear it?"

I shook my head. "I don't know what you're talking about."

"It's the way the Calusa knew a thousand years ago. The way they knew their nightmare was coming. On this coast, waves roll ashore about eight every minute. But that thing out there, that storm, it's gaining mass, sucking things up. It's giving the waves big shoulders, making them slower. Hear the difference? Now we're getting five, maybe six waves a minute. The Indians always knew. They were brilliant in their way."

I told him, "If it keeps coming, you need to have *No Más* hauled. What do you care, you've got the money. Or get the hell out of this shallow water. You don't want to be anywhere near Pennekamp or Key Largo. All this coral."

He looked at me, his bright blue eyes sober and alive. "No

man. I've been waiting for this for a while. If it happens, if it
really happens. Hell! Charles gets near enough, *No Más* and
me, we're sailing into the eye."

"Dog-tor Ford! I have a message to call you at this number." The German accent of Dieter Rasmussen was unmistakable. Still, with all the noise in the bar—the *Mandalites* were
listening to Jimmy Buffett and arguing about water spouts—it
was tough to hear.

There was also zero privacy.

Dieter told me he was aboard his Grand Banks trawler,
Das Stasi, and I could reach him there.

I jogged up the steps to the apartment. I saw the rumpled
sheets on the couch bed and thought of Nora as I picked up
the phone.

A nice independent lady. There seem to be fewer and
fewer of those. Spirited and smart, too.

"Doctor Ford! It is so surprising to receive the call from you,
yah! We don't even have the conversation here at the marina,
now we are talking on the phone." Rasmussen's tone was
jocular, but there was a goading edge to it. I didn't blame him.
I didn't actually avoid him at Dinkin's Bay, but I'd never gone
out of my way to sit down and have a talk with the guy. Everyone liked him. Everyone said he was a lot of fun; generous
and brilliant, as well. But what everyone didn't know was that
his boat had been named after the small, very select intelligence service that had once operated in Germany. I found that
off-putting.

"We're both very busy guys. And Dieter? Call me Marion. Or Doc. Okay?"

"That we are busy, we both know that is not the reason we do not talk." He was laughing. "Even so, I am glad to finally have this opportunity to speak with a man who, I suspect, was once so famous in so many private ways."

There it was. Exactly why I'd dodged one-on-one conversations with the guy. Not that I was surprised. Sanibel is a very popular vacation and retirement island among the intelligence community worldwide.

I said, "Tell you what, Dieter. When I get back, we'll sit down and exchange stories. Right now, though, I could use your help. You really are a physician and psychiatrist?"

"Oh yah, yah! I was the foremost psychopharmacologist in Munich and am licensed to practice and do research even in this country. You are having emotional problems?"

I smiled at that, then laid it out. I told him about my conversation with Ted Bauerstock, trying to reduce my concerns to the simplest elements. I told him about Dorothy Copeland's grave. I asked about manic fixation; told him about the totem and the gold medallion.

He said, "You are asking me if it is possible for a very evil man to fool all the very best people? Yah, of course! I can tell you frightening stories, terrible stories, about some of my own patients. But I can do more than this for you. You say this man was institutionalized in North Dakota?"

"I was told he attended a very strict boarding school there. I was never told that he was institutionalized."

"That is easily enough found out. There is one very, very fine facility there if money is not a problem. It is full-time treatment and behavior modification, and I guess you could call it a boarding school in a way. Some people have spent years there. I will contact my colleagues. They will know my work and will talk to me."

"You can ask them about Ted Bauerstock?"

"No! That would be a breach of ethics; illegal as well. But I can ask for their case histories on certain manias. Part of my research, understand. If your suspicions are merited, I will find this person as easily as you would pick out his photo. The symptoms are as unmistakable as fingerprints. His name will never be mentioned."

"He's on the verge of being elected to a political office. So maybe it's about time someone dug into his background. We don't need psychopaths in the state senate."

Dieter laughed. "But why not! Psychopaths are the politicians of your country's future—and your recent past."

I didn't care for his flippant attitude. "Call me overly patriotic, Dieter, but I find it offensive when foreigners criticize my country while they're drinking our beer, sleeping with our women and getting rich."

"It is not a criticism! My dear Ford, at a time when our most personal behavior can be scrutinized instantaneously, only those who lie automatically and without remorse will rise in the political ranks. Why? Because only they have nothing to fear!" He chuckled at my discomfort. "I will get the information for you. A day, maybe two. That's all it will take. Do you have a fax number? An e-mail address?"

I gave Rasmussen the Mandalay's fax number, but when I started to thank him, he interrupted. "Wait! I want something in return."

"If you're talking about billing, I can pay you. That's not a problem."

"Not money. I have plenty of money. It is something else. An explanation."

I waited, feeling increasingly uneasy.

Listened to him say, "Nearly fifteen years ago, a member of the Communist organization, Students for a Democratic Society, disappeared from a bar in Aspen, Colorado. The night he disappeared, there were members of U.S. Naval Intelligence in that same bar. With them was a member of SEAL Team One, along with a representative from Studies and Operations Group, your top secret organization. The name of the bar was The Slope. That man's body was never found. Another SDS member was also targeted to be killed. This was in retribution for the bombing of a Naval facility in San Diego."

I said softly, "I'm familiar with this story, Dieter."

"I know that you are! I skied in Aspen last winter. The name of that bar has changed, but the picture is still on the wall of you and your SEAL colleagues. You were there that night because one of the men killed in that bombing was your close friend. I have two questions: Were you with Naval Intelligence? That is unclear. Or were you the SOG member?"

I spoke carefully. "I was never in the military, Dieter."

"Yah, I knew it! The SOG member in the bar that evening, he was very gifted. Very famous in the craft, a, how do you say, *der Attentaeter.* He was a man who sometimes went by the name of North. Did much work in Cuba. So my second question is this: Why haven't you? Why haven't you extinguished him?"

"Who?"

"You *know* him. *Him.*"

I said, "I am completely lost. Is any of this supposed to make sense?"

"Of course you don't understand me. But please, answer."

"Did you sail all the way to Dinkin's Bay just to ask me strange questions?"

He thought this was hilarious. I listened to him roar. "Yah! It was a consideration! I knew it must be an interesting place, the two of you at one small marina. But your answer! Why was this second Communist subversive not extinguished?"

Looking through the apartment's sliding doors, out onto the boat basin, I could see Tomlinson aboard *No Más,* sitting cross-legged on the cockpit locker. He was eating fish; had a glass of red wine balanced on the stern coaming. He appeared to be talking to the glass. Talking to his wine? Yes, no doubt about it. He looked like a stork with dreadlocks. He seemed to be really enjoying the fish.

He'd baked the entire snapper, yet hadn't invited me to dinner? I'd loaned him my fine Loomis rod to catch the damn thing. Come to think of it, he hadn't even *thanked* me.

I said, "Dieter, I have no idea what you're talking about.

But, if I did, I'd say the party in question, the Communist? If he doesn't start being a little more thoughtful, his days may be numbered."

It was nearly sunset. Because he knew I was still expecting more calls, Jack, the owner, told me I was welcome to carry around the restaurant's portable phone. "If you're down here to help Della, we want to take care of you any way we can," he told me. "This place may be kind of strange and funky, but we're family."

Trouble is, they couldn't find the portable phone. Then Salina remembered that Tomlinson had carried it out to his boat and never brought it back.

I asked her, "Where is Tomlinson?"

She became evasive and amused. "Tommy-san? Oh . . . I think, but I'm not sure . . . it may be that Betty Lynn took him over to her trailer to, you know, show him around." Laughter. "Like Jack said, we're trying to take care of you boys."

Betty Lynn, the stocky deep-south blonde who couldn't fit safely into a tank top, so had to wear a jogging bra beneath her *Mandalite* waitress outfit.

Tomlinson. He had always been extremely selective about liaisons until the mother of his young daughter had married a Boston politico. It had put him in an emotional tailspin. Since then, he'd demonstrated the jaunty sexual abandon of a lovebug.

I walked out the dock to *No Más,* stepped aboard, swung down the companionway steps and there, on the wooden door to the ice box, was the beige telephone handset.

As I reached for the phone, it rang. I picked it up and heard Salina's voice say, "Doc, honey? Man's on the line, he says he wants to speak to you."

Then I heard Detective Gary Parrish's voice. "Yeah, Doc honey, it's me. You got a minute?"

Tomlinson had left the uneaten portion of the fish out on a wooden platter covered with aluminum foil. He'd baked it with onions, fresh chilies, lots of mushrooms, and he'd made fish gravy.

Despite his many oddities, the man is a fine cook.

I removed the foil, stooped, got a fork and began to eat, as Parrish said, "Only thing I've had time to do is try and find the girl's runaway daddy, Dart Copeland. Wanted to ask him a few questions. You see him whispering to Mr. Bauerstock? But when he walked away from that funeral, it's like the man disappeared. You expect me to know anything else, you're too impatient for this kind'a work."

I said, "Oh? My luck's been a little better."

I told him what I could about my conversation with Bauerstock. Without going into specifics, without breaching the confidentiality I'd promised, I presented a very clear image of who wanted the totem badly enough to exhume Dorothy: Ivan or Ted Bauerstock. Perhaps both.

Parrish whistled, "Man, the chance to take down Ivan Bauerstock. That snobby rich man, he got the overseer attitude. I can see it when he looks at me. Wouldn't I love to put the bracelets on him." He paused for a moment. "But if the man knew where the wooden carving was buried, why'd he bother having someone rob Mrs. Copeland's trailer?"

"I don't think they *did* know at first. Della's address was on file with the city cemetery, so she was easy to find. She hadn't sold the carving, hadn't donated it. They could have searched their computers on that, too. So the reasonable assumption was that she'd kept it. I think one other person knew where the totem really was, the big guy who was at the funeral. The guy with the red face, Frank Rossi. When Ivan or Ted dropped the word, Rossi probably told them about the grave."

Parrish chuckled. "That reminds me, man. We got a report this other big white guy from the funeral beat the Johnny-cakes outta two of the local crackheads. One of them Tony Rossi, Frank's boy. 'Bout ripped one'a their ears off, put the other one in the hospital. Families decided not to press charges. Who knows why? You wouldn't know anything 'bout that, man?"

I said, "I know enough about Frank Rossi to not much care." Then I told Parrish what he'd done to Della, adding, "So after he robs her, he date-rapes her. A woman who's absolutely crippled by grief. He and his son aren't going to get a lot of sympathy from me."

Parrish said, "You eatin' something?"

I told him.

"Man oh man, fish gravy and mushrooms. That's Bahamas soul food, man!" Then he said, "We got that goin' on here now."

"Bahama's cooking?"

"*No.* A version of it, date rape. Only worse. We got the

whole staff workin' on this one. That's why don't expect me to be doin' much about Mr. Bauerstock and his politician son. Thing is . . . wait, tell me something first. Anybody else around to hear you and Teddy talkin' about how much his daddy wants that carving'?"

"No."

"Then it's his word against yours. All the people on Mr. Bauerstock's payroll in this state, how you think that'd go? So I best spend my time tracking down this very bad man we got roamin' around the Everglades."

"The date rapist, you mean? Any man who rapes a woman should be put away for life. Or killed. Or chemically altered. You'll get no argument from me. You can't work both cases at the same time?"

"It's worse than date rape, man. I told you about the three women disappeared? We finally found one of 'em. She must'a put up a hell of a fight. Jumped out of her abductor's car while it was moving, but she chose the wrong time 'cause he was on the Marco Bridge when she bailed. That's a very long fall."

I said, "Dear God," picturing it. "How old was she?"

"She was twenty-four, on vacation down here from Columbus. Medical examiner says she had a drug in her, this new drug come up here from South America from what the natives there call the Borracho tree. It means 'drunk tree.'"

I said, "Borracho, *Jesus.* I'm familiar with it." The drug made from the leaf of the Borracho tree is *scopolamine.* I knew about it because, south of Cartagena and off the Rosier Islands, locals boiled skin off the roots and dumped the liquor into calm backwaters to stun immature tarpon which they then sold in the markets. Colombia is one of the few places in the world that considers tarpon to be a table delicacy.

Shamans there also used it to induce waking trances in their patients. An individual under the influence of Borracho is unaware that the dream they seem to be having is actually real. They can be ordered to engage in sexual or illegal acts without their consent or knowledge. They are also extremely suggestible.

I also knew about *scopolamine* because it was used for interrogation and subjugation in the world of international espionage.

"You think Mrs. Copeland feels bad 'bout her daughter? Listen to this. Man, I had to call this girl's parents on the phone, tell them we'd found their missing child. Then stand there beside her father when the medical examiner pulled the sheet back for him to ID his dead girl. Know the worst thing?"

I had a terrible feeling of dreamy premonition as Parrish added, "The man who got the drug down her. He'd already hurt the girl bad before she jumped. He'd taken her eyes out; probably used his fingers, the medical examiner said. I had to tell the daddy the truth about that. It happened while his child was still alive."

I said, "How do you know she jumped out of a car?"

"What you mean? 'Course she jumped out of a car. How else we find her floating under that bridge?"

"A boat," I said. "She could have jumped from a boat."

Twenty

Tomlinson stood at the top of the companionway steps, looking in. For no reason that made sense, the individual ropes of his beaded hair created streamers of colored light as they swung back and forth. He said, "Uh-oh, uh-oh, holy *shitzky*. What you been eating there, Doc?"

"Some of your snapper. Thanks for inviting me, by the way. Yes, I'm being sarcastic. It's excellent." I touched a fist to my chest. "But I think it's giving me heartburn." Then I said, "Whew! Is it hot down here? All of a sudden, it seems really warm." I tried to stand, then sat down quickly on the settee cushion. *No Más* seemed to be dancing around in the wind.

He came down the steps fast, held his palms outward. "Okay, first thing is, stay calm. I'm here by your side. I'm not going anywhere; not a thing in the world to be afraid of. Some consider me an expert in this field."

"Are you nuts? I've got to fly. You know where Ted Bauerstock's ranch is? We need to get up there right away. Take the truck, bang on the gate till they let us in. I think the girls could be in trouble."

He put his hands on my shoulders. "You're in no condition to go anywhere, compadre. What you're feeling right now is very typical. Mild panic, sweating, mild heartburn, all symptomatic. Especially the panic. It's to be expected on your first journey."

I was sweating and burping. Colors through the companionway door had gotten much brighter: molecularized purples and fruity pinks. As the boat rocked back and forth, the mast created a metallic slash in the tissue of burning, sunset sky. It was an opening large enough to swim through.

"Doc, there's something I need to tell you. Before I do, I want you to promise me something. Please don't hit me. I've seen you hit people. I'm much too fond of my nose to risk it. Plus it makes my eyes water and it looks like I'm crying. It would be embarrassing. I cry too much as it is."

"Hit you? I don't have time to hit anybody. I've got to get to Marco, find that ranch." I tried to stand again. My legs had turned to water. I looked down at my boat loafers to see orange streaks scoring the leather. Then my brain, in rapid succession, transferred the outline of the loafers onto a leather hide hanging on the wall, then onto a cow that was sprinting away from a bald-headed cobbler who was chasing the animal, thread and needle in hand.

I sat again. Forced myself to be calm, and said, "Tomlinson, something's happened to me. I'm not sure what. But my brain has begun to . . . has begun to." I realized that I was focused on the telephone sitting atop the icebox. The phone was melting. As it did, drops of beige plastic turned to black and jumped around like grease on a griddle. "My brain, Tomlinson . . . it's my brain. It isn't translating information the way it should."

Now my heart was pounding, and sweat was streaming down my face. I felt my friend's hand pat my shoulder, trying to comfort me. "It's okay, Doc, after I explain, you'll understand. What I want to tell you right off is this: psilocybin mushrooms are illegal in forty-nine of the fifty states. Know what the good news is? Florida is the fiftieth state. So it's *legal,* rest your mind about that. We're not breaking any laws. What you're feeling right now is legal. Isn't that great!"

I couldn't believe what I was hearing. "Are you saying that the mushrooms on the snapper are psychedelic mushrooms?"

"Shrooms we call them. Friendly little guys who know just how to mix with a natural chemical in the brain. Think of them as tour guides. It's a chemical called *scrotonin.* Kind of a cool, masculine name, huh? It's *fun.*"

I was looking at him, trying to remain calm. "Oh *shit.*" Then I said, "Okay, okay . . . I would never have consented to this. But I've got to deal with it, so . . . so when I see something crawling around your neck . . . something that appears to be a scarlet boa constrictor—like now, for instance—I should assume it's bad information altered by chemicals?"

Tomlinson pulled the snake away from his neck, and it became a Vietnamese flag, red backing, single yellow star. "Yep, see! It's really just a scarf."

"Right, that explains it. File this away, Tomlinson. If you ever do this to me again, leave psychedelic food lying around, I will personally grab you by the neck . . ."

I lost my train of thought. Realized I was gazing at the shell mobile hanging from a locker. It really was rather pretty. Nice earth colors on scallop shells that were wonderfully formed with precise ridges. Reminded me of Arizona where I'd seen petroglyphs on red stone high above Tempe . . .

My wandering inattention startled me. I straightened myself and said, "Help me out of this damn boat. I need to get up. I'm going topside and try to make myself puke. Is there an antidote?"

"An *antidote?*" Tomlinson was shaking his head, slinging colors against the bulkhead. "Doc, you know how to take the fun out of everything."

"I want this to be over. I *hate* it. Isn't there something I can take to make it go away?"

"You're speaking, like, heresy, man. Good shrooms are hard enough to find as it is. Why would anybody want an antidote?"

Five minutes later, Tomlinson pressed the phone to my

ear, saying, "Put a smile on that mug of yours. Guess who just answered her cell phone? I explained things to her. She understands."

I heard Nora's voice say, "Doc? Are you okay?"

My heart was still pounding in my ears and I was hyperventilating. "Are you at the ranch? Are you with Ted? I want you to get out of there right away. I mean it. Get Della and run."

She was laughing. "Oh sweetie, I wish I was there to see you. Marion Ford on psychedelics! I don't think the world's ready."

"Please, listen to me. I'm probably wrong, but if I'm right—"

"You're not right. Believe me. The shrooms are getting to you, babe. I've been through it. Just hang on, stay calm, you'll be fine and so will I. Ted's one of the nicest men I've ever met. I'm going to work in his *campaign*. Don't worry, though. He doesn't have your magnetism. But he's genuine. He's making cocktails for Della and me right now."

"Don't drink it. Don't eat or drink anything he gives you."

"*Marion*. Calm down. Depending on how the hurricane goes, we'll be home tomorrow. I want you to take some long slow breaths. I'm not going to hang up until you feel better."

"Are you there with him alone?"

"No. His father's here, too. What could be safer?"

Did that make any difference? I couldn't analyze it; couldn't make my brain function properly. "You have your cell phone? You have the number here?"

"Of course."

I was shaking my head; couldn't seem to clear it. "Okay, here's what I'd like you to do. Indulge me, okay?" I had my billfold out. Found Gary Parrish's card with his home number scribbled on the back. "The moment we hang up here, I want you to call Detective Parrish. Do it in front of Ted and Ivan, make sure they know what you're doing. Talk to Parrish or leave a message. Tell him where you are, who you're with and when you plan to leave."

"Marion, there's no need!"

"I'm asking you to do it as a personal favor, Nora. Please."

"It would be so rude."

"Blame it all on me. Tell them I'm crazy, obsessive, whatever you want. Neither of them will have any trouble believing that."

Her tone softened slightly. "It would make you feel better?"

"Yes, absolutely. Promise me you'll call Parrish immediately and I'll feel a hundred-percent better. It'll let me concentrate on dealing with this damn drug that's in me."

"If that's what it takes to give you some peace of mind, I'll do it. But, believe me, I'm not in any danger. With the security system they've got at this ranch, I'm probably the safest I've ever been."

"I'm going to wait right here by the phone. I expect to hear from you in no less than ten minutes."

A few minutes later, the phone rang and I heard Nora's voice say, "Okay, Jimi Hendrix, I got Parrish's recorder. I left a detailed message. That ought to put a smile on your face."

"Did both Bauerstocks hear you?"

"I made the call from the great man's own desk. I don't think Ted approves of you. He said he thought you were a bit obsessive."

"Uh-huh. I don't like you being there. I don't trust either one of those guys."

Nora's voice was intimate and patient. "I know what you're going through. Relax. Enjoy it. The first time I did shrooms, I was panicky and goofy as hell. So hang on, I'm here for you. I won't be happy unless I see you tomorrow. There! That ought to take the panic away."

The last thing she said to me was, "Oh, Marion. You are such a big lug!

Tomlinson said, "Know what we could do? Hop in the truck, drive up the island to Card Sound. Stop at Alabama Jack's, have a couple beers. Sit outside and maybe a saltwater croc will come along. I haven't seen a croc in a couple years. That'd be a nice break. Not many tourists go through Card Sound. Or maybe Ocean Reef. Have a cocktail at the pool bar and meet some rich girls."

It was just before dusk. I was jogging, stopping to do push-ups, deep knee bends, trying to increase my heart beat and hurry the chemical through my system. We'd run along Marina Road among mangroves and gumbo limbos past Poisonwood to A1A, then south, facing traffic on the divided highway. Jogged past the Koni Kai and a Tom Thumb convenience store; running on the road's shoulder, white coral rock crunching beneath my feet like bone.

I said, "Last thing I need is alcohol in my system. Are you *nuts?*"

It seemed as if Tomlinson didn't hear. "Or we could drive down to Summerlin, hang out with Bob and JoAnne Boast at Sherman's Marina. I haven't been there in a while. Or hell, shoot the wad, go clear to Key West, man. Sit under the ficus and play checkers with my old buddy Shine Forbes. Then stop by Blue Heaven, or the Green Parrot."

Tomlinson was struggling to keep up, running in sandals, still wearing his black Hawaiian shirt with the hula dancer on the back. I couldn't bear to look at her. The pinks and greens of her skirt were so penetrating they hurt my eyes. Also, if I looked at her for more than a second, she became a live person, attached to Tomlinson's back but openly lascivious.

"How long did you say this crap lasted?"

"If you're lucky, seven, maybe eight, hours man."

"And if I'm not lucky?"

"Four hours tops. Your journey will be over."

"I can't believe you actually *enjoy* this feeling."

"Man, it's like watching Disney films, but on the inside. I can't believe you *don't.*"

We'd left the marina when I realized that I was becoming introspective to the point of catatonia. Running seemed to be the thing to do. I was carrying the black briefcase, my left hand pocketed inside, holding the wooden totem. I hadn't mentioned it to Tomlinson, but touching the totem, feeling the hard curvature of wood beneath my hand, gave me an irrational sense of peace that I attributed to the very powerful hallucinogen circulating through my brain. It reminded me of Dorothy. But . . . why would that matter?

"Or we could stop at the Paradise Pub. They got pretty good food."

I interrupted him. "Are there really pineapple streaks in the sky, or is that just more bad data?"

"No, man. Those streaks are real. The sunsets here, that's one of the good things about the Keys. With all the colors, it's like being on shrooms half the time anyway. Even when you're straight."

"Good, good, okay. What about the rainbow stripes down the middle of the road?"

"I'm afraid that's the toadstool God pulling one of her little tricks."

I said, "Uh-huh, that's what I thought. I'm starting to understand. It's like code. I have to unscramble everything. At least my stomach's feeling better. So maybe that's not a bad idea, go somewhere and get something to eat."

"The munchies, I hear you. See? Now you're getting *into* it. . . ."

That night, dizzy, exhausted, passed out on the couch in the Mandalay's apartment, I was awakened once again by an abrupt tug on my ankle. The fishing line outside, broken by a late-night visitor, popped once, then twice.

I'd been immersed in a dream so real in terms of awareness and visual details, and so emotionally powerful, that it seemed I had the very real choice of staying in that dreamy world, or of returning to reality.

Had it not been for the fishing line pulling at my ankle, and what it meant, I would have chosen to remain as long as possible in that place of imagination—for it *had* to be imaginary, fabricated, no doubt, by the lingering effects of the psilocybin mushrooms circulating in my brain and my heightened susceptibility to Tomlinson's suggestions.

In the dream, I was wearing clothing not of these times. It was rough-woven, hand-loomed. There was some kind of weapon strapped to my hip, something heavy. I could feel it thump my left leg as I walked.

It seemed a comfortable, familiar feeling; a weapon so customary that it did not require inspection or definition.

I was walking through a stone chamber with a vaulted rock ceiling framed by rough-cut beams. There were windows in the walls without glass. Through the windows were muddy streets where oxen pulled wagons. Beyond were gray moors. There was an oak forest so green it appeared to be black.

I could smell the mud. Could smell lichen on bare rock.

It was cool, nearly cold. Half of one wall was a fireplace. Stones dissipated the heat. There was a bough of evergreen, like a good luck charm, tacked above the hearth. I crossed a hallway, then another. I knew the building well. At a set of double oak doors, I stopped and tapped. Heard a woman's voice say, "My love . . . ?"

It was a voice that I had never heard. It was a voice that I've known forever.

Then she was there, dressed in white crinoline that touched the floor, long blond hair hanging to her waist, material clinging to her body, her arms held out to me. Her face was luminous in golden light, a woman so beautiful that seeing her caused me to linger upon detail: lighted portions of chin and cheek, strong nose creating shadow, perceptive eyes unaware and uncaring of her own beauty. Her voice was a kindred chord as she said, "I've waited so long for you, my dear. So many, many years. Now, finally, you've come back to me. . . ."

Then we were lying together on a feather bed beneath a canopy of royal blue. Being able to hold her, to touch her, to turn and touch my lips to her pale cheek, seemed to neutralize all that was hurtful in me. Negated a universe of uncertainty, a lifetime of confusion and solitude. I could feel her warm breath; hear the fragile beating of her chest against mine. She was real. My skin was against hers. I was no longer alone.

Into my ear, she whispered, "I have tracked you through the ages, just as you've searched for me. In small ways, through other good people, we've touched briefly, briefly. But I know that it's never been enough, my dear, because it's never been enough for me. It is why people like us are alone even in a crowded room, even in an intimate bedding place. We are waiting. Forever waiting.

"But take comfort in this, dearest: I will find you. We are

always of one heart, one mind, and I will find you. Love is religion, not emotion. It requires a leap of faith. Remember that. Have faith in me. There are so many destinations, so many way points, but we *will* arrive on the same small island once more. On that island, we will make ourselves free. Never lose hope."

Feeling a delicious sense of well-being and contentment, I turned to her, braced on one elbow, looked into her dazzling blue eyes; eyes that would be forever familiar on the distant rim of memory, and I leaned to kiss her. . . .

Which is when I felt a violent tug on my ankle. Then a second tug on my ankle, monofilament fishing line cutting skin.

As sometimes happens in dreams, that strong, physical sensation imposed itself and became part of the dream—a rope being roughly constricted—but now the rope was around my girl's neck, hurting her, pulling her upward and away from me, as my big hand reached to stop her . . .

It was Dorothy's face, though older. Looking at me were Dorothy's water-clear eyes.

I sat up so violently that I rolled off the couch.

Waited there, crouched on my knees, listening.

Had the fishing line really been broken? I found my ankle and gave it an experimental pull.

Yes, a person was out there.

Then I heard a metallic sound at the door. A key? No. Some kind of lever, a crowbar perhaps. Someone was trying to break in.

I studied myself for a moment. Confirmed that I was still dressed. Apparently, I'd passed out in my clothes. I reached and found the sap I'd made, right where I'd left it the night before. Then I stood, my head pounding. I felt like vomiting. I spit onto the carpet, then went out the open glass doors, moving very fast and quiet.

This time, it couldn't be Nora. It was someone coming for me, coming for the totem.

I peeked around one corner, then the next: I saw a big man standing there, something in his hands. Very wide shoulders, a belly. No facial features at all. I realized he was wearing a ski mask.

No doubting his intent.

I watched him lever the bar into the doorjamb and lunge. The door popped open. He went in quickly.

I swung around the corner and stepped in behind him, close enough to smell his sweat and the metallic tobacco stink of him. He must of heard me or sensed my presence because he started to turn. As he did, I sapped him once low on the head, just behind the ear.

I didn't hit him hard. It's not like the movies. Hit a man behind the ear with much force and you will kill him. Or he will spend the rest of his life in a hospital attached to complicated machines.

The intruder went down hard enough to make the walls shake. He started to roll toward me, and I sapped him again on the left shoulder, this time much harder. He gave a whistle of pain, then lay still at my feet in darkness.

He almost certainly wasn't unconscious. It is a predictable reaction: twice clubbed, a man feigns unconsciousness so that he won't be clubbed a third time.

I closed the door, hit the light switch and picked up the crowbar he'd used to jimmy the door. A big man with dark, hairy hands, wearing tan coveralls and a green ski mask.

I nudged him with my foot. He didn't move. I stepped on his fingers, increasing the pressure until he finally yanked his hand away.

He was conscious, all right.

"Take off the ski mask, but stay on your belly."

He did.

It was Frank Rossi.

Twenty-one

You pull this shit on me, pal, you don't know who you're dealing with." Rossi had a voice like his son, only a stronger New Jersey accent. Same mindless vocabulary, too.

I'd used the duct tape to tape his arms behind him. Now I was taping his legs, but only temporarily.

"You don't let me go right now, asshole, I know people. Important people. I'll have you killed."

I said, "Gee, that's the first time anyone's ever said that to me. In English, anyway."

"That some kind'a joke? A funny boy, real funny. You'll see. You'll see what happens to you after you let me go."

The color of his face changed slightly when I said, "Frank, I'm not going to let you go. I'm going to kill you. Any advice on how to get a tub like you to sink?"

I dropped the weight of my knee onto his neck. When his head arched upward, I taped his mouth. As I did, I thought of the way he had manipulated Della Copeland, stealing the medallion, then getting her drunk and forcing her into bed.

I made several more wraps with the tape, intentionally sealing off one side of his nose.

He began to wiggle, fearing that I was going to suffocate him. I had no intention of doing that. But I wanted him to experience the fear. I wanted him to know what it was like to be overpowered and controlled.

"Save your breath, Frank. You'll need it."

I went through his pockets. I found a length of woven cord—apparently, he'd planned to tie me up—along with Winstons, car keys bearing a Mercedes's logo, billfold and a palm-sized Colt Mark IV .380. A nice little weapon. I popped the clip. Fully loaded, too. One round already in the chamber.

"Frank, how'd you know? It's *exactly* what I wanted."

I took the car keys and went out the glass doors, swung over the railing and dropped down to the ground. If someone was out on the street, waiting in Rossi's car for him to return, I didn't want them to see me coming.

No, he was alone. I found his car on Marina, pulled off the side of the road. What a dope. That was like advertising, telling the cops he was sneaking around.

I drove the car to Shell World's deserted parking lot, left

the keys in the ignition, opened the hood as if it were broken down, wiped off my prints and jogged back to the Mandalay.

I cut the tape binding Rossi's legs, got him to his feet and said, "We've got about an hour before first light. What you say we go for a boat ride, just you and me?"

His eyes grew wide and he began to shake his head furiously.

I added, "You're right. I almost forgot. I need to take along an extra anchor. A belly like yours, you're going to be really buoyant."

There was less than a quarter moon drifting through clouds above a black, windy sea. Lots of wind and getting worse.

The moon made me think of the wooden totem, the designs on it. The gold medallion, too, though I'd never seen it.

Once I'd gotten Rossi into the boat, I taped his legs again. Now he was lying on his back, head at my feet, squeezed in between the console and the gunwale. I had the bow trimmed down, running as smoothly as a small boat can run in a rolling sea. Even so, big waves caused his head to bang on the deck.

"Kind of rough out here tonight, Frank. Look on the bright side. You don't have to make the trip back."

I ran out the mouth of Rock Harbor, almost due south. Ronrico Key was a dark elevation against a black sky. Out on Hawk's Channel, I could see the green four-second light off Mosquito Bank and the red flasher off Hen and Chickens Reef. Beautiful place to dive, all those big corals. Hit either reef and you'd kill your boat. Even a skiff that ran as shallow as mine.

But I wasn't going nearly that far.

I ran in darkness, seeing only the reddish glow of my compass. I turned on my VHF radio as I did; switched down to Weather Channel 2, Key West, where I heard a computerized voice say: ". . . small craft warning is now in effect for Dry Tortugas to Key Largo and Florida Bay. Waves inside the reef, two to four feet; eight to ten feet outside the reef."

There was an electronic pause.

"The latest advisory issued by the National Hurricane Center at Miami places the eye of Hurricane Charles slightly south of Isle of Pines, Cuba, at latitude 17.6 degrees north, longitude 85 degrees west, moving northwesterly at thirteen knots. Winds have been measured at one-hundred-twenty-five knots and gusting stronger, barometric pressure at 27.80 and falling. Charles has been upgraded to a Category Four hurricane on the Safir-Simpson scale. Computer analysis projects that it will follow a low-pressure system through the Yucatan Channel into the Gulf of Mexico where it will be driven eastward by a ridge of high pressure. The Center expects to issue a 'hurricane watch' within the next twenty-four hours for the west coast of Florida, Cape Sable to Tarpon Springs. Be advised that a 'hurricane watch' is defined as . . ."

I punched off the radio.

It was coming.

About a quarter mile from Ronrico Key, on the bay side, I dropped down off plain and switched off the engine. I found the duct tape and began to tape my extra anchor to Rossi's head. As I did, I said, "We need to make this quick. There's a hurricane out there."

His eyes were wide in the moonlight, terrified.

"Frank, I've got good news and bad news. The good news is, you're only a couple hundred feet from land. The bad news is, it's straight down. But there's one other option. Maybe you'd rather talk for a while?"

I only had to thump Rossi twice with the sap before we developed a pattern. I'd ask him a question. When I had the tape recorder going, he would then repeat the question with robot precision, and answer the question fully and honestly.

My voice would not be on the tape.

The first time I caught him in a lie, I lifted him by the belt, got him up onto the casting deck as if to throw him in. He began to beg. Then he began to cry, his whole body shuddering.

Despite what Tomlinson says, I am not without feelings. It is a pathetic thing to hear a mature man cry. But when I began to feel sympathy for Frank Rossi, I reminded myself what he'd done to Della . . . and then to Dorothy.

Rossi did not lie to me again.

With me holding the small tape recorder near him and out of the wind, I listened to him say, "Did I dig up the grave of Dorothy Copeland? The answer to that is yes. I didn't see the harm, she's dead, right? I had one of my men drop the backhoe near the cemetery. We had some sewage pipes in the

area to replace anyway—I'd been awarded the city bid on it—
so I decided to get to it a little earlier, that's all. I was aware
that my primary employer was interested in purchasing a
wooden carving that was buried with the girl. I mean, who's
it gonna hurt? The carving wasn't doing her no good. If the
cops hadn't come, I'd a buried her back, no problem. It's not
like I was being disrespectful. The thing about breaking into
the gal's trailer, I didn't do that. It was probably the big colored guy, the football player, or one of his other flunkies. Oh,
something I forgot . . . Ivan Bauerstock, he's my primary employer."

I listened to Rossi say, "Did I steal the gold Indian medallion? Did I rape Della Copeland? Well . . . look, those are
really strong words. Now, I *did* con her out of the medallion,
I admit that. You grow up the way I grew up and, hey, it's a
tough world, pal. People dumb enough to get conned deserve
it in my book. So the woman's not real bright. Who you
gonna blame for that? *Me?*

"About the other thing, the rape thing, definitely no. I
wouldn't say what I did can be called rape. Yeah, I got a bottle of wine down her. Maybe I put some grain alcohol in it, I
really can't remember for sure, but who hasn't done that, pal?
It's true she kept telling me no when I tried to get her dress
off. Kept saying she didn't want to. But lots of times I've had
women say no, but then they end up saying yes. How's a guy
supposed to know?"

I found his nervous, locker room laughter nauseating.

A few moments later, I listened to him say, "No, I don't

have the medallion. I sold it to my primary employer, Mr. Ivan Bauerstock." Then: "Look, pal, I can't talk about that. I really can't. Believe me, you don't want to know the truth, 'cause they'll come looking for you. Seriously. You talk about political juice, pal? Fucker's got tons of it."

I had to get Rossi up on the casting deck and nearly rolled him into the water before I taped him saying, "How did I become involved with my primary employer, Mr. Ivan Bauerstock? Just for the record, in case the wrong person hears this, I got the whole story written down at my attorney's office, and he's been instructed to mail my sworn statement to the DA's office if anything weird ever happens to me. Like if I just disappear. Keep that in mind."

I had to thump him a third time before he said, "Okay, okay, the way I got involved with the family is, I like to collect Indian artifacts. Bauerstock, he's the same, only I didn't know that at the time. This was like fifteen years ago. The Bauerstock family, they got a lot of property on Marco and back in the 'glades, Indian mounds all over the place. The estate on Marco—it's called Indian Hill—I'd go up there and dig. Not with permission, understand. I'd climb the fence. If they'd seen me, they'd of called the cops. It was no skin off their nose, but property owners, they're bastards like that.

"This one afternoon, it was about the same time of year, October, I climbed the fence like I always did, and I was digging and sifting on the highest mound when I heard a girl's voice out of nowhere say, 'You won't find anything there, mister.' Turned and here's this teenage girl standing there looking at me. Kind of a pretty girl with blond hair. She's dressed up like she's going to church. Yellow dress, white gloves. In fact, that's what I figured 'cause it was a Sunday. She says, 'You're digging in the wrong place.' Something like that, and I figure she's being a smart-ass, so I tell her to fuck off, get the hell away from me. So what's she do? She smiles at me and drops this beautiful little Spanish chevron bead into my hands—had to be four hundred years old and worth a hundred bucks even then. She says, 'I hope this makes you happier,' or words kind'a close. Then she walks away."

I listened carefully, trying to remain relaxed and in control as Rossi continued, "Next time I see her, it's like half an hour later. I'd walked to the top of the highest mound, and I was looking down through the gumbo trees and there she is again. Only this time, Bauerstock is with her. He was doing something to her. It looked like he was hugging her, but from behind. I couldn't figure it out, so I kept watching. There was something weird about it, almost like they were dancing, kind of swaying back and forth. Then I realized, the girl was tied to a rope. It was tied around her neck, and Bauerstock was holding her arms down, using his weight. What he was doing was killing her. And he did. He murdered the teenage girl, then he started to play with her a little bit. Reminded me of a cat. But then his old man come along and stopped him. I watched for a while, then I left."

I punched off the recorder, my hands shaking, "It was Ted Bauerstock."

"Hell yes, it was Ted. He's a freak."

"Then *say* it. Say his name!"

Rossi had played it smart and cool. After watching the murder, he'd backtracked, climbed the fence and returned to the cheap motel where he was staying. He got a pen and paper and wrote down everything that he'd seen. He made copies at a Winn-Dixie, stopped at the first law office he came to, sealed his statement in an envelope and got a signed receipt for it.

He waited a couple of days before he telephoned Ivan Bauerstock.

"What got me was, the old man was like, it's no big deal. Like it was just another business matter he had to take care of. He's always treated Ted like something in a trophy case. I asked him once how much he figured he'd paid out to keep the kid's record clean. The way Mr. Bauerstock looked at me, I knew I better never ask him anything like that again. Ted does something, it's never mentioned, so it's like it never happened. One thing I learned early on, pal, money's all that matters in this world. Money and power. You got money, you can get away with anything. Murder, drugs, you name it."

Rossi went for the money: a long-term deal. If Ivan Bauerstock set him up in the contracting business, guaranteed him work, Rossi would never mention what he saw that day.

"It's played out good for both of us. I worked my ass off, pal. I made a bundle and I made it on my own. Old man Bauerstock, he couldn't have gotten better or for less. Then it turns out I got the thing in common about hunting artifacts. We get a new development project, first thing we go after is the burial sites. See? Kind of adds a little fun to the job."

I switched off the recorder before I asked, "Ivan Bauerstock is the collector?"

"No. Well, he buys stuff for his kid, but Teddy's the one. He's crazy about artifacts. His dad says it's 'cause he used to screw their colored maid, who was like a voodoo woman or some such thing. She had a big influence on him. Teddy collects artifacts like he's starving for the stuff. Wears the shit, prays to it for all I know. He's nuts.

"After the thing with the girl, him killing her, the old man sent him off to some private loony farm. Then kept him in very strict private schools after that, making sure he didn't get into any more trouble. As long as Ted stays righteous, the old man gives him anything he wants. He made it through college okay, been practicing law for his dad's companies, no problems that I know of. So he's like rehabilitated. But he's still nuts. Lately, it's that wooden carving. Ted was putting all kinds of pressure on his old man. He *had* to have it. Their luck had been running kind of bad, the old man's businesses, too. We find them that wooden carving, or maybe another gold medallion, that was supposed to change their luck. Give them more power, whatever. Ted even tracked down the girl's father, thinking maybe he had the same gift for finding stuff. But Dart Copeland, he's a bum, a drunk. Talk about nuts? Ted hired him anyway 'cause the guy had unusual eyes."

Still lying on the deck, Rossi stopped, tried to turn and get more comfortable, but couldn't. "So that's about it, pal. What you say, you cut me loose, then we go on back and have a beer? One day, we'll probably laugh about this shit, huh? A tough guy! Come down here to rough you up a little and I run into another tough guy. What're the fucking chances?"

The recorder was off. I placed it in the black briefcase, stepped over Rossi and stored the bag in a dry locker. "Where's the Bauerstocks' ranch? How do you get there?"

"Easy, only I don't try going in there without an invite. They got fences, cameras, the whole world. Security you wouldn't believe. You know where Port of the Islands is on the Tamiami Trail, east of Naples? They own about a thousand acres west of there, but that's the road you take in. Get within a mile of the mansion, though, someone will stop your car."

"What about by water?"

"Water? What'a you mean, water?"

"How hard would it be to go in there by boat?"

"By boat, yeah, I hadn't thought about that. The back way, you mean. They got water access. A river cuts in behind their place, and it's connected to the long canal that leads in from the islands. I can't remember its name. Hey, pal? You gonna let me go now, right? I cooperated. I'm gonna have to move out of Florida now that I spilled the beans. Maybe even outta the country, because of it. But, hey, I told you everything you wanted to know. I was honest."

In the vertical rod holders bolted to the console, between my fishing rods, I keep a stainless scissors. I reached for the scissors now, held it for a moment, then touched the point to

Rossi's neck. "You watched that girl die. You did nothing to stop it."

"Hey! What was I supposed to do? The man was on his own private property with a girl I'd never even met. It wasn't none of my business."

I said, "So she deserved it. That's what you're saying."

"The girl who died? Who knows? Maybe she got smart-ass with Teddy. It ain't my problem." Rossi was looking up, into my face. There was more light now, a pale dawn rising, and he could see what was in my eyes. "Hey, wait a minute, pal. I don't like what you're thinking. Wait . . . *don't*. You got no reason to blame me. Really, I'm begging you. Don't kill me, *please*."

With a slash, I cut the tape that bound him to the anchor, then I cut the tape around his legs.

"Get out of the boat."

"What?"

I repeated myself.

"Jesus Christ, you're not serious. It's gotta be a quarter mile to that island, and with my hands tied?"

"Get out of the boat!"

I grabbed him by the belt and throat, lifted him and threw him over. Watched him thrash and splash for a moment . . . until he got his feet under him, then he stood.

"Fucking water's only three feet deep! You bastard, you fucking lied to me!"

I said, "You got conned, Frank. So you're not very bright. Who you going to blame? *Me?*"

I told him he could wade two miles to Key Largo where his car was waiting at Shell World. Or wade to the island and hope to flag down a boat. He was still screaming at me when I started my engine and left him.

Back at the Mandalay, Reefer Vinny, one of the locals had already popped a sunrise beer. He was wearing a T-shirt that read, *Think Globally, Drink Locally*. When I told him I'd been out by Ronrico Key, he became concerned. "Watch your step out there, Captain. You didn't know? They should note it on the charts. Someone released a bunch of circus chimps there years ago when they got too big and mean. A deserted island, what's the harm? they figured. Plenty of wild monkeys around the Keys, islands full of them. But these chimps, they bred. That's why no one goes there. They're big. There's not much to eat, and they hunt in packs."

Twenty-two

Tomlinson said, "Just because Ted had some emotional problems when he was younger, it doesn't mean he's crazy now. I myself spent a year or so in, well, let's just say a confined, safe environment."

I looked at him sharply. "You ever murder anyone?"

In his expression, I could see the question jolt him; could see that it hurt. He said softly, "I think you know the answer to that. I think you've known for a while."

We were in the upstairs apartment, and I was packing. I was also hitting the redial button on the phone, trying to contact Detective Parrish, trying to warn Nora.

It was a little after eight a.m.

Parrish didn't answer. I got an infuriating recording when I dialed Nora: "*The Cellular-One customer you have called is unavailable or has traveled outside the coverage area. . . .*"

I said, "Once again, I don't know what you're talking about."

He ignored the evasion, looking at me. "There are things I've done in my life that I will regret for eternity. There is no absolution. None. Not from outside or from within. Some things make me wince, others make me want to cry. I try to make up for those sins as best I can."

"Ted Bauerstock doesn't strike me as the crying type. Della and Nora need to get the hell out of there. If I can't get Parrish in the next twenty minutes or so, I'm leaving. I'll have to go by boat."

"You already spoke to the Sheriff's Department?"

"The woman on the desk treated me like a crank. Mr. Bauerstock is dangerous? She laughed at me."

The apartment's dining table was made of glass and chrome. On it was a fax I'd found tacked to my door when I came up the steps from the fueling dock. It was from Dieter Rasmussen. At the top of the first page he used precise block letters to note: *This is consistent with the man in question.*

There were four pages. Some parts were more telling than others:

Date: (Confidential)
Place: St. Elizabeth's Hospital
Fargo, ND

This is a report of a psychiatric observation requested by the sole parent of patient 05715 and approved by Circuit Court Judge Amos Johnsleur. The examiner is the head of a team of psychiatrists that has examined the patient over a four-week period. All procedures were videotaped.

The patient is an adolescent male who is 17 years old. He is 75 inches tall and weighs 185 pounds. . . .

. . . The patient also underwent several batteries of psychological examinations including Rorschach and Meyers-Briggs tests. An abnormality was found in the EEG, the PET scans and the CAT scans.

Tests confirmed a distinct abnormality in the right amygdala portion of the subject's brain. Studies showed that the patient's amygdala did not respond to a series of actual news photographs of individuals who were about to be shot or burned or who were falling. Victims included children and women. This battery of photographs produces marked electric activity in the amygdala of normal subjects. Perhaps because his intellect was measured at 160 on the Stanford-Binet Test, the subject was immediately aware of the proper response. He voiced compassion for the victims, even while his brain registered none . . .

. . . Commentary: The subject was also found to have very low levels of noradrenaline. Lack of noradrenaline causes under-arousal and is associated with predatory violence. It is also possible that some of this patient's behavior may have been shaped by trauma in his late infancy and by his nanny during childhood.

The subject claims that his earliest memory is that of watching his father choking his mother. Since the mother died from a self-inflicted gun wound when the subject was three, this incident may well be apocryphal.

Between the ages of three and fifteen, the subject was raised by a Colombian female who, the subject says, practiced shamanry or witchcraft. The subject is very resentful of his father's apparent sexual relationship with the woman. The subject does not admit it, but it seems likely that he also had sexual encounters with the woman.

This woman apparently shaped the subject's religious beliefs which have manifested themselves in a series of fixations. Fixation is often associated with religious fervor. The strangest of these, though, is that the subject maintains his "power" through certain objects, and that it would "strengthen his own soul" if he ate the eyes of certain animals, although he maintains he would never do this. . . .

At the bottom of the final page, Dieter had written: "Dr. Ford, The human brain is especially vulnerable to such defects. During the last 1.5 million years, it has tripled in size. Any organ that changes that rapidly is increasingly prone to genetic error. There will be more and more of these people, yet society allows their defective genes to be passed on through conjugal visits in prison!"

Now I put a small bag over my shoulder. "Keep trying to call. I'm going to load the boat."

"It's going to be rough out there."

"I'll run backcountry, cut up through Whitewater Bay and the islands, hug the beach and stay in the lee. It won't be bad at all. The hurricane's still five or six hundred miles away."

Tomlinson had already agreed to take my truck, drive up to Sanibel and board my windows. The Florida Keys were no longer in danger. I'd asked him to release my sharks just in case.

"Can you do me one more favor? Go down to the bar, ask around, see if you can borrow or buy some goggles. The kind the motorcycle guys wear."

"Goggles?"

I went toward the door. "Yeah, for the first time, I think I'll open the throttle. See what my boat can do."

I idled beneath the bridge off Largo Sound, my Yamaha burbling like an alcohol dragster, then jumped to plane and was doing a spooky seventy miles an hour within seconds. By the time I hit The Boggies and crossed into Florida Bay, I was doing seventy-five; I could feel the squirrely, dancing feeling of air beneath the hull. The wind was gusting fifteen to twenty out of the southeast, piling water deep on the flats, so I ran a rhumb line course to Flamingo, not worried about bars or channels. I had to back off quite a bit because of the chop, especially in the open stretches, but I pushed it as hard as I could.

To the west and south were tentacles of rain suspended from thunderheads; a veil of squall to the north. I seemed to be at the very center of watery solitude, cloaked by the silence of my boat's velocity.

Hurricane Charles was pushing weather out ahead of it,

flattening pressure obstacles, causing sea birds to cauldron over land. As a hurricane grows, it gathers momentum, sucking in smaller storms as it rotates, feeding on a sea vaporized by tropic heat. The increasing disparity between pressure inside and outside the eye causes it to rotate ever faster, discharging rain, lightning, tornado appendages, spinning like a dust devil in the wake of a delivery truck.

As I steered, I tried to still my fears for Della and Nora by doing some mathematical calculations. It is an old trick. Our brains are segmented into halves. Primitive characteristics, such as emotion, are stored in the right hemisphere. Math is on the left. It is impossible to do math and be frightened at the same time.

Okay, so calculate the fastest estimated time of arrival for a storm traveling at thirteen knots that has to cover five to six hundred miles. A knot is 1.2 miles per hour, so convert thirteen knots and you've got . . . a little over fifteen miles per hour. Therefore, in a very worst case and unlikely scenario, Charles could travel one hundred fifty miles in ten hours, five hundred miles in a little over thirty hours.

But storms rarely travel straight lines. They slow down, they stall, they regather their strength over water, lose strength over land. This one would probably do what most do: bang back and forth between pressure ridges and plow ashore somewhere between Pensacola and New Orleans.

When I slowed at Flamingo, the rain finally caught me: a silver torrent with droplets that stung like pellets from an air rifle. In such a storm, you wear a foul weather jacket not to stay dry, but to avoid contusions. Even with goggles down, I couldn't see. So I pulled into temporary dockage at the National Park Marina, used the bathroom, dropped coins into the pay phone and heard, *The Cellular-One customer you have called is unavailable or has traveled outside the coverage area. . . .*

"Damn it!"

Dropped in more coins and heard, "Gary Parrish speaking. Calling me at home, on my day off, this better be good."

Detective Parrish said, "You got a tape of who saying what?"

I repeated myself.

"Holy shit, man, you serious. Teddy Bauerstock, I thought he was one of the good ones. You sure about this, Ford? Goddamn it, you better be sure 'cause it'll be your head and my job if you're not. How you know Rossi wasn't lying, making up all that shit?"

"Take my word for it. Rossi was in no position to lie."

"Oh goddamn, that's just great. You beat another confession outta someone. That ain't gonna stand up in no court."

"I never expected it to. You're the cavalry, I'm just the messenger. Have the right people listen to the tape, you'll come up with the evidence. All I care about now is making sure Nora and Della are safe. You got Nora's message, right?"

"Yeah, man. Couldn't figure out why she was laying all the information on, now I see. I don't care how crazy Teddy is, he knows she's got the cops involved, he's bound to be a good boy."

"Oh, he's crazy. Wait till you hear the tape."

Parrish began to chuckle, "I hope to hell you made more'n one copy. Something happen to you, man, I'm gonna miss out on a lot of fun. Arrest Teddy Bauerstock for a fifteen-year-old murder, hot damn!"

"Don't worry, I made several." I had, too. Tomlinson had one copy, and I'd addressed two to myself at Dinkin's Bay, asking Jack at the Mandalay to mail the envelope. "You want, I'll meet you at Port of the Islands; we can get into Bauerstock's ranch by boat. Go the back way."

"The back way? That back-way, back-a-the-bus shit went out with Kennedy, man. I'll meet you at Port of the Islands, but we'll take my squad car. Go in with the blue lights flashing, you want. One more thing, Ford—where's Rossi? He's okay, isn't he? You didn't kill him. I don't want to have to arrest you, too. But I would. Don't doubt it."

"Last time I saw Frank Rossi, he was a couple miles from Key Largo, walking. He looked fine. But I think the smart thing to do would be drive into the Bauerstock ranch, make sure the women are okay, then back way off. *Way* off. Use the tape to build a case, take your time, depose the right people, then nail him."

"You think even a cop can drive onto their estate without reason? That man, he's famous for being a hermit. *Nobody* goes onto his property 'less he wants 'em."

"I want to do things right, that's all."

"Bullshit, man. You just gave me probable cause. We need

to march in there, catch the rich man when his guard's down. Make Teddy listen to the tape, look in his eyes before his daddy's attorneys get involved. That's what really screws things up, a killer who hides behind his attorney. 'Member my brother O. J.? Both of us hear what Teddy has to say, we got two witnesses ready to testify in court. You and me. Rattle the rich boy's cage, see what hits the floor.

The rain had slowed; storm clouds had created a corridor of light to the west. I said, "Know what, Gary? You may be right."

I stopped only once before I ran the channel past Panther Key into the Ten Thousand Islands and Faka Union Canal. It was off Lostman's River, a confluence of oyster reefs, mangroves, dark water. I sat there idling in the white storm light, watching a spiral of frigate birds circling the deserted ranger station. A frigate bird is prehistoric in design; it has the reptilian aerodynamics of a pterodactyl, and the long rubbery wings of a bat. There were hundreds of birds, black scissor shapes ascending and turning, creating their own slow tornado.

For some reason, an unexpected voice came into my mind: *I told you about her eyes, too, Dad! They're amber, the color of a cat's eyes.*

Ted Bauerstock speaking of Nora.

I touched the boat into gear, and shoved the throttle forward. . . .

Twenty-three

You tell Mr. Bauerstock or Ted, either one. You tell them Detective Parrish is here with Doctor Ford for the second time, and we ain't waitin' no longer. I think they'll invite us right on in."

We were sitting in Parrish's unmarked squad car, a white Ford, a shotgun racked in a standup clip between us. I'd met Parrish at Port of the Islands, then tied my skiff at a public access dock a quarter mile or so from the guardhouse where we now sat. The first time we'd pulled up, the guard had told us that Mr. Bauerstock was in an important meeting, no way he could see us, but if we came back at three, that'd be fine.

I found the hour delay maddening, but Parrish was right when he said, "What you want me to do, bust in there without a warrant, get us arrested for trespassing?"

Now we were at the gate for a second time.

The guard shelter was a single roofed room, common to most gated communities. The only difference was, this narrow road could be sealed off by an electronic, steel-mesh gate, surveillance cameras positioned on galvanized posts high above.

The guard, in his gray uniform, went into the room, picked up the phone, then came back out carrying a handheld metal detector. "You can go in, but you got to leave your weapons here. It's an insurance thing, liability."

Parrish chuckled, said, "Liability? I'm a sworn officer of the law. You think I'm handing over my weapons, you can kiss my black ass." He was wearing rumpled brown slacks, a white shirt with the sleeves rolled up. He didn't look like a cop.

The guard didn't seem to know what to do for a moment. "Then I need to see some identification." When he'd handed Parrish's billfold back, he said, "What about the other gentleman? Is he a police officer, too?"

Parrish slapped the steering wheel. "Jee-sus Christ!" Looked at me. "Ford, you ain't carrying a weapon are you?"

Actually, I was—the little Colt I'd taken from Rossi. I had it in the briefcase with the totem. Both were too valuable to leave on a boat. But I said, "Why would I need a weapon when I'm hanging out with a cop?" hoping the guard wouldn't ask to search me.

He didn't.

We drove a quarter mile through sawgrass and sabal palms, the road snaking back and forth. Then there was high pasture land, Brahma cattle grazing, everything industrially fenced. Then much higher fencing, where I was surprised to see exotic animals, mostly African. There were ostriches, several water buffalo dozing in the mud, some kind of delicate horned animal, kudus, maybe. Off by themselves, a pack of hyenas sat beneath a banyan tree, staring at us with their telescopic eyes, testing our odor with their noses. No state is infested with more dangerous exotic feral species, plant and animal, than Florida. Bauerstock, apparently, was trying to contribute his share.

Parrish said, "This is what I heard about the man. He like to go big game hunting, but he does it on his own property. Never invites guests over, just does it all by himself. That's probably why they got the thing about guns back at the gate. Delivery people come in here and take potshots at his lions and shit."

Now I could see the house, though at first I thought it was some kind of manufacturing plant. It had the size and geometric harshness; a massive square building of stucco so gray that I wondered if the psilocybin mushrooms were still affecting my color perception.

Truth was, they probably were.

"No one ever gonna call the big man tasteful. That fucking thing looks like a shopping mall."

Except for the red tile roof, the porch, the black Humvee sitting outside the five-car garage, it did, too. A shopping mall is exactly what the Bauerstock home resembled. Some careful landscaping; the same sanitized open space, lots of galvanized light poles and a concrete blockhouse down by the river where there was a dock. The main house sat atop a massive mound that had been cleared and sodded; several acres of Bermuda grass bolted down with a sprinkler system.

We rounded a final curve and Parrish said, "Well, looky, looky there. All our eggs in one basket. Two white ones, one great big brown one. Man, am I looking forward to this!"

There was a pavilion of tile and wood on the shore of a small lake. The lake was as round as a moon crater, the water inside a stunning purple rimmed with green: a *cenote,* fed by an underground river. Sitting at a table beneath the pavilion were three men: Ivan Bauerstock, Ted Bauerstock and B. J. Buster. They were wearing swimsuits and robes, except for Buster, who was letting his muscles show.

By the time Parrish parked and we were getting out, Ted was already at the car, a big smile on his face, hand outstretched. I heard him say, "You just missed the girls. Nora and Della, they headed back to the Keys not half an hour ago!"

I stared at him until he took his hand away. I said to him, "We need to have a little chat, Teddy."

I noticed that Buster was shepherding my movements. He

always kept himself between me and his two employers. He did it quietly, trying not to draw attention, but there was no doubt what he was doing. I hadn't realized how huge the man was until I was next to him. Not tall, but double-wide from his hands to his head, trapezius muscles pyramiding up to his tiny ears.

Now he sat between Ted and myself at a glass-topped table beneath the pavilion, Ivan Bauerstock and Parrish across from us. Bauerstock in his white robe, silver hair darker because it was wet; his metallic eyes stoic, showing nothing as Parrish lighted the cigar he'd been offered. Parrish, at least, seemed to be enjoying himself.

In the center of the table was the little tape recorder, everyone staring at it but Ted, who seemed bored. He kept looking out toward the line of trees, which marked the river bank where the Hinckley was moored. He did a lot of heavy sighing, too, showing his impatience.

We all listened to the voice of Frank Rossi say:

Then I realized the girl was tied to a rope. It was tied around her neck, and Bauerstock was holding her arms down, using his weight. What he was doing was killing her. And he did. He murdered the teenage girl, then he started to play with her a little bit. Reminded me of a cat. But then his old man come along and stopped him.

Ivan reached, punched off the recorder with a long finger as Ted began to laugh.

I heard the first warning sounds of anger roaring deep within me as I said, "You think that's *funny?*"

"Dr. Ford, Detective Parrish, let's be serious. You really believe that old drunk's story? My father and I, we tried to *save* Dorothy. I *liked* her. You know what it is, fellas? It's like a few years back, that housewife accused my father's political friend, you know who I'm talking about; she accused this very great man of rape. People can say anything. We're easy targets, for God's sake." He began to laugh again. "We all *know* he didn't do it, and now I'm in the same situation."

Parrish blew a cloud of smoke Ted's way. Said, "Do we?"

Ivan Bauerstock wasn't laughing. He was still staring at the recorder. "How many copies of this tape are there, Dr. Ford?"

"Several. I took all the precautions. Let me guess, Mr. Bauerstock, next you'll ask who else's heard the tape, or maybe who was with me when Rossi confessed. It doesn't matter. Frank Rossi's talked once; he'll talk again. There's no statute of limitations on rape. You think he's going down just to save you? He doesn't strike me as the selfless type."

Ted began to say something, but Ivan cut him off, saying, "Shut up, Teddy." Then Bauerstock lifted his eyes; looked into mine and said, "You realize, of course, if this terrible lie gets out, my son's political career will be ruined. That would be a tragedy, Dr. Ford. We have great plans for Teddy. Tallahassee, then Washington."

"Dad, don't worry about it! Talk to your friends at the network. All I've got to do is get on camera and tell people I didn't do it. They'll believe me. You *know* they'll believe me. Set it up so we turn the tables. I've been falsely accused. Isn't it about time that innocent people like me fought back? Make it work to our advantage. Why are you getting so upset about this bullshit?"

Bauerstock was still staring at me. He touched his hand to the recorder and said, "How much, Dr. Ford?"

"Pardon me?"

"How much money? Or maybe you want a job. Or maybe there's a special project that you would like funded. How about your own fully computerized research vessel? We've *got* the technology. It's a straightforward business proposition: How much to destroy this tape and to tell us where the other tapes are?"

I said to Parrish, "I'm trying to remember. When someone tries to pay off a private citizen, is it called bribery or extortion?" Which made Parrish grin through the cigar smoke.

"We don't have a lot of time, Dr. Ford. We're due at Naples Yacht Club by eight. We're having our boat hauled, put on a flatbed and transported inland. There's a hurricane coming, you know. How much do you want?"

I noticed a lean, dark woman walking down the mound toward us. She reminded me of the striking Indio women of South America, with her long black hair, though older. She appeared to be feeling her way, hands balanced outward. I realized that she was blind, but very familiar with the route. As she drew nearer, I realized the woman had no eyes.

I slid away from the table and stood. "Bring back Dorothy

Copeland, Bauerstock. That's my price. Bring her back to life. I think you're insane, and I think your son's a freak. Let's get the hell out of here, Gary."

Looked to find my briefcase and saw that B. J. Buster was holding it to his chest, smiling at me. He had a surprisingly high, adolescent voice: "That ain't a very nice thing to say, Doctor whoever you are." I turned to Parrish, and saw the sudden tension in his face as I reached for the bag. When I did, Buster latched onto my wrist with fingers as blunt as hammers, twisted and catapulted me into a cement column. I hit spine-first; so hard that, for a moment, I teetered on the hazy, bright world of unconsciousness.

Trying to get up off the tile, I saw Buster coming at me, grinning. Saw Ted Bauerstock behind him, ripping at the briefcase, then hold up the totem. Heard him yell, "I've got it! I've finally got it!" as Buster grabbed me beneath the chin and lifted me off the ground.

With both of his hands clamped around my head and neck, I could hear vertebrae pop as he pulled my face toward his. "The man ask you a real simple question, you best answer. Now you go 'head an' tell Mr. Bauerstock where them other tapes are. Hear?"

When I tried to pry his hands away, Buster threw me into a post again. I got up quickly, but when I tried to tackle him, he caught me by the head and shoulders, and slung me into another post. I caromed off the cement, down the hill toward the lake.

The man wasn't just strong, he was discouragingly quick. Attacking him from the front wasn't going to work.

He came walking toward me, in no hurry at all, already reaching for me, but, this time, I ducked under his hands, buried my fingers in his throat while I tried to lock his left arm behind me. He knocked my hand away without much effort, then turned and came at me again. "You can make it easy, you can make it hard. But you gonna tell Mr. Bauerstock where them tapes are."

I glanced away for just a moment—what the hell had they done to Parrish?—and Buster was on me, heavy arms squeezing the wind out of me, his face so close to mine I could smell his sour breath. I head-butted him in an explosion of blood. Then head-butted him again. Felt his nose collapse beneath my heavy, frontal bone. He didn't let go, but it loosened his grip enough for me to slide under his arms and lock my hands around his waist.

I spread my legs slightly, lowering my center of gravity, and began to drive him backwards toward the water. If I got him into the water, he wouldn't have a prayer. He seemed to realize that. He used his big fists to pound at my head and neck, but I kept driving.

There was a stretch of man-made beach; very deep sand. I lost my footing there and went tumbling over him, glasses cockeyed on my head. Even so, at the edge of the beach, I could see a set of fins and a mask—Ivan or Ted were snorkelers, apparently. I grabbed the mask as Buster got to his feet, and fit my fist into the glass plate like a sort of glove. When he leaned toward me, I clubbed his face hard, then punched him twice more, once under the heart, then the side of the throat.

It dropped him to one knee, his face a mess.

I stepped forward to finish him when, behind me, I heard, "Hold it! That's enough. You stop right *now,* Ford. I'll take it from here."

I turned to see Parrish approaching, what looked to me a 9mm Glock in his right hand. He still had the cigar clamped in his teeth.

Ted and Ivan Bauerstock were a few steps back, walking.

I was breathing heavily and bleeding. "Damn it, Gary! What the hell took you so long?"

He had a little smile on his face. "What, miss a good fight? See Mr. B. J. Buster get a butt-whooping, I'd pay money for that. You handle yourself pretty good, Ford. Got some nice moves on you."

Behind him, Ivan Bauerstock said in an eerily calm voice, "Detective Parrish, I'm afraid we've got a problem. I'm afraid Teddy's been very bad again."

Parrish said, "Uh-oh. Been a long time since I heard that, Mr. Bauerstock."

Buster was dusting sand off his arms, stopping occasionally to spit blood. "Why you tellin' the man that, boss? After what I saw? You be speaking to a cop, my ass goin' to the joint, too."

"You're well paid, Mr. Buster."

"Um-huh, you gonna be paying me for a long time, so don't be runnin' off the mouth to no cop."

Parrish said, "B. J. was here?"

"I'm afraid so. And let's face it, Doctor Ford has become a liability, too."

I watched numbly and threw my hands up as Parrish pointed his weapon at my face . . . then swung it suddenly toward Buster and shot him twice in the chest. Buster went down in a fetal position, kicking, moaning.

Parrish shrugged at me, saying, "How you think I afford that cabin in Colorado, live with all those rich skiers?" as Buster began to cry, "Oh man oh man, I'm hurt! I'm hurt bad!"

Parrish stood over him for a moment, Buster staring up. "You got to help me, brother. Swear to Christ, you got to call an ambulance. Leave me with these two, they'll feed me to them fucking hyenas! That the truth! Put my eyes in the re-frigerator and haul me out there to the fields."

Parrish extended his arm and shot Buster once again, this time to the head. Turned to Ted Bauerstock and said, "You feedin' people to the jungle animals now, Mr. Ted? Whatever happened to your hee-bee-jeebie hobby, them water burials?"

Twenty-four

Parrish turned and pointed the pistol toward me, holding it at my face, standing close enough he couldn't miss. Wind coming off the river, across the lake, whipped the cigar smoke away. "I believe Mr. Bauerstock asked you a question. I figure the drunk hippie, he got one of the tapes. At least, you'd a let him hear it. But what'd you do with the others. Or maybe there *ain't* no others."

Ivan Bauerstock had returned to the shade of the pavilion. He'd found his glasses and was holding the totem in the light, inspecting it while Ted Bauerstock bent over Buster's body.

When Bauerstock noticed what Ted was doing, he called, "Teddy? *Teddy.* You get away from him right now!"

Ted stood. He seemed to be holding something in his hand, but hiding it, as if he didn't want anyone to know. He wore the self-satisfied sneer of a child who knew he could get away with whatever he chose. "I was trying to *resuscitate* the man."

"No you weren't, goddamn it! Don't lie to me. Get rid of that thing. Throw it in the water immediately and go wash your hands! Listen to me, mister—I will *not* have it in the house."

His hand still cupped, Ted began to walk toward the boat. "You're imagining things. You're *always* accusing me."

Bauerstock made a gesture of frustration and dismissal. "*I* can't do anything with that boy," then leaned toward the small brown woman and yelled, "I hope you're satisfied, you pathetic old bitch."

Parrish was listening to them, seeing it out of the corner of his eye, as I said, "Do you really want to be associated with this filth? They're sick, you know. Insane. You don't know the difference between right and wrong, anymore, Gary?"

"Right and wrong?" He seemed amused. "Man, them's just words, like . . . like Chevy or like see-gar. Rules is what rich people break just to show the rest of us there's a boundary. They decide what's right." He took the cigar from his mouth; looked at it with appreciation. "Know what those people decided? Power ain't sick and power ain't wrong as long as you got enough of it. Mr. Bauerstock here, he's got plenty. This only the third time in fifteen years he ask me to help him, but the man pay me in cash every year, right on time. To me, Doc? That's somethin' righteous." Parrish thumbed the hammer back, his expression changing. "I believe I asked you a question about them tapes. Where are they? You got exactly five seconds to give me an answer."

My mind was scanning frantically for a way out. "You're going to kill me anyway."

"That's right. I'm gonna kill you anyway."

"Then I'll talk. I'll tell you."

A soft, slow smile of awareness came on Parrish's face as he said, "No, you ain't. You just using your brains to buy time," and he leaned toward me slightly, straightening his arm, and I collapsed into the sand just as he fired—*thWAP*—and scissored his legs out from under him as the gun fired twice more.

From the distance, I heard the voice of Ted Bauerstock yell, "Don't shoot him the face!" as I rolled onto Parrish, fighting to control his hands. I smashed his jaw open with a glancing fist still gloved by the heavy mask, but he kept his arms moving, swinging them around, firing randomly—*thwap, thwap, twap*—so close to my head that I was deafened, ears ringing. I had to get some distance between us.

I shoveled a handful of sand toward his eyes, rolled to my feet, sprinting hard toward the lake and dived, pulling myself deep into the water as the trajectory of bullets traced scimitars nearby.

I'd noticed a dock and diving platform on the other side

of the lake. It was maybe sixty, seventy yards away—not an easy distance when wearing shorts and a shirt. I didn't swim fast. I swam with long, slow strokes, conserving my air. Glided until I'd nearly stopped before I stroked again. Didn't matter. I couldn't make it the whole way.

I surfaced to grab a breath and Parrish was already shooting at me—now standing on the dock that was my destination. Slugs were slapping the water so close that I could feel the explosion of compressed air as they slammed past my head . . . then I felt a stunning impact that nearly somersaulted me in the water. I'd been hit. . . .

I swam downward, downward, feeling the dreamy unreality of shock. I touched my hand to the area of my right ear, a throbbing slickness. No, I hadn't been shot in the head. My glasses were gone and so was the skin off my ear. I realized the face mask I'd carried had slid far up my arm. I pulled it on and cleared it, looking toward the surface: a lens of light above, a blurry gray sky beyond.

Parrish was waiting up there. Surface, and I would die.

I pivoted and looked below.

What I saw was surreal; a scene from a nightmare.

The interior of the *cenote* was shaped like the mouth of a volcano. The sides were sheer, dropping quickly to thirty or thirty-five feet, the green boulders there creating a second, narrower rim.

On the lip of that rim, spaced at random, were four . . . no, five decomposing bodies attached to the bottom by cement blocks and anchor chains. Enough flesh and clothing remained to maintain buoyancy, so that the bodies floated upright, arms above their heads as if on crosses.

There were also two cars, both of which had snagged on the ledge as if hanging from a cliff.

One of the cars was black and rusted, had moss growing on it.

The other was a white Honda that I recognized immediately.

It was Nora's car, air bubbles still escaping toward the surface. . . .

In training, we used to play a game. Dump the spent tanks and work your way to Destination X by finding and breathing trapped residual balloons of oxygen we called air pockets.

Anyplace people dive, you will find air pockets. With conventional tanks, a diver uses less than ten percent of the air he inhales. The rest is exhausted through the regulator as waste, then vanishes on the surface or is trapped in little caverns of rock, there for the taking by an air-starved swimmer.

A great place to find really big air pockets is a sunken boat . . . or plane . . . or car.

I swam down to the car, already aware that someone was inside. The car was tilted forward, its back axle caught on a limestone ridge, the front of the car hanging over the purple abyss. Windows were open.

I got a good grip on the right, rear window and pulled myself down. The glass of my mask had cracked badly, was leaking water. I had to clear it again before I could see the back of a woman's head, short dark hair undulating in the *cenote*'s updraft.

First things first, though. I turned and looked up into the car, then pulled myself through the window far enough so that my face was pressed against the roof molding and the rear windshield.

There was air there. A couple of cubic feet, anyway. Enough to last several minutes. I hung there breathing, resaturating my lungs, then looked as I touched my fingers to the woman's hair and pulled her head back. I had to fight the reflex to vomit and an overwhelming horror.

It was Della Copeland, not long dead. But her eyes were gone.

This had been a nice woman. She'd worked at a place where people loved her. More importantly, she was Dorothy's mother.

Where was Nora?

I looked. Nowhere in the car. I took another few bites of air, then looked outward through the clear water. Was hers one of the anchored bodies?

No. . . .

Judging from their streaming hair, there were three woman and two men, skeletal heads showing mandibles and teeth, cavernous eye sockets tunneling out from pale flesh. One of the men had black, Indian hair; cheap slacks, a white shirt, a red cigarette pack showing through.

Darton Copeland.

Ted Bauerstock had managed to murder the entire family.

The second man was the diver Bauerstock had mentioned. The man, he said, who'd gone down but never resurfaced.

No wonder. The diver was chained by the ankles, still in his dry suit. Considering the circumstances, it wasn't much of a surprise. Not in this graveyard. No way they could ever let him leave after what he'd seen. They'd lured him in with money, used him, then murdered him. The fact that a supposedly experienced cave diver hadn't used a dive partner had made no sense. Now I understood.

The diver's mask was pulled down around his neck, a black hole the size of a dime in his cheek; a black hole the size of a half-dollar on his neck. Entrance and exit wounds. He'd been shot from above, or maybe while he was kneeling. His buoyancy compensator vest had been slashed too . . . but the BC was built around the black modular walls of a closed-circuit, multigas system known as a rebreather.

The ridged hose of the regulator floated higher than the diver's head.

What were the chances there was still oxygen left in the tank.

Probably pretty good. One of the big advantages of a rebreather is that you have a much, much longer bottom time than with a standard, open-circuit scuba rig.

I'd trained with one of the earlier systems, a Drager—a chest-mounted rig. Unlike the newer systems, it was used for shallow-water diving only.

Could I figure out how the thing worked?

I didn't have much choice. I had to try.

I hyperventilated until the car's air pocket was nearly spent, then I swam across the black abyss. Got a grip on the dead man's elbow. The first thing I did was grab the regulator hose and check the valve on his mouth piece. If the valve was open, the system was flooded and ruined for me or anyone else. I'd have to surface and take my chances.

The valve was closed.

Next, I found the standard scuba single-hose pressure gauge. The needle was on zero. He was either out of air, or his tanks were shut off. Attached to the rebreather pack were two spherical canisters slightly smaller than volleyballs. The canister to his right should have been for oxygen, the canister to the left for a diluent gas, maybe helium.

I reached behind him, turned the valve on the oxygen tank and watched the needle jump to 700 psi. On a standard open-circuit system, that wasn't much air. On a rebreather, it would be good for a couple of hours.

I fitted the regulator into my mouth, opened the valve and snorted out through my nose; snorted again, hoping to hell not to taste caustic soda lime.

Nope, the air was good. Just to be certain, I pulled off the computer panel Velcroed to his wrist. Held the ON button down until the LCD screen activated. Saw that it was 4:09 p.m. October 5 and that I was at thirty-nine feet with 708 psi oxygen remaining and an onboard diluent gas supply that was fifty percent maximum.

This guy had been doing some serious deep diving.

I also saw the heads-up light was reading a cautionary yellow, so I hunted around until I found the bypass valve and dumped a little oxygen into the system. I watched a bead of green light replace the yellow, now indicating I was getting an approximate number of oxygen molecules in the mix of gas that the unit was computing.

I floated there for a moment, breathing easily. I didn't have to worry about them seeing bubbles on the surface because a rebreather exhausts almost none. My mask was still leaking badly, so I took the dead man's, cleared it with no problem.

What else did he have that I might be able to use?

The knife scabbard strapped to his leg was empty. They'd probably taken that before they killed him.

There was a small strobe light tied to one of the three pockets on his vest. I couldn't imagine why I'd need that. I opened the first two pockets and found nothing but a tiny bottle of Clear Mask. I opened the third, saw something gold and shiny. . . .

I reached, felt a hard surface that was smooth, warmer than the water, and I pulled out a medallion made of gold, the cross and concentric circles similar to those on the totem. At the top, through the hole, was a broken clasp, one link open.

The diver *had* found it. But why hadn't he told them? Why hadn't he turned it over and got the bonus? I remembered Ted telling me that the reward his father had offered was way too small. Maybe the diver decided to try and sneak the thing out, make a lot more money by selling it on his own. Or maybe . . . just maybe the diver realized that they would never let him leave their property alive, and so he kept it as a bargaining chip . . . but had never been given the chance to bargain.

❧

I floated there, admiring the medallion; its weight and color and density. It was a stunning piece of jewelry. There was something almost hypnotic about the way light clung to the designs. But while I was holding it between thumb and forefinger, inspecting it, my grip on the diver's elbow slipped . . . which caused my right hand to automatically scull for balance . . . and the medallion fell from my hands.

I watched it for a sickening moment as it fluttered toward the black hole below, glittering like a fishing lure.

Then I switched off the regulator's valve and was after it, swimming hard, hard, everything a blur but that golden flash. I caught the medallion just before it went over the rim into darkness.

Once I had the regulator in my mouth again, breathing easily, I put the medallion into the pocket of my fishing shorts. No more admiring it until I was safely on the surface.

Nora would get a kick out of seeing the thing. I would present it to her with flowers and a bottle of champagne, perhaps.

If she was still alive. . . .

It crossed my mind that Bauerstock or Parrish might be the extra-careful types. With all the bleeding my ear had done, they had to assume I was dead. But most bodies float. They might find another set of snorkel gear and take a look through the clear water, try to figure out why my body had yet to surface.

I decided I'd better hide.

I unstrapped the rebreather, mounted it on my own back, Velcroed the ruined BC across my chest, then released my breath so that I would sink. I descended down the wall, over the limestone rim into darkness. Felt the familiar sensation of stepping over an underwater wall—the sensation of falling, falling in slow motion.

I drifted downward until the computer panel told me I was at 60 feet. Hunted around until I found a comfortable rock outcrop where I could wedge myself and relax.

Negative buoyancy is an advantage of a closed-circuit rebreather. At this depth, zero decompression time was another benefit. Closed circuit meaning that nearly a hundred percent of the system's gas supply is used. Each time I exhaled, my air was exhausted through a soda lime filter that scrubbed out carbon dioxide, then recirculated wasted oxygen back into the system. Gases were added depending on my depth and when the volume dropped below a certain minimum value. As long as the batteries that ran the onboard computer were good, I could stay down for a couple of hours.

Hopefully, I wouldn't have to stay that long.

Water transmits sound more efficiently than air.

Ted and Ivan had an appointment in Naples, a pretty Gulf Coast city that was more than an hour away by water.

They would *have* to start their boat, and I would hear them.

An hour and eighteen minutes later, according to the computer board, they did.

Twenty-five

I surfaced cautiously, still wearing the rebreather. Came up beneath the dock, peering out. My teeth were chattering, my fingers puckered. Wind was in the trees, showing silver in the tops of palms, blowing sand across the lake.

There was someone in the pavilion, a lone figure.

The old brown Indio woman sitting there in her dark dress.

She cupped her hands around her mouth and called something, her words muffled by the wind. She tried again, louder. I realized she was calling out in Spanish: *They are gone!*

Who was she speaking to? No way she could know I was there.

Apparently, she did, though, because she stood and began to find her way toward me, hands outstretched, feeling the air.

Heard her say: *I have been waiting for you.*

If a woman without eyes knew where I was, there was no fooling anyone else they'd left behind, so I dropped the scuba pack and scrambled up the bank. When a man climbs fully dressed out of a pool or lake, he frets about mundane things: sopping billfold, credit cards, treasured leather belt. I had something more pressing on my mind.

I touched my pockets.

The pendant was still there.

As she drew closer, I saw that she had something in her hand—my glasses. I'd lost them on the beach, but how had she found them? As I put them on, she said again, "I have been waiting for you."

I said, "Everyone's gone?"

"Yes. Everyone."

"Your name's Bella."

"Yes. And yours is Ford."

"How do you know that?"

"I know more than you realize, big man. I know they tried to kill you but couldn't. I know that you swam into the eye of the earth and stayed as long as a fish. If your power is so great, perhaps you can destroy them. You found the amulet? The golden god?"

"I didn't find anything. I don't know what you're talking about."

"Of course you did. You need not lie. I want to help you. I can feel the power of the amulet in you, but believe what I say: use it, but do not cling to it. Free yourself of the golden god the moment you are finished. It is evil and it will consume you."

I looked down into her face. Even with the wrinkles and sun damage, I could see that she had once been very beautiful. She kept her eyes closed tightly—a touching vanity. I asked, "The other woman, the younger one named Nora, did they kill her?"

"No, I do not think so. He gave her the drunken potion to make her useful. He likes to use his women before he eats their souls."

In place of Borracho to describe the drug, she used a chilling Spanish phrase, *cadavere vivo.*

"Then she must be on the boat."

"Yes. The girl and the large black man, the policeman. Both will be killed before they reach the city if you do not hurry. The policeman, I do not care about. But the woman, it would be a good thing, very powerful, if you could save her. There is a spirit in her. I felt her strong presence when she arrived." The woman began to walk toward the pavilion, signaling me to follow. "Come. I have something that may help you."

She handed me a leather snap-open case. Inside was a

20cc glass syringe, very old, and a heavy-gauge, beveled hypodermic needle. The syringe was full of a dark liquid.

"Borracho?" I asked.

"Yes."

"I'd rather have a gun."

The old woman smiled slightly, the contracting of facial muscles allowing me a brief glimpse into the white orbits which once held her eyes. "If there was a gun they did not lock, do you think they would be alive now? You will need a boat to go after them."

I said, "I've got a boat."

"I know. But they moved it so no one would become suspicious. The black man moved it there."

She gestured toward the river.

I said, "You're certain there's not a gun around? The old man's a hunter. If he keeps the guns locked, I could break in. Just show me where he keeps them."

She was shaking her head. Her expression said, *Impossible.* "He locks them in a steel safe. The safe is one whole wall of his study. It has a knob that clicks. Only he knows the way in."

What was I going to do? Finding them wouldn't be enough. I'd have to stop them. There was one other possibility. I said, "What about chemicals? Do you have a gardener's shed? A maintenance shed? The sort of place they would store gasoline, poisons, that sort of thing."

"If you want to poison them, why not use the drunken potion?"

"That's not exactly what I have in mind. Can you show me?"

I followed her across the lawn to a concrete building the size of a garage. I had to use a brick to smash the lock off. I flipped the light switch and stepped into stale air that smelled of fertilizer and paint. I began to lift cans and jars from the shelves, looking at labels. It is no longer true that it is easy to make a bomb from common household products. However, it is *very* easy to make a lethal variety of explosives from chemicals and propellants purchased legally from a garden supply store. On the shelves, I found a particular mix of nitrate fertilizer, a bottle of ammonia, plus a very common kind of acid used for cleaning metals. I found a large thermometer, the mercury still in it. I found a bottle of ethyl alcohol, a box of coarse salt and a squirt bottle full of soap. There was a five-gallon can of gasoline, a couple of kerosene railroad lamps and several Mason jars that probably once held paint thinner.

It was no longer a question of, could I mix together an effective explosive? The question was, what kind of explosive did I choose to make? And which would take the least amount of time? Explosives come in three basic forms: high-order explosives which detonate, low-order explosives which burn, and primers, which may do both. Nearly all combust so rapidly that large volumes of air are displaced faster than the speed of sound, and so a sonic boom occurs.

I wanted the boom. Hopefully enough to shatter the windows on a fast-moving yacht. Maybe even a little fire. And it had to be an impact explosive because I didn't want to have to mess with lighting a wick in the wind, on a moving boat.

To the woman, I said, "Go to the house and bring me a bottle of iodine and a box of baking soda. Hurry! And a bucket of ice. Don't forget the ice." I'd already placed three Mason jars by the bag of fertilizer on a bench next to the acid.

"Have you cut yourself? I'll bring a first-aid kit."

I touched my ear. I was still bleeding a little, but that's not why I needed the iodine. I said, "A first-aid kit might come in handy, too."

I flew through a blur of mangrove switchbacks; twisting hedges of green that created ponds and creeks, one linked to another through a hundred miles of wilderness. The words of the old woman kept echoing in my head: *He likes to use his women before he eats their souls.*

In his note, Dieter Rasmussen had warned of human anomalies. Bad genes, flawed brains. Remorseless liars, strengthened by their own pathology, who were destined for success.

Teddy Bauerstock would do very well in Tallahassee. Tomlinson had said it and believed it—all his instincts, his intuition demonstrably wrong. So had Della, one of the women Bauerstock had killed. So had everyone else the man had ever met, probably.

But he had not fooled me.

I found strange comfort in that. Inexplicably, that small triumph brought the face of Dorothy Copeland once again to memory. A lovely face with a mild, wistful smile, silken hair hanging down.

Then she was gone, a momentary nexus left in my wake.

The Hinckley had about a half-hour headstart on me. I had to catch them before they got near civilization. I had to get their yacht stopped in a place where no one could see what I was going to do. My boat was more than twice as fast, true, but, once I got into the Gulf, the growing waves would neutralize that advantage.

So I would stay in the backcountry just as long as I could. I'd gain a lot of time on them because Ted or Ivan—whoever was running the boat—had almost certainly taken the much longer route, out the channel past Panther Key, into open water. No one is going to run a half-million dollar vessel through the unmarked backcountry of the Ten Thousand Islands, even if it doesn't draw much water. The region is too remote; has too many reefs of oyster and rock. Make the wrong turn, run aground hard enough, and you could be stranded for days before another vessel happened by. Even with a cell phone or a VHF radio, help is hours away.

No, Bauerstock wouldn't risk that. Particularly with a hurricane bearing down. That's what I told myself, anyway.

As I drove, I turned the VHF radio volume full on and switched to Weather Channel 3. Heard that Hurricane Charles had already slipped through the Yucatan Channel, and was being levered toward the Florida coast by an Arctic high-pressure ridge. The ridge was steering the storm like rails beneath a freight train. Predicted landfall was somewhere between Naples and Marco.

The computerized voice told me, ". . . two hundred and ten miles off Marco Island, the air temperature is seventy-six degrees, water temperature eighty-two degrees, wave heights unavailable. National Hurricane Center at Miami places the eye of Hurricane Charles . . . slightly north of the Tropic of Cancer, moving northeasterly at fifteen knots . . . expected to make landfall at approximately noon tomorrow. Voluntary evacuation is urged for residents of all barrier islands, Siesta Key to Marco Island, Goodland and neighboring areas. A mandatory evacuation notice may be issued for Marco Island, Everglades City and Chokoloskee. Winds have been measured at one-hundred-thirty knots and gusting stronger, barometric pressure at 27.50 and falling. Charles may be upgraded to a Category Five hurricane in the next advisory. . . ."

I punched off the radio, feeling an irrational anger toward whoever the fool was who decided to replace a human weatherman with a digitized voice. The phonation was so badly coded that it sounded like a drunken polka king who'd been filching tranquilizers.

No, it had been a group decision, more likely. Individuals are rarely so misguided. Because the voice was difficult to understand, I hadn't been able to decipher the exact location of Charles, nor how many miles the storm still had to cover before it reached the coast. Computer profiteers like Ivan Bauerstock would've applauded the transition to something that was programmable. Maybe that's why it made me so mad. . . .

I swung in close to Dismal Key: a ridge of black trees rimmed with swamp. Said a silent greeting to the old hermit who once lived in a shack on the high Indian mounds there, Al Seeley.

Al lived without phone, power or running water, just him and his little dog. He painted, he read books. He had a sharp intellect and an appreciation for the ironic. He loved to tell the story of a hermit colleague who came to Dismal Key determined to build a bomb shelter. He spent hours in the heat and mosquitoes digging through shell until he said, screw it, let global warfare do its worst. He was tired and in need of a beer.

Heading out to sea only hours in advance of a Category Five hurricane, Al would have found that ironic, too. There was no place safer than the high mounds of his island.

I busted out of the mangrove gloom at Turtle Key and went pounding through whitecaps, steering toward a sunset horizon that was a firestorm of smoldering clouds and tangerine sky. Big, big seas and lots of wind. I banged my way toward Coon Key Light: an offshore tower built of metal and wood that marked the back entrance to Marco and then Naples.

In these seas, Ted or Ivan would have to take the back way to Naples. No way they'd run outside the islands and risk the surf at Big Marco Pass. They would see the light tower on the radar screen, and they would steer for it. Or maybe the marker was already programmed into their Loran and autopilot system. Either way, the thing was nearly twenty-five feet high and impossible to miss. If I kept my skiff close enough to the tower, that's all their radar would pick up.

My boat would be invisible until I decided it was time for them to see. . . .

I began to think I'd missed them. Or that they'd taken the more dangerous, outside route. I sat in my skiff, the engine idling, rolling in the heavy seas. I could feel each wave gather mass beneath the boat. Could feel it lift and thrust me skyward before I slid back into a green trough. From the top of each wave, I could see around the horizon. What I saw was not reassuring. I was the only boat for miles. No Hinckley. No *Namesake*.

Where the hell were they? Could I have gotten that far ahead of them? Or maybe they'd already passed Coon Key Light and were on the Intracoastal to Naples.

Or maybe, just maybe, they'd stopped back there in the Ten Thousand Islands to dump two bodies. . . .

I had no choice. My best chance of intercepting them was to sit right where I was.

I watched a sunset that had no sun. The world became lemon-bright, as if seen through yellow glasses. A horizon of copper clouds sailed northward and then curled west. The clouds moved in horizontal bands, one above the other, striations of blue sky showing through. I was seeing the front rim of a hurricane, spinning in slow motion over the earth's curvature. Fog drifted down out of that copper rim, moving toward me as a wave, and then I realized it wasn't fog, it was a misting rain. The rain swept across the water in panels of silver, soaking me, dripping off the poling platform of my skiff.

The lemon world became purple . . . then charcoal . . . then gray, as I waited.

Behind me, the solar switch was activated and Coon Key Light began to strobe every four seconds. Wind blew the light across the water in streamers of green, along with the stink of bird guano.

I'd missed them. Unless they'd run aground, or they'd had engine failure, there was no way it should have taken them so long to get to Marco.

So what was Plan B?

Plan B, I decided, was to get to Naples Yacht Club as fast as possible, and maybe catch them there. Get the law involved somehow, make them search the boat.

I'd been holding my skiff bow into the sea. But now I nudged it into gear and began to turn. I waited until I was atop a wave to complete the turn—which is when I noticed the shell of a dark hull wallowing on the horizon, not more than a mile away.

It was the Hinckley.

Twenty-six

Detective Gary Parrish was not a blue-water sailor. Judging from what I saw, he wasn't much of a sailor at all. As I made my first pass, I could see him on his knees, hanging his head over the transom and vomiting. He'd made quit a mess on the big golden letters: *Namesake*.

I approached the Hinckley from head-on. If someone is chasing you, they approach from behind, right? I ran at an angle as if I was going to pass them port to port, just as cars traveling opposite directions pass. In this failing light and at a distance, they wouldn't recognize me. There was no color or detail. They would probably just think me some crazed flats fisherman trying to get his skiff back to Everglades City before the big storm hit.

Something else to my advantage: in heavy weather, men standing huddled in a cabin acquire tunnel vision. They don't look out the side windows, they seldom look behind. They stare hypnotically through the slapping windshield wipers and see little else but the glow of their own red and green running lights.

Namesake already had her lights on, obeying the laws, not wanting to attract any attention. The white anchor light was mounted on the antenna stem atop the cabin, which is why I could see Parrish and the mess he was making so clearly.

I was running without lights. Which is why it was unlikely they would notice me.

But Parrish hanging over the stern was an unexpected component. If I swept in close and lobbed one of my Mason jars at *Namesake,* he would see me. He'd hear and feel the small explosion and see me very clearly for several seconds, at least, as I blasted past. Plenty of time for him to draw his weapon and empty a clip at me.

The chances of a nauseous man hitting a moving target with a 9mm in heaving seas were not good. Still, all it would take was one lucky round.

If possible, I wanted to eliminate Parrish before I attacked. I needed to do it quietly, without attracting the attention of Ivan Bauerstock, whose silhouette I could see in the computer glow of electronics. He was sitting in the yacht's helm seat, head pushed forward as if straining to see through the rain.

Where were Ted and Nora?

No sign of them.

If they were aboard, they had to be together in the cabin below deck. It was an unsettling possibility—no, *probability*— that sickened me. It also underlined the need to hurry.

I passed the Hinckley a couple hundred yards to seaward, then swung in behind them. Jumped the wake and turned into their jetstream contrail, throttling, closing the distance between us.

Had Parrish noticed?

No. He was still retching. He appeared oblivious to everything around him. I could see the top of his head and shoulders clearly, heaving up and down. He was such an easy, unguarded target that I was tempted to ram *Namesake* from behind. Any small impact would have flipped him off the back of the boat. That's exactly what I would do if my first attempt to snag him didn't work.

As I bore down on them, I took the heavy Loomis baitcasting rod from the standup holder. It was still rigged with the Bomber lure that Tomlinson had been using. I tested the reel's star drag; tightened it. Tested it a second time and tightened it even more.

Shifted the rod to my right hand, which rested atop the throttle. I was closing distance at twice their speed, planing in fast. I expected Parrish to lift his head at any moment and see me, but he didn't. I was forty yards behind them, then twenty, then ten. When the bow of my skiff seemed almost on top the teak dive platform off *Namesake*'s stern, I pulled the throttle back, and matched her speed, wallowing in her exhaust stream. I pressed my hips to the wheel, holding course, as I cast the plug toward Parrish. The first cast was long and banged on the deck behind him. I yanked the plug back, reeling furiously.

Parrish looked up, alerted by the sound, or maybe the breeze that the lure created as it flew past his head.

Then he saw me. In the stormy dusk, with the aid of the anchor light, I could see the man's expression change. It went through abrupt transitions: puzzlement . . . awareness . . . shock . . . horror. He looked at me, then recognized me. Gary Parrish did not want to believe what he was seeing.

I had the lure back and I cast again, thumbing the line so that it wouldn't backlash.

I saw his grimace of surprise when the lure hit him just below and to the side of his neck. I saw his face contort with pain as I struck hard, arching my back, burying the gang hooks into his cheek and throat. Parrish's right hand flew up to pull the plug away, but he only managed to bury the hooks in his palm, disabling himself.

With my left hand, I turned the wheel sharply as the rod bowed, the spool and level-wind feeding line now, monofilament burning the skin of my thumb as I jumped the big boat's wake once again, surfing away at an angle, still feeling torque and the big man's weight in the butt of the rod. I glanced astern and I saw, for a grotesque microsecond, Parrish's face being dragged through rollers behind me, his eyes wide, his mouth thrown open in a soundless scream as he fought to free himself.

I turned my eyes away, still holding the rod. I held fast, not looking back until the line broke; nearly lost my balance when it did. Then I reeled in the excess line and stowed the rod in its holder.

My attention turned once again to *Namesake* as my skiff lunged ahead into the waves.

Ivan Bauerstock hadn't noticed that Parrish was missing. More likely, he'd noticed but just didn't care. He'd probably figured the man had fallen overboard. They would have to kill him one day anyway, and what could be easier to explain than an actual accident at sea?

I could see Bauerstock still sitting at the helm seat as I swept in for a second pass. He wasn't looking in my direction. Didn't yet know I was in pursuit, judging by the way he behaved.

I'd stopped just long enough to take all three Mason jars from the cooler and wedge them between my ankles. I'd dealt with enough explosives to be reasonably confident at least one of the jars would detonate if it impacted hard enough against the hull of *Namesake*. I'd also dealt with explosives enough to know not to ever, ever trust them. Particularly concoctions made with anything less than laboratory-grade chemicals.

This time, I approached from the mainland, coming fast out of the darkness as if to ram them on the starboard side. At the last instant, I throttled back, turning hard toward *Namesake*'s stern. I waited a moment to get my balance, then I threw the Mason jars one after another, holding them like footballs, giving them all the velocity I could.

There was so much adrenaline in me that the first jar spiraled over the bow; missed everything. The second hit the cabin trunk just aft the side windshield, but didn't detonate. The third jar hit the cabin right outside where Bauerstock was sitting and it *did* detonate, but with such an impotent little *whoof* that I was surprised Bauerstock heard it.

He did, though. I saw him jump. He also saw the blue alcohol and ammonia flames riding soap bubbles harmlessly along the side deck; harmless because the fire burned at a temperature much too low to ignite wet fiberglass.

Bauerstock didn't know that, though, and I watched as he slowed the big Hinckley to a crawl and came out onto the deck carrying two fire extinguishers.

I didn't hesitate. I already had my anchor ready, cleated to a few yards of line—the most primitive of boarding hooks. Now I swung in behind the yacht; put my bow against his stern as if attempting to push him out of the way. Touched a toggle switch, turning on my navigational lights, then tossed my anchor over his transom. Removed the ignition cord from my belt and left my engine idling as I crabbed forward onto my skiff's casting deck, fighting for balance. I timed a lifting wave and swung over onto *Namesake,* then stood to see a very surprised Ivan Bauerstock staring at me. I heard his frightened voice say, "My God, it's . . . it's *you.* I thought Parrish killed you!"

I stood there using the gunwale for balance before I answered. I said, "That'll be the day." Then I began to move toward him. There was so much wind and wash of heavy seas that I had to yell to be heard. "Where are they? Where's Nora?"

Bauerstock was backing away. "Listen to me, Ford. You can't blame me for my son's behavior. I have nothing to do with his private life."

"Where *are* they? Where's Nora!"

"Teddy's going to be a very important man. If you can overlook the last few weeks, we can help you tremendously down the road. Whatever you want!"

Bauerstock had backed into the white helm seat. He was still holding one of the spent fire extinguishers. When I reached for him, he swung the metal canister hard at my head. I caught his arm, locked my fingers under his chin until the fire extinguisher clanked upon the deck. Then I pulled his face close to mine. In a voice hoarse with anger, I whispered, "I don't blame you, Ivan. I just don't *like* you."

He tried to fight as I swung around behind him, and began to push him toward the water. He was yelling, "I can pay you, I can pay you! Don't do this to me, *please*."

I got my right hand on his belt, my left hand in his hair, then I ran him toward the transom. He gave a terrible soprano yelp as I lifted him airborne and vaulted him overboard.

Ivan Bauerstock was still screaming at me as we idled away, his words indistinguishable in the wind.

The door through the aft bulkhead was locked from the inside.

Someone was down there, hiding in the cabin.

I lifted myself between the companionway entrance and used both feet to kick the door open. It took awhile. The boat was solidly built. Finally, the door shattered, brass hardware flying.

There would be no surprising Ted now. He'd be waiting.

I squatted and looked down the steps into a beautifully appointed cabin. I got a whiff of something as I did: a metallic, human odor that I couldn't identify. The room was dimly lighted; had a candle softness. Music was playing through the built-in sound system. Willie Nelson. The place might have been set for a romantic dinner but for the storm outside.

I looked beyond the dinette table and stainless steel galley to the cushioned V-berth, and felt a sickening panic at what I saw there. A human figure lay motionless beneath a sheet. A pillowcase covered the head, as if draped for execution.

There was a black swash of blood on the sheet. More blood on the pillowcase; heavy in the area where the face would have been.

Where the hell was Ted?

Because there was no other option, I swung down into the cabin. The moment my feet hit the deck, the door to the toilet came flying open. I didn't react in time and felt a tremendous impact as someone clubbed me behind the neck. He clubbed me again, grunting with effort, and I went down on one knee. I got my elbow up and blocked the next blow, saw a pair of bare feet braced on the deck. I reached, yanked and rolled hard. Felt his body weight collapse on top of me. I wrestled myself into control, pulling my fist back to flatten the nose of Ted Bauerstock . . . but instead I was looking into the tear-streaked face of Nora Chung.

I froze, my fist poised a few inches from her chin, as she whispered, "Doc? *Doc!* Oh, thank God! Thank God it's you!"

I got to my feet and pulled her up. She was wearing only a white bra and panties, blood on both. She'd used a fish billy to club me, and now I retrieved that, too. She was shaking, seemed on the verge of hysteria. I sat her in the settee booth and kissed her forehead, then cheek, trying to calm her.

"Where's Ted?"

She made a gesture that asked for a little time to get herself under control. It appeared as if she might faint. "This can't be real. Doc, are you sure this is real? Is this really happening? I can't tell the difference anymore."

She was probably still suffering the effects of *scopolamine.* "Did he give you something? Did he make you drink something or give you a shot?"

Nora's expression became savage and she looked at the motionless figure beneath the sheet. "Him? You mean that son-of-a-bitching animal? He gave me a shot, yeah. He gave Della one, too, before he strangled her. Know what he did? He ate one of her eyes. I saw him. He made me watch. Like it was a grape. Then he raped me. And he kept on raping me. I had no choice, Doc. You have to tell the police. Lot of times they don't believe women, but I had to do it. I had to make sure he could never hurt me again."

I patted her back for a moment, then went to the V-berth and pulled the pillowcase away. Ted Bauerstock lay there blinking up at me, recognizing me, his pupils gigantic. He still hadn't moved and I had to lean to hear his weak voice as he gasped, "I'm paralyzed. The bitch stuck a needle in my neck. You've got to get me to a hospital."

I looked at Nora. She sat there tapping her fingers together, very nervous. Her speech became accelerated. "He thought I was unconscious. I grabbed the needle when he turned his back. After that . . . after that . . ." She began to cry. ". . . I'm not sure what happened after that."

I pulled the sheet down, looking at what she'd done to him, then covered him as Bauerstock whispered, "She's going to jail for this. I'll make sure of it. She'll never have a free day."

I said, "Jail? Teddy, the lady ought to get a reward. Or a bounty. After what you've done?"

"I don't know what you're talking about. I haven't done anything wrong. I'm running for the senate—"

I put my hand on his mouth, silencing him. I didn't want to hear it. After a moment, I said, "You need to answer one question. If you expect me to help you, it'd better be the truth. Why did you kill Dorothy?"

"I'm not answering anything. I need a doctor."

"No answers, no doctor. Why'd you murder that child?"

The smile that grew out of his mouth was infuriating. "Honestly?"

"If you're capable."

"Because it felt good and . . . I *like* it. The power."

"That's what I'll tell the cops."

The smile widened. "No . . . won't happen. They won't believe you. They never have. They never will."

I said, "For them to believe you, Ted, they've got to hear you," and I dropped the pillowcase over his face.

When she'd calmed down, I said to Nora. "You're safe now. You didn't do anything wrong. Get your clothes on. Did Ted bring the wooden totem aboard?"

She nodded. Her face was pale; wet with tears. She looked very fragile in the cabin light.

"Find it and bring it with you."

I touched my pockets as I went toward the steps. The gold medallion was in one. The syringe the old woman had given me was in the other. If I sold the medallion and the totem, the Egyptian cat and the rest of the artifacts, it would make a sizable scholarship fund. Or maybe donate everything to the museum. One way or another, keep the name Dorothy Copeland alive.

Topside, I made sure my skiff was still in tow, then seated myself at *Namesake*'s helm. I touched the LCD window of the Cetrek autopilot. I saw that it was keeping us on a flawless heading of 312 degrees, directly at Coon Key Light, but at the very slow idle speed of only three knots.

The yacht was equipped with a steering wheel, but also some kind of computer-type joy stick that I didn't know how to operate. I disengaged the autopilot, turned the wheel and the yacht came around. I pointed her bow out to sea. Felt

Nora come up beside me and lean her warm weight against my shoulder, as I listened to the robotic voice from the VHF radio say, ". . . Hurricane Charles continues to move northeasterly at a speed of eighteen knots, with sustained winds measured at a hundred thirty knots. Charles is expected to make landfall at ten a.m. tomorrow. Mandatory evacuation has been declared for Marco Island and the neighboring cities of . . ."

I switched off the radio and said, "You remember how to run my boat?"

She nodded.

"I'm going to help you get aboard, then cut you loose. I want you to follow me until I get this boat up to speed, but not too close. Pay attention because I'm going to jump. I'll blink this boat's running lights twice to warn you, then go over the port side. It'll be on your left. All you have to do is put my skiff in neutral. Don't worry about finding me. I'll swim to you. Can you do that?"

Nora's voice had regained some strength, and I felt like hugging her when she said, "Of course I can do it. I'm not an invalid, for God's sake. Don't treat me like one."

I was experimenting with the autopilot, learning how it worked. I also had both radar screens on, watching the scanning arm show blobs of islands, nothing else. I figured out that the Doppler was also linked to the computer screen built into the console, and I accessed a perfect satellite picture of the storm: a red vortex less than three hundred miles away.

That gave me an idea. I touched the cursor to the center of the hurricane, and punched the exact heading into the autopilot, 225 degrees. I clicked on *Auto-track* and then *Engage*. Waited for a moment, then felt the autopilot take control of the steering, running directly southwest toward the target I had designated.

"What are you doing?"

I said, "Teddy likes eyes? His computer's got him headed for a big one."

A few minutes later, with Nora trailing me in the skiff, I throttled the Hinckley up to a jarring twenty knots. I made sure the servo-systems were vectoring properly. Then I jumped overboard into the black water.

A little after 9:30 that night, Nora and I dragged ourselves through the wind, up the highest Indian mound of Dismal Key. We had flashlights, tent, mosquito netting, sandwiches and beer, each of us muling bags. We were soaked, exhausted.

I'd tied my skiff in the mangroves with a spider webbing of lines to hold her. Even if the storm surge was more than fifteen feet or higher, we'd be safe and so would my boat.

The walls of Al's shack were still standing, the screen broken out of the windows. But I didn't want to be inside a building, not in a wind that was expected to exceed a hundred miles an hour. It took me a while to find what I was looking for, but I finally did: a room-sized hole dug into the shell mound, the ironic hermit's bomb shelter. It wasn't far from the key lime and avocado trees that grew there. The hole would provide windbreak enough that the tent would survive. Even if the tent didn't, we would.

That night, cuddled together to stay warm, Nora said into my ear, "I don't know which part of it's a dream, which of it's real. It's the drug. I can still feel it, but it's wearing off. I can't believe what I did to him."

I said, "I think you're imagining things. What do you think you did?"

After she told me, I pulled her closer and said, "You're not the one. I did it. Your brain mistranslated. It happens all the time in dreams. When I ate those mushrooms, the same thing happened to me."

"Are you positive?"

"I'll swear to it. Besides, he deserved it."

She moved her face onto my chest. "I would love to believe that."

"Then do."

Hurricane Charles hit the next morning. Stick your head out the window of a car doing sixty, then imagine what it would be like to try the same thing at a hundred-twenty. Once and just once, I poked my head up above ground level. It was like being sprayed with an industrial sand blaster. Lips and cheeks flutter; the eyes blur. I got a momentary glance at boiling storm clouds. High overhead, I saw a full-grown Australian pine go tumbling past. The tree had to be a couple hundred feet or more in the air. Mostly what we did was hold tight to one another, soaked and cold from driving rain, our eyes closed in the freight train rush of wind.

The sound is what surprised me most. The sound of wind was deafening, numbing.

Then, at a little after eleven, it stopped; everything stopped. The wind, the noise all gone. I crawled out of our threadbare tent and looked through broken trees. In the eye of a hurricane, there exists an illustrative calm, as if to underscore the energy of the storm just passed, the power of the storm to come.

I looked down into a bay that had been drained of water. Along with beer bottles and the lapstrake of ruined boats was a litter of pottery shards, whole bowls and shell tools: the detritus of a people who'd survived storms on this island for thousands of years.

Then I looked up into the sky, pausing to study the unexpected cirrus formations. The clouds formed concentric circles within concentric circles. At the center of the smallest circle was a starburst cross of sunlight that illuminated ice crystals in the high ionosphere.

I took the gold medallion from my pocket, handed it to Nora. She looked from the sky to the medallion, then back to the sky. She was nodding. "I think so. Yes. I can see it. The designs, they're like a storm etching. But how could Dorothy have known? Someone with that kind of gift, I wish I could have met her."

To the west, drifting above Ten Thousand Islands, was the ghost of a crescent moon.

I said, "Me, too."

Epilogue

On Friday, a little more than a week after Hurricane Charles joined the ranks of Donna, Andrew, Floyd and other killer storms that have hit the Florida coast, I sat in the reading chair by the north window of my stilt house, next to my telescope and shortwave radio.

I was listening to the pretty lady say, "Know what we should do, Ford? Load the boat with enough supplies for two weeks, and sail down the coast to the Keys. Do it up right. Jars of caviar. Cases of beer and wine packed in ice. We'll make a survey of deserted islands. Find some private little coves to anchor. Bake ourselves in the sun during the day. Look at the stars at night until we feel dozey. Do lots of swimming and running. I've got a new red thong bikini that you won't believe. In fact"—her smile was well known and good to see— "in fact, I won't need to wear much of anything most the time."

I'd begun to reply when I felt the familiar vibration of big feet slapping on the walkway outside. I'd been sorting my mail as I listened to the lady, had finally gotten around to the big, unopened stack. At a marina, the week following a brush from a major hurricane is a busy week, indeed. I was placing bills in one pile, correspondence in another. Now I put the stack aside and stood. I looked through the window to see Tomlinson approaching. He was wearing a new blue Hawaiian shirt—it had surfboards all over it—and he was carrying what looked to be a rolled-up newspaper.

Coincidentally, I'd just opened a letter addressed to me in Tomlinson's unmistakable hand. The postmark was dated September twenty-first, which made no sense. He'd left for Key Largo on the day of the fall equinox, September twenty-third. Why would he put something on paper when all he had to do was boat over and tell me what he wanted to say?

I glanced at the first paragraph:

Dear Doc. I write to you from the future because, skeptic that you are, it will be years before you are sufficiently enlightened to understand why, very soon, I hope to introduce you to the mushroom goddess. She is the only path back to your own lost love. . . .

More New Age ramblings. That was all I needed to see. I folded the letter, dropped it on the table for later, then went out the door to intercept Tomlinson. I paused on the way to stoop and give the lady a kiss on top the head, felt her give me a pat on the backside in reply.

"Doc, you read the paper today?" Tomlinson was already talking as he came up the steps to the top platform.

I waved him into the lab as I said, "I never read the papers. You know that."

As he brushed past me, taking a seat at the stainless steel dissecting table, I could smell the strong odor of patchouli and the must of cannabis. "The cops finally sent divers down. They found the bodies, just like you said. You were the anonymous source they mention, right?"

"Of course."

I was also the anonymous source who'd told authorities to search Ronrico Key for the remains of Frank Rossi. If there were remains to be found after the monkeys got through with him. I did it for his relatives, not for him.

Tomlinson shook the newspaper. "Then you ought to read this. They got a whole piece about it in here. And still no sign of Ted or Ivan. The boat, nothing. Vanished. Both their estates flattened, all those animals roaming the 'Glades. At least it's stopped them from developing that island, the one with the Indian mounds. For now, anyway." He looked at me with his wise and haunted blue eyes. "You hear about the two park rangers attacked by hyenas? Man, Florida is some wild state. Just keeps getting crazier and crazier."

I held my hand up, palm out. "I don't have time right now. There's a lady in there waiting on me. All I asked you to do was talk to Dieter, find out how Nora's doing."

Dieter Rasmussen had arranged for Nora to spend two weeks of treatment at a state-of-the-art rape and trauma retreat that was among the finest in the south.

"He said she's doing great. Getting stronger every day. They don't let them call out the first week, so she should be able to call you on Monday or maybe Tuesday. Hey, Doc—" Tomlinson turned his eyes to the floor, then cupped his forehead in his hand. "I need to keep saying this till you know I mean it. I want to apologize again."

"You already have, and that's enough. Forget about it."

"I can't, man. I feel like crap. I was so wrong about Ted. I feel responsible and guilty as hell. My intuition is almost always right. I was sure he was a good man."

"It was the drugs. I told you before all this started. They're screwing up your judgment. You've cut back, right?"

He smiled, then began to chuckle; a warm, weary chuckle as if amused by himself. "Oh, sure, you bet. But I'm still drinking beer. You coming to the Cotillion?"

Through the lab's big windows, I could see Jeth and Mack lugging a big Igloo cooler out to the docks, getting ready for the traditional Friday, end-of-the-week party.

As I held open the door for Tomlinson, I said, "I wouldn't miss it. I told JoAnn I might actually try dancing. Who knows? Maybe I will."

I went back into my house to find the pretty lady standing, waiting for me. Dr. Kathleen Rhodes, tall, chestnut-haired and articulate, and without football player. The two hadn't lasted long, just as O'Rourke had said, and when Pete had told her how pitiful I'd looked in his office, she'd decided that maybe I'd learned something, after all. And she was right: I had.

She took me into her arms, holding me, then turned her face in a way so that she would be easy to kiss. But I did not. I hated what I as going to say next, but I knew if anyone was going to understand, it would be Kathleen.

Instead, I took her by the shoulders and steered her back to her chair. "Kathleen, I am flattered beyond words that you drove all this way just to surprise me. And I would *like* to get together again. But not now. Not for a while. For one thing, I have a friend who's . . . who's been sick, and I need to be here in case she calls. Plus, I had Tomlinson release all my fish before the storm hit. So now, I've got to restock my aquarium, and that's going to take weeks. It's weird, but—" I stopped, wondering if I should tell her. Then decided, what the hell, why not. "The weird thing is, I didn't realize how attached I'd become to those animals. My bull sharks, especially the immature tarpon. They're just fish, I know, and I'm not speaking of any great emotional investment, but still—"

The woman stood and touched her finger to my lips, silencing me. She had a nice smile on her face and gorgeous brown eyes. She was shaking her head as if perplexed but pleased, as she said, "Ford, you've changed. There's something very different about you."

"I don't know what that would be, Kath."

"For one thing, look at you. You're wearing a Hawaiian shirt with a hula dancer on the back. Never in a thousand years would I expect to find you wearing something like that. That's just not you."

"It's Cotillion night, big party. Plus, we're going to 'Tween Waters, sit around the pool bar and talk to the guides. I borrowed it from Tomlinson."

The woman stepped toward me and touched her hand to my chest. "And this. You don't wear jewelry. Marion Ford wearing gold around his neck? You told me you despised jewelry."

On a woven rope cord, covered by my shirt, I wore a golden locket in the shape of a smiling full moon. I touched my hand to the pendant now, feeling its warmth; a thing to be worn occasionally as a reminder of someone.

I said, "This? It was a gift from an old friend."